I0687596

# THE DOVE

*Wings of the West Book 2*

KRISTY MCCAFFREY

The Dove

First Edition published by Whiskey Creek Press, 2005.

Second Edition published by K. McCaffrey LLC, 2014.

Cover by Earthly Charms – earthlycharms.com

Author Photo by Hannah McCaffrey – hannahmccaffrey.weebly.com

E-book ISBN-13: 978-0-9976651-4-7

Print ISBN-13: 978-0-9976651-5-4

kmccaffrey.com

kristy@kmccaffrey.com

# BOOKS BY KRISTY MCCAFFREY

## Wings of the West Series

The Wren

The Dove

The Sparrow

The Blackbird

The Bluebird

The Songbird (Novella)

Echo of the Plains (Short Story)

The Starling

The Canary

The Nighthawk

The Swan

The Falcon (Coming Soon)

## Stand-Alone Novel

Into The Land Of Shadows

## Short Story Collections

The Crow Brothers Collection

The West: A Romance Collection

## Long Novellas

Alice: Bride of Rhode Island

Rosemary

Blue Sage

The Peppermint Tree

A Mirthful Wish

## Contemporary Adventure Romances

Deep Blue

Cold Horizon

Ancient Winds

Sapphire Waves

Cobalt Sea (Coming Soon)

"I...commend McCaffrey for the historical accuracy of her stories...a phenomenal read that I'd recommend to anyone who enjoys historical romance, with a hint of the other." ~ Jonel Boyko, Reviewer

"Ancient Hopi and Havasupai legends have a new voice in McCaffrey. Her inspired writing made her main character's mystical journey into another realm entirely believable and kept the pages turning long into the night." ~ City Sun Times

### *The Blackbird*

"With dastardly villains, plenty of action, a strong heroine, surprising twists and turns, and a sexy cowboy, all underlined by a sensual love story, this historical western romance has something for everyone." ~ Janna Shay, InD'tale Magazine

"A steamy, intelligent historical fiction set in the Arizona desert where the harsh environment matches the characters who populate it. Can two wounded souls find each other and flourish? Find out in Kristy McCaffrey's hard to put down, fourth book in the *Wings of the West* series, *The Blackbird*." ~ Chanticleer Book Reviews

### *The Bluebird*

"The reader will find themselves often sitting on the edge of their seats...a quick and exciting read!" ~ Belinda Wilson, InD'tale Magazine

"...a fast paced read with a depth to the characters and the story that kept my interest from the first page to the last..." ~ Jo, Romance Junkies

*To my parents, for allowing me to write all night when I was a child.*

*And to my first edition editor, Karyn Cheatham,
for making the story better.*

# CHAPTER 1

*New Mexico Territory*
*July 1877*

"The whores are much prettier up that way." The toothless Mexican smiled wide as he pointed up Pacific Street.

Logan Ryan considered the comment as he tied off his horse and approached a two-story building with the name WHITE DOVE SALOON painted with flowery white flair on a red background. He hitched a boot at the bottom of a well-worn step and rested hands casually on his hips.

Claire Waters couldn't possibly be here.

Maybe the Mexican, reeking of whiskey, had misunderstood him. *You lookin' for a Waters woman? Sí, you find one there.* Logan was sure this was the building the man had fingered.

He pushed his hat back, aware of the fast approach of nightfall, both by his weariness and with the increased activity inside the saloon and behind him on the dusty street. Cigar smoke and the unruly voices of the men inside filled the air.

Las Vegas was a bustling town on the Santa Fe Trail, last stop before reaching the town of Santa Fe, and with so much traffic—traders, merchants, ranchers, and the military from Fort Union—an abundance of saloons and dance halls was to be expected. Maybe the Mexican had simply assumed Logan was looking for a good time.

He climbed the steps, keeping his exhaustion at bay with the anticipation of finding Claire Waters. He'd ridden in record time and had stopped for only a few hours at Fort Sumner to check up on Lester Williams, the ranch hand who had brought Claire home after her brief stay with Logan's folks at their SR ranch. Lester's telegram —stating that he was too ill to return—had prompted Logan to check on the older man who'd been with the Ryan family for years and was more than a ranch employee. Thankfully, Lester's health was much improved and he'd soon be able to return to Texas, but he'd been bedridden with a fever for more than a fortnight. It concerned Logan that Claire might also be sick. What if she was wasting away from some mysterious illness at this very moment?

The batwing doors to the saloon flew open with a piercing squeak. A blur of black silk and bare flesh slammed into Logan. Before he could steady the sweet-smelling bundle, the woman fell back on her rear end with a firm thump.

With curves in all the right places and an eyeful of cleavage that would tempt any man, Logan's eyes slid over the woman in silent approval. Although he'd never been one to dally with saloon girls, the thought suddenly had merit; the intensity of it surprised him. He leaned down and offered to help the woman—obviously one of the pretty whores the Mexican had mentioned—to her feet.

"Sorry, miss. Are you all right?" He glanced into the saloon, half expecting a randy customer to be right behind her.

As the woman raised her eyes to his, the green depths triggered recognition and shock. Air drained from Logan's lungs as surely as if she'd barreled into him again.

"Claire?" He was stunned. The black hair had thrown him. Claire Waters had long tresses the color of the sun.

Her eyes widened. "Logan? What are you doing here?" Her panic was plain to see.

"Looking for you." He ignored the sharp stab of disappointment over what her attire and disguise implicated—that she wasn't the quiet and reserved woman he'd come to know at his folk's ranch. Truth was, he hardly knew her at all. But he'd wanted to see her all the same, and had come full of worry and expectation.

"Why? Is something wrong? Is Molly all right?" She ignored his hand and stood on her own. Logan watched as she hastily smoothed the tight bodice that showcased her attributes in a way that set his teeth on edge. What had been nearly irresistible to him a moment ago was now displayed for any and all to see. He didn't like it.

Logan reached up to brush aside the long dark strands impeding his view of Claire's face, but she hastily shifted the wig herself. Reluctantly, he let his hand drop.

"No, nothing's wrong," he answered. "And Molly's fine. But we got word at the SR that Lester was ill, and I wanted to make sure *you* were all right."

"Lester's sick?" she asked. "I had no idea. He was perfectly fine when he...dropped me off in these parts. Does he need medical attention?"

Logan frowned. When he'd spoken with Lester, the man was uncertain of Claire's exact whereabouts—he'd dropped her outside of town three weeks ago at her insistence, then had headed southeast to Fort Sumner. He said Claire had convinced him all was well, with her home only a short distance away; so he'd let her go, not altogether certain he should have, but soon after he'd begun to shake and shudder, barely able to sit his horse before succumbing to the fever.

Logan should have been the one to accompany her back to Las Vegas, but when Claire had decided to head home the timing couldn't have been worse. His pa and the ranch were gearing up for the spring roundup, and Logan couldn't shirk his duty to his old man.

"No. He's doin' fine." He couldn't understand why he was both glad and bothered by her concern for Lester, a flash of jealousy surprising him.

Claire stared at him from under a hideous black mop and a dress he suspected would have to be cut and peeled from her body to remove it. Was he volunteering for the job?

Swearing under his breath, he took a moment to decide how to proceed. The facts were plain to see—Claire was a prostitute. He should be able to accept that. Many women sold themselves to survive. But it didn't make him feel any better that other men had touched her.

"Are you alone?" she asked.

"Yeah. Cale rode with me until Fort Sumner, but then headed to Arizona Territory." He hadn't seen much of Cale Walker since their younger days in Texas; Cale had joined the army at the same time as Logan's brother Matt. Although Logan had returned home more than a year ago—leaving his post as a deputy in Virginia City—Cale, no longer a U.S. soldier, had remained in the territories bounty hunting. The revelation two months ago that Cale was, in fact, the brother of Molly Hart—Logan's sister-in-law—had drawn their lives back together.

"I hope he's well."

Logan nodded.

"You came all this way to find me?"

"I came to check on Lester." He looked into her apprehensive eyes, framed with dark lashes despite her natural blonde hair. He'd forgotten how lovely she was, how much he had enjoyed suppertime at the ranch simply because she was sitting across from him. "And I came to check on you, too."

She watched him and her graceful lips parted as if to say something while uncertainty played across her face.

The loud roar of men arguing about a card game made Claire jump.

"Is someone bothering you?" Logan asked.

With a hand to her chest, she appeared bewildered. "No. Why would you say that? Actually, I'm really in a great hurry. It's been wonderful to see you. Please send my best to Molly." She ran past him and disappeared around the corner.

Logan stared after her, shocked by her sudden departure.

Knowing he couldn't return home with so little information—Molly would tan his hide for not *visiting* longer, although he had no idea how he would break Claire's situation to her—Logan strode forward to find her. He nearly fell backwards when she appeared on horseback from around the side of the saloon.

"What're you doin'?" he demanded. "Molly's gonna want more than a hello and a goodbye from you."

"I don't mean to be rude," she said, attempting to control her gelding, the old horse looking a might cranky. "But one of the women inside is in trouble. I need to go for help."

"What kind of trouble?" It wouldn't be the first time he'd gotten into the middle of something he shouldn't.

"She's sick. Bleeding." Claire's gaze flicked from the street to the saloon. Logan wondered why she was so worried someone would see her. And there was that god-awful black wig. His instincts told him the woman inside wasn't the only one in distress.

"Her condition is beyond my abilities," Claire added. "I need to go for someone."

"The town doctor?" Logan could accomplish that.

Claire shook her head. "He won't come here. None of them will. There's an Indian woman who lives in the hills. She'll help."

"I'll go with you." He retrieved Storm. The brown mare moved eagerly despite the days of riding she'd already endured.

"You don't have to," Claire replied. "I've been there hundreds of times."

"With the way you're dressed, I'd be surprised if trouble didn't find you and knock you on your pretty backside again. I think once is enough for tonight." He swung atop his horse. "I'll follow you."

Logan wasn't certain, but he thought he saw a flash of gratitude in Claire's gaze when she realized he wouldn't take no for an answer. With a nod, Claire kicked her animal into a gallop and led them into the dark alleys behind Pacific Street, then quickly into the moonlit wilderness of the Sangre de Cristo Mountains.

WHEREVER THEY WERE GOING, it wasn't close. Logan found it difficult to mentally mark the terrain since one spot seemed much like the next—loose rocks, occasional clumps of cactus, and endless clusters of pine and juniper. The branches scraped and clung to his arms and legs. While only a minor nuisance to him, he could imagine how scratched and bruised Claire would be at the end of their hasty, uphill ride. Scantily clad, she was nothing but a distraction to his own mental terrain, the dancehall dress she wore hiked up around her shapely thighs, covered enticingly with dark red stockings. But the woman was determined and continued moving steadily ahead.

Logan's mind drifted briefly to when he first met Claire. She had arrived at the SR Ranch with Molly Hart, whose folks had been old family friends of the Ryan family. Ten years' prior, a shocking raid on the Hart Ranch had resulted in the deaths of Robert and Rosemary Hart, with strong evidence that their second daughter, Molly, had also been murdered. The grisly discovery of a young girl's body—mutilated and burned beyond recognition—had left little doubt in the minds of Logan and his family. But a twist of fate spared Molly and put her into the hands of the Comanche, with whom she lived for many years until she was able to return home. Logan's folks welcomed her with all the fanfare of a long-lost daughter, and his brother Matt fell hard—surprising everyone when he gave up his rough-riding Texas Ranger days to marry her. But for Logan, Molly's return had meant something else. It had brought Claire to the SR.

Traveling alone, Molly had journeyed through New Mexico Territory in her bid to reach Texas and the home she hadn't seen in ten years. Through sheer luck and serendipity, she found Claire in a desolate arroyo outside Albuquerque, beaten and left for dead. Molly nursed her back to health, then brought her to Texas.

Logan garnered this information from Matt—Claire had never spoken of it during their brief acquaintance, and he'd never been of a mind to pry. With their initial introduction a bit awkward, it should hardly have surprised Logan that Claire never really warmed to him.

The first night Molly and Claire stayed at the SR, Logan's ma had put Claire in his bedroom, thinking he wasn't due back till morning. He'd been scouting beeves on the south ridge and he'd all but resigned himself to sleeping under the stars, but deep into the night he'd returned to the main house looking forward to a soft bed and a big breakfast. As he always did, he'd climbed into bed as naked as the day he was born, startled to find the warm body of a woman already under the sheets. Claire fought him like a mountain cat, scaring the hell out of him. But, in all honesty, she'd also caught his eye in a way a woman hadn't in a good long while.

His recollection of the memory brought one thought to his mind. If Claire was parading around as a whore, why did her behavior in Texas contradict it? Before he headed back to Texas, Logan would sit the black-haired beauty down and have a heart-to-heart with her. First and foremost, he wanted to find out why none of this added up to a consistent hill of beans.

The wig jerked from Claire's head and snagged on a tree

branch. Logan grabbed it easily as he rode past and waved it at her as she looked back, clearly dismayed.

"Got it," he said, pleased to finally see the pale mass pinned atop her head in a tight bun. He'd like to see it down, just once, before he left. *Yeah, and the sun'll rise in the west.* He'd best watch his intentions with this woman. His ex-fiancée, Dee Griffin, had taught him that good intentions and a good woman didn't necessarily go hand in hand. As much as he'd tried to please Dee, she'd still skipped out on him without a goodbye or even a *go to hell.* Anything would have been preferable to her silence and cowardly escape in the arms of another man.

The horses broke through the trees to an open, grassy area and a small adobe building came into view on the far side. Smoke rose from a chimney and a pale light flickered through the one and only hazy window. Claire slid from her horse before the animal completely stopped. Her fancy boots with ridiculously high heels hitched in the dirt and she fell to the ground with a startled gasp. Before Logan could dismount and help her, she was up again, hobbling toward the cabin.

"Tia! Are you here?" Claire pounded on the door. Logan came up behind her as it opened.

A short, robust Indian woman greeted them, a frown etched on her face.

"Tia, thank God," Claire said quickly, out-of-breath.

The woman inhaled sharply. *"Palomita?* Is that you? Everyone say you are dead."

Claire nodded quickly. "I know."

Clearly shaken, Tia reached a hand to Claire's cheek. "Oh child, I prayed that *Sin-o'-Wap* got possession of your soul, that you went to the Happy Hunting Ground. My heart has been broken for you."

Claire leaned down and hugged the woman. "I'm sorry I didn't come to see you sooner," she whispered. "I was afraid to involve you, that Sandoval or Griffin might see me, that they might hurt you."

She returned her gaze to Tia. "It's all so confusing and I'm not sure who to trust, but I need you to come with me. It's urgent, or I wouldn't have come. Ellie's bleeding something fierce and I don't know how to stop it."

The mention of the name Griffin caught Logan's attention. The connection seemed farfetched—he'd looked for Dee in the days and weeks after she left him, but the trail had been difficult, ultimately drying up in Denver. By then he'd been fed up with women, and life in general. He'd backtracked to Nevada, resigned his deputy position in Virginia City, and headed to Texas, finding refuge with his folks and the day-to-day labors of running a cattle ranch.

"Her woman's bleeding?" Tia asked.

"Like that, but worse. Much, much worse." Claire's voice ended on a sob.

"*Sí*, I come." Tia poured water on the flame in the small beehive fireplace—steam and a sharp hissing filled the room—then retrieved a large leather bag. As she exited the cabin, she noticed Logan. "And who are you?"

"Logan Ryan, ma'am." He tipped his hat.

Tia suddenly grinned. Despite the white that streaked the two black braids hanging down the sides of her face, and the crinkling of skin around her eyes, she appeared young, almost giddy. She craned her neck back. "You are so tall. But you watch *Palomita's* back?" She nodded and continued before he could answer. "It is time someone watch over her. It is time you have come."

"It's not like that," Claire cut in.

Tia smiled. "Maybe not for you." She held out her stubby fingers to Logan. "You can call me Tia Anita."

As he clasped her hand, Logan was aware of the Indian woman's curiosity but it didn't bother him. He sensed her strong affection for Claire. "Do you have a horse?" he asked.

"*Sí*, but he is very slow."

9

"You can ride with me," Claire said and urged her toward the two animals waiting behind them.

Tia waved the notion aside. "Reverend is too old to carry the both of us. Look at him, he is tired already. He will mosey to town, and we will be lucky to arrive the day after tomorrow."

Logan ran a hand down the horse's snout. Reverend's grayish hide was long and unkempt, but his eyes were a clear deep black. While it was obvious he wasn't accustomed to constant, vigorous exercise there remained a fire in him nonetheless. Logan nodded in silent approval, sensing the horse's scrutiny much the way Tia had sized him up moments ago.

Claire surrounded herself with creatures of opinion; perhaps the reserved blonde beauty had convictions as well. Logan was struck by a sudden desire to know her better. While he'd thought of her often since her departure from the SR and had come here with the intention of finding her—although until now he wouldn't have admitted it—the truth was more of a problem than he needed in his life. Instead of coming face-to-face and finding her less attractive, less intriguing, less interesting—she was only more so.

And possibly a whore to boot.

His knack for picking women was priceless.

"Claire can ride with me," Logan said and helped Tia onto Reverend. Then he mounted Storm, grabbed Claire's hand and hauled her up behind him. He snatched the wig from where it rested on the pommel, twisted his torso around and pushed the black mass onto her head.

"Thank you," she murmured, her hands brushing his as she tried to reposition the disguise.

"You look better as a blonde." Claire's look of confusion—the result of a simple compliment—brought a smile to his lips once he faced forward again. She clearly wasn't schooled in the ways of a saloon girl. Logan felt the first ray of hope that maybe all wasn't as it appeared.

"Do you know the way?" Tia asked.

"You'd better go first." He didn't want to risk getting them lost. No doubt every minute counted where this woman Ellie was concerned.

"Hold on," he said to Claire. He grasped both of her hands in his and pulled her snug against his back. It was for her safety, he told himself.

And if that wasn't a load of crap, then he didn't know what was.

# CHAPTER 2

A shudder snaked down Claire's spine as the screams filled the small room. Ellie Hicks sobbed and gasped for breath as tears streamed down her face and mixed with the sweat that drenched her body. No pale wallflower, Ellie was a woman in her forties, well-seasoned from years of selling her body to any man who offered. Claire had never seen the stalwart, unemotional woman so broken, her silver-red hair plastered in a tangled mass along her cheeks and neck. And the blood. God, it was everywhere.

Claire closed her eyes for a moment to steady herself. What use was she to Tia if she couldn't hold herself together? She wanted to be a doctor, of all the crazy dreams, and her reaction to Ellie's condition dismayed her.

"More blankets," Tia said.

"The pain," Ellie moaned as she lay back against the pillow. Even her lips were drained of color. "Am I gonna die?" she wailed.

"Shush," Tia quieted her. "You will not die this night."

Claire met Betsy Williams in the hallway. "I need more blankets," she told the young, brown-haired woman.

"Is she all right?" Betsy asked, her eyes wide with concern.

The girl had been at the White Dove for five months, serving drinks and helping with general upkeep. Eventually Claire's mama expected all the women to service customers via the second floor, but Claire wondered if Betsy truly had the temperament for it. Perhaps Maggie Waters was getting soft in her old age. Only one other time had Claire's mama let a girl off the hook, and that had been Claire herself.

On her sixteenth birthday Claire had dreaded the foregone conclusion that she would have to earn her living the old-fashioned way, but her mama had given her a reprieve due to Claire's skills with healing and medicines. During the past three years, Claire had done her best to help the women at the White Dove, but recently her mama had expressed displeasure that her daughter helped any whore who came to the door.

Claire reached out and squeezed Betsy's arm. "I hope so. Can you bring the blankets?"

The girl nodded and returned quickly with the request. "If you need me..."

"I'll let you know," Claire replied. "It's best if you and the other girls keep things running downstairs. We wouldn't want to alarm any of the customers." The truth was, with only Louisa Pérez and Alice May providing additional entertainment of late, the customers simply weren't coming around like they had in the past. Claire could only conclude that with Ellie out of commission and Maggie gone, the men were taking their business elsewhere. Southern Charm was only a short walk down the street and Claire knew the proprietress, Belle Mason, employed at least a dozen girls.

Claire closed the door and helped Tia clean Ellie, piling the bloody sheets and cloths in the corner. Although the mattress was a loss, they covered it again with a new blanket. Ellie gripped painfully onto Claire's shoulders while Tia accomplished the job.

Tia ushered Claire to the other side of the room and said quietly, "I think she lose a babe. Her body try to help, but not fast enough." She leaned down, pulled a rawhide bag from her satchel, and handed it to Claire. "Take these *cuipa de sabina* and make a pot of tea. It will help push the babe out. She bleed too much. No time."

Claire nodded and left the room. She took the back staircase to the kitchen, relieved to avoid the saloon, despite the sparse number of customers. Louisa, one of the White Dove's more popular attractions with her exotic Mexican looks and expertise behind closed doors, had lamented over the decrease in clientele more than once. Concern over the financial state of the establishment, as well as her mama's absence, weighed more and more on Claire as each day passed. The girls told her Maggie had taken Jimmy—Claire's younger brother—to Cimarron. Since a trip north wasn't out of the ordinary, Claire had kept a low profile while awaiting their return, wanting to explain in person why she'd stayed away as long as she had. She ignored the twinge of bitterness that her mama was somehow responsible for Sandoval overtaking the stage that day. The memory of how he'd pulled Claire from its interior while Jimmy screamed for her—fighting to save her as only a reckless eight-year-old dare against a group of armed men—still echoed despairingly in her mind.

As Claire entered the narrow kitchen, she caught a glimpse of her hand—a disturbing sight of blood-stained skin and fingernails rimmed in dark outlines. A wave of fear washed through her, and she wondered if becoming a doctor wasn't in the cards for her. She was certain the men in town who hung out a shingle and treated the population in general didn't have hands that shook like leaves in a thunderstorm. Blinking back tears, she took a steadying breath.

The stove was already hot; Claire had stoked it earlier when Ellie's condition had worsened. She scrubbed her hands as best she could with soap and a bristle brush, splashing water onto the wooden countertop around the wash basin. In haste, she grabbed a white cloth hanging from the wall and dried her hands. She retrieved a large teakettle from a shelf and filled it with water from a bucket near the back door. As she struggled to lift the heavy cookware, a very masculine hand came from behind and immediately relieved her arms of the burden. Startled, her gaze locked with Logan's blue-green eyes. Her heartbeat picked up considerably.

"How's Ellie?" he asked.

Claire watched as he effortlessly placed the kettle on the cast-iron stove. He opened the hinged door below to check the fire, to which he added several pieces of wood from a stash in the corner.

"Not doing well," Claire replied, wondering why her voice sounded so different to her, deeper and more cautious than usual. She felt spent, in more ways than one. And Logan's sudden attention was almost enough to push her beyond the breaking point.

He had found her on the steps of her mama's saloon, dressed like one of the women who spent much of their time horizontal, or sitting upright if she was to believe Louisa. That thought made her face burn. She had no firsthand knowledge of such things, but Logan's eyes on her made her realize he thought she did.

While the idea shamed her, it was, surprisingly, equally matched by a fierce desire to explore Logan the way Louisa and the other girls claimed to do with the men who patronized them. The longing was so sharp it staggered her. Claire stepped back and gripped the edge of the one and only table in the room.

*What kind of woman did Logan choose for a bed partner?*

Tall and broad-shouldered, he all but consumed the enclosed space of the kitchen. She truly had never expected to see him again, a notion that had nagged at the back of her mind many times since she had left Texas.

He moved toward her, his hat casting a shadow across his face that was both familiar and unreadable. She well remembered the way his dark brown hair curled slightly at the nape of his neck, how she would find him watching her from time to time during her stay at the SR, how his gaze had made her mind wander to possibilities never before imagined.

He loomed closer, and she leaned back involuntarily as his hand came to her cheek. "You have blood on your face," he said quietly. Very gently he rubbed a spot near her nose with the pad of his thumb, his hand warm where it touched her.

Unable to find her voice, Claire stared at the dark blue collar of his shirt, the top buttons undone and revealing tan skin and a hint of chest hair that likely went farther down. A prospect she would certainly never know.

Moving his hand away from her, he carefully lifted some of the black hair trailing over her shoulder from the wig that was making her head itch like wildfire. "We need to talk," he said.

The kettle began to boil, throwing a thick line of steam above the stove. Claire rushed toward it but Logan was two steps ahead of her; he took the towel from her hand and lifted the heavy pot. She found a white porcelain teapot, the ceramic lid clanking loudly as she fumbled with the cookware. *Damn my shaking hands.*

She deposited a handful of the cedar shavings Tia had given her into a piece of cheesecloth, haphazardly tied it then placed the bundle into the teapot. Standing far enough back so as to avoid accidentally touching Logan, she waited as he poured the water. In an effort to occupy herself she located a battered wooden tray and placed a tin cup and the brewing tea onto it.

"This may take a while," she said and glanced at him. Why in the world did his presence unnerve her so much?

"I'll wait."

Claire was about to say he shouldn't, that she was certain he had better things to do than linger around for her, but she knew she wasted precious time. Ellie needed the tea.

She nodded, lifted the tray and left the kitchen, sensing Logan's eyes on her. Although glad to see him, she was thoroughly confused by her reaction.

When she entered Ellie's room all thoughts of his dark gaze and broad shoulders left her mind as she faced the arduous task of delivering the woman's stillborn child.

———

A SLIGHT TAP at the door roused Claire from her exhausted slumber in a chair near Ellie's bed. She immediately checked on the woman; thankfully she still slept. They had bound her abdomen with bandages several hours ago and it appeared to be working—her excessive bleeding had stopped. Tia slumbered on the floor, a faint snore signaling her location at the foot of the bed and near the window. She lay flat on her back, and Claire thought the position looked terribly uncomfortable. Through the white, threadbare curtains a light blue sky signaled the coming of a new day.

Louisa leaned inside. "Ellie, she is better?"

Claire rubbed her stiff neck and wondered at Louisa's ability to appear lovely and composed so early in the morning, her shrewd pitch-dark eyes gazing from a flawless complexion. The black-haired woman had obviously not been to bed—except for business, Louisa's regulars were a loyal group—since she still wore the same attire from the previous night, a red silk dress that accented her brown skin and had been sewn by the Mexican woman herself. Claire's disguise, a tight-fitting black gown she looked forward to shedding, had also been designed and stitched by Louisa.

Claire stood, reminded again of the plunging neckline that emphasized her breasts, the pale skin a sharp contrast to Louisa's sultry beauty. A part of her, so miniscule she hardly acknowledged it, had enjoyed squeezing into the disguise, had enjoyed the revelation that she was a woman and was built of the same features as any other female. She viewed the human body in terms of healing, or as a means of male satisfaction—never had she considered her own attributes as something beautiful, something desirable. *Had Logan appreciated any of what he'd seen?*

It shouldn't matter what Logan thought.

"Yes," Claire replied.

"I must bother you. All the clients, they leave except one, and he only ask for you." Louisa pressed her full lips together as she shook her head. "I told him you no take customers this night, but he no leave. I offer myself—many times—but he say no. I'm thinking," she gave a coy smile, "you must give the dress back."

Tired, Claire's mind could only focus on two things—Logan was still here, and Louisa was working her charms on him, a thought that made her feel unbelievably jealous. She had never before been envious of Louisa's curvaceous body or easy sexuality, but one thought of her working Logan over made Claire feel threatened.

She moved past Louisa and paused in the doorway. "You're certain he's alone?"

"*Sí*. But you no go like that. You need wig."

Claire nodded, not wanting to explain why she *didn't* need it. "Send him to Maggie's room."

Louisa cast a surprised glance her way. Claire decided not to set her straight.

She could have met him downstairs in the saloon, but her gut told her a private meeting would be better. She wouldn't have to compete with Louisa for Logan's attention. And while she could have taken him to the room she occupied behind the White Dove—a separate cabin Maggie had constructed for both Claire and Jimmy— the thought of inviting him into her personal space disquieted her.

Claire walked to the end of the hallway and entered her mama's room where a layer of dust covered the bureau and nightstands, the bed neatly made with a white lace coverlet. She unpinned her hair and scratched her scalp, wondering what she should say. She could explain everything—her whole damn life, in fact—but she doubted Logan wanted to hear it. Better to say as little as possible. He was sure to be leaving for Texas in no time at all.

With the door ajar she heard his boots on the wooden floor. A flutter of anticipation engulfed her.

———

LOGAN TAPPED on the open door, removed his hat and stepped into the room. Claire sat in a chair at the foot of the bed still wearing the tight black dress, her exposed shoulders and the swell of her breasts skimming his mind like a tantalizing breeze on a hot summer day. With hair spilling down to her waist, she was, despite the dress, a vision of everything natural and straightforward, a woman that would fill a man's world and connect him to life in the most basic sense. The vision unsettled him while at the same time his mind took a mental count of the money he had on him, wondering just what her price might be. Shit, he was in trouble.

"I can't believe you're still here," she said.

Sunlight poured in from the window behind her and illuminated her hair with a golden hue. His wish about seeing her hair down had just been granted. How many more wishes were likely to come true?

"Yeah, well, I don't normally hang out in saloons all night." He closed the door, leaned on it, and crossed his arms. "How's your friend?"

"I think she'll be all right. You really ought to get some sleep yourself. Did you come straight from Texas?"

He nodded and noticed the dark circles under her eyes. She needed rest as well.

"How's your family?" she asked.

"They're doing fine. Matt and Molly got married."

"They did?" Her eyes widened in surprise.

A smile turned up the edge of his mouth. "There was definitely no stopping it. Just took 'em awhile to come around."

A wistful expression crossed Claire's face. "I'm really happy for them."

"What's going on here? Have you always worked in a place like this?"

Her smile vanished. "I've been at the White Dove since I was a little girl."

Shocked, Logan didn't know what to say. He'd dealt with his fair share of fancy girls and harlots during his watch in Virginia City— the mining town had been overrun with saloons, dance halls, and brothels—but it didn't prepare him for the knowledge that Claire had lived, *still lived,* such a life.

He forced his mind to focus on something else. Her safety.

"Are you in trouble?"

"Why would you ask that?"

"Just a hunch."

Claire pushed a hand through her hair and looked at him with a serious expression. "I'm as fine as I've ever been." She raised her arms to take in the surroundings then let them drop to her sides. "I know what you must think."

"You have no idea what I think," he replied and wondered why she got to him. It wasn't just the physical attraction, though God knew she appealed to him in every way possible—from the swell of her breasts to the flare of her hips to her unforgettable golden hair. But beneath it all was something else; he had a strong intuition there was more to Claire than was obvious. For that reason, he should push her to tell him everything—why she was a prostitute, why she continued to live a life like this, why she was in trouble. But did he really want to get that close to her and risk his heart yet again? Common sense told him no.

"I hope you'll use...discretion when telling your folks about your visit here," she said. "They were very kind to me."

"You could come back to Texas." The words were out before he realized it. "I'm sure Molly would be happy to see you again, and my ma could help you find something productive to do."

A flash of Claire's astonishment was quickly hidden behind a glazed look of regret, and if Logan hadn't been watching her he would have missed it.

"Thank you for the offer," she said slowly. "But I have obligations here."

When she stood, Logan's thoughts went unwillingly to the bed. Extending this meeting in tangled sheets, however, would only make matters worse. He knew that. But the thought was there all the same.

"Will you be leaving today?" she asked.

"I suppose so." He had no reason to stay except for the woman standing before him.

"Tia will probably be awake now, and I'll be needing to get her home."

As Claire closed the distance between them, Logan felt a twinge of disappointment when she reached for the door behind him. He thought she might reach for him. *Damn, I must be more tired than I thought.*

"I'll take her," he said. The words stopped Claire in her tracks. A small victory, which brought her less than an arm's length from him and gave him a brief moment to memorize the incredible green of her eyes. "You look exhausted. Why don't you get some rest." The urge to kiss her was strong. "And you'll always be welcome at the SR."

Her eyes filled with tears and he would have touched her if she hadn't lowered her face, effectively shutting him out. "I'd be most grateful for your help with Tia. And please give Molly my best on her wedding."

Reluctantly, he stepped aside as she reached for the doorknob. Hesitating, she brought her gaze to his. "Have a safe journey home," she added.

And for a second time Logan watched Claire walk out of his life.

# CHAPTER 3

"Why do you call Claire *Palomita?*"

Logan rode beside Tia as they passed the brown adobe structures that constituted many of the buildings in Las Vegas. Several had porticoes, while others had additional floors. There was wealth in the town alongside poverty, and the White Dove appeared to fall somewhere toward the downside. As he waited for Claire last night, he'd noticed the dilapidated state of the saloon and the limited offerings from the bar. This morning, he glimpsed the weeds and bushes that had overtaken the establishment outside.

"The first time I see her," Tia said, squinting against the bright, morning sun, "I see a little dove. Claire, she was young, maybe eight or nine winters. I find her out there." She gestured toward the mountains. "She was so quiet, so still. A dove come and sit with her. Together they stay a long time. I think how odd the picture. But it not odd now. That is always Claire. Closed." Tia pointed to her head. "Thinking. There is something about her. You can see it." With more fervor, she added, "You can *feel* it."

Logan glanced at the stout Indian woman. "Maybe," he murmured.

Tia smiled. "Why you here, Logan Ryan?"

"I was worried about her," he answered truthfully. "But she doesn't seem interested in someone doing that."

"*Palomita* hide her true self."

"Yeah," he said, "doesn't everyone?" He studied the red and green chilies hanging from the wooden porch beams of the homes they passed, the peppers swaying in the wind. Hispanic boys and girls ran back and forth, playing in the bright day.

Tia laughed. "What the matter with you? How far you come to find her?"

"From Texas."

Tia nodded, never urging Claire's old gelding to go any faster. The slow pace didn't seem to concern her, so Logan settled in for the ride. Perhaps she could shed some light on Claire's situation. No sense beating around the bush.

"How long has Claire been a prostitute?"

Tia raised an eyebrow then clucked softly. "Is this what stand between you?"

For a moment, Logan was speechless. Tia made it sound so trivial; in Logan's mind it was anything but.

"It's just a question," Logan replied. He ran a hand through his hair then repositioned his hat.

Tia chuckled and shook her head. "I usually no stick my nose in other people's business, and especially not into *Palomita's*, but I cannot think why she drive you from her. Her view of the world is shaded by her time at the White Dove." Pausing for effect, she said, "Claire no sell herself." She jabbed a finger at his chest. "If you think hard, your heart already know it."

Logan blew out a relieved breath. Damn, but it'd rankled him mightily the idea of her working for hire. "Then why does she stay?"

"Maggie Waters always have much ambition. She come to town many winters ago, with Claire, her daughter, so young and sweet but with too much wisdom in a child's eyes. Maggie had no husband so she sell herself and make good money, but not enough. Soon she hire girls and sell them too. Then she open the White Dove. *Palomita* is a respectful daughter, she stay because it her duty."

"Where is Maggie?"

"Three full moons have passed since Maggie return to town with only Jimmy."

At Logan's questioning gaze, Tia added, "He Maggie's other child, born here. I hear rumor that Claire in trouble. I go to Maggie and demand to know, but she in no good shape. Her spirit cry and I know it bad."

"Who beat Claire? Sandoval? Griffin?"

Tia gazed at him, her expression closed and rigid. "Is that what happen?" Her neutral voice couldn't mask the flash of anger in her eyes. "Maggie never say." Tia looked away and muttered something unintelligible then turned back. "If I guess, I say it Raul Sandoval. Griffin a snake but no like to dirty his hands. I no ask Claire on this morning, I rejoice in her return. I not understand Maggie, but with Claire gone her heart was broke. She leave with Jimmy...don't know. But I must believe that she would thank a god she does not worship to see her daughter live again."

They moved beyond the town and to the foothills—Logan rode behind Tia on the narrow trail. Upon reaching her small home, Logan swung down and offered assistance as she dismounted. A figure emerged from the cabin.

"Jack!" Tia squealed and moved quickly to embrace the man. He wore a tattered old suit, the dark cloth lightened from sun and dust, and his long black hair covered his shoulders like a spider web. His oversized black hat all but shielded his face and Tia's as they shared more than a friendly reunion.

"Where you been?" he asked and leaned back to have a look at her.

"At the White Dove," Tia answered. "Here, you meet Logan

Ryan." Without waiting for an answer, she grabbed Jack's arm and dragged him back to where Logan stood discreetly out-of-sight.

"You can call me One-Eyed Jack," he said and smiled. He offered his hand.

Logan shook it. "Nice to meet you, sir."

A patch covered one of Jack's eyes and he smelled distinctly of liquor, but his gaze was warm. And shrewd. A copy of the Bible poked out of one of his coat pockets. Logan suspected the image of an Indian who lacked intelligence and blindly followed the tenets of the Christian faith was one Jack *wanted* to project. Never show your truest self. That seemed to be Claire's style, too. And it was a tactic Logan had used often enough during his deputy days. Perhaps he and Claire weren't so different.

"I have good news." Tia grinned. "*Palomita* lives."

Jack stared at her in surprise. "You've seen her?"

"*Sí*. She is well, and safe. Logan Ryan is here to help her."

"Well then, young man," Jack said, "it's right fine to meet you. It near broke our hearts when we got word she'd disappeared. The talk about town had her dead and buried."

"So it would seem," Logan replied. "Claire mentioned a person by the name of Griffin last night. A man or a woman?" He thought of Dee with her brown hair and smoky gaze, his memory of her appearance distorted with the passage of time. But some recollections only grew more vivid in the remembrance. Dee had always cut short an argument with the promise of a bedroom dally, blinding him, plain and simple.

"*Señor* Griffin...a man," Tia replied. "He and Raul Sandoval are close. Where one is, you'll find the other."

"What's Griffin's first name?"

"Frank," Tia said.

Hadn't Dee mentioned a brother named Frank? Maybe. Logan couldn't recollect for certain. "Does he have a sister?" he asked.

"A sister?" The Indian woman thought for a moment. "It is

possible. Many moons ago I did see him with a woman, but she was on the arm of that pond scum Luttrell." Jack nodded at her words, clearly in agreement.

Dee had left Nevada in the company of a man named Teddy Luttrell. A flash of anticipation coursed through Logan, not unlike the sensation he'd always felt when putting a fugitive behind bars.

"What did the woman look like?" Logan asked.

"Dark hair, much like Griffin."

This was the strongest lead he'd had since her disappearance from his life. He had long since cut his losses and stopped searching for her. Was there any point in a confrontation now? Could any explanations she offered make up for the sting of her betrayal?

"Do you know this woman?" Tia asked.

Logan hesitated. "Of a sort." He didn't feel inclined to rehash his past.

Tia shook her head. "If she is a Griffin, do not trouble yourself with her."

Easier said than done. But Logan kept his conflicted interest in Dee to himself. "Where's Luttrell now?"

"Dead," Jack said, his tone without inflection. "Happened last year, in the winter."

So much for leads. Dee was probably long gone by now.

"It was a might suspicious, Luttrell's death," Jack said. "No wounds, so the rumor was he'd been poisoned. But as far as I heard, no one paid for the crime."

Logan pushed aside a brief wave of concern for Dee. Whatever she'd been involved in was by her own choice. As soon as she had left him, his responsibility to her had ended, yet...

"Come inside," Tia said. "I make you and Jack some tea."

"I'd best get on back," Logan replied.

"It just for a short time." Tia tugged at his arm. "Come. I have something to show you."

Reluctantly Logan let Tia push him into her cabin while Jack smiled from behind. Logan stepped inside and waited for his eyes to adjust. Various types of willow baskets covered several shelves along the walls. On the floor, near the beehive fireplace, was an urn-shaped basket covered with a coating of piñon pitch. Logan thought it was probably a water jug and was proven correct when Tia used it to fill a cast-iron pot.

In a large basket near the door were several items made of rawhide and decorated with yellow, blue, and green beads. Logan saw what looked like purses of various sizes, armbands and moccasins. Tia probably made the items herself and sold them in town. From what he could see, the craftsmanship was excellent.

He and Jack sat on colorful blankets—mixtures of blue, brown and red—on the dirt floor while Tia stoked the fire and heated the water. After a short silence she brought them two steaming cups of liquid in discolored brass cups. She handed one out to Logan then changed her mind, giving him the other cup instead.

"Thank you," Logan said.

"Tia." Jack's voice had a tone of reprimand to it. "What are you doing?"

"What do you mean?"

"What kind of tea did you give to Mister Ryan?"

Tia cocked her chin and put hands on her hips. "Birthroot," she finally replied. "It is a fine tea," she defended. "It bring *Señor* Ryan good luck *and* it protect his teeth."

Logan raised an eyebrow. It was the first time a woman had ever been concerned about his teeth. He felt a sudden urgency to finish his cupful of the bitter brew and be on his way. If his instincts were right, Tia and Jack were about to start arguing.

"You're not using it as a love potion?" Jack asked.

Logan choked on his mouthful. "Pardon me?" He stood and continued to cough.

"No." Tia stared at Jack. "It not a love potion." She turned her gaze back to Logan. "But if it were, who you fancy? And do not say that Griffin woman."

Logan stared at Tia. He'd always considered himself a smart man with the ladies. But then, there'd been Dee, so all those smarts must have deserted him for good because otherwise how could he have missed the fact that Tia was sweet on him.

To buy some time, he said slowly, "Who would you like me to fancy?"

Tia stared right back at him then slapped her leg and started to laugh. "*Señor* Ryan, you a funny man. Jack, he thinks *I* want him." She shook her head and chuckled to herself, then leaned close. "I with Jack, you see. But what you think of Claire?"

Logan let out a relieved breath and spoke honestly before he thought better of it. "She's a hard woman to forget."

Tia silently agreed. "Here." She handed him a small, wood-carved figure. Logan rolled it back and forth across his palm and saw that it was a likeness of a bird.

"Claire made it when she a child," Tia said. "She give it to me but I know it not meant for me. You take it."

The childish carving intrigued him, as did the link it represented to a younger Claire. But it didn't seem right that he should keep it. "Why don't you give it back to her?" He tried to hand the figure to Tia, but she wouldn't take it.

"No. It not for her either," Tia said. "You keep. If you don't want it, you bring it back. Deal?"

Logan paused, then slowly nodded in agreement. Tia was determined and it didn't seem worth the effort to belabor the point. Claire had probably forgotten about the carving as soon as she'd given it to Tia. He ignored the feeling of connection he felt while holding it—a connection to the woman who had created it.

"Deal," he agreed.

Tia smiled. "At last Little Dove is spreading her wings."

Logan glanced down at the carving again. It wasn't just any bird Claire had chiseled. It was a dove.

---

IT WAS late in the afternoon when Claire checked on Ellie again. Thankfully, the woman still slept. Claire went downstairs and acknowledged Louisa and Betsy as they cleaned tables with rags and buckets of water.

Glad to be dressed in her own clothes again—a colorful Mexican skirt and white blouse—Claire moved behind the bar and retrieved a leather-clad ledger from a locked cupboard. She'd found the key in her mama's room several days ago and had already flipped through the pages on two different occasions, attempting to understand the entries. She sat on a stool, laid the book on the bar, and tried to make sense of it again.

When her mama took Jimmy and headed to Cimarron, she'd left Ellie in charge, and with less than fifty dollars in petty cash. While the White Dove was bringing in money nightly, a quick deduction showed that within the next week or so they would barely break even. Liquor supplies were low, and for the first time Claire wondered if there was a mortgage on the property, although she could find no evidence of one in the ledger. Her mama had always taken care of any and all things related to the business. Even now, Claire was reluctant to dig too deep into the financial situation of the White Dove, fearing her mama's reaction when she eventually did return, but with Ellie recovering upstairs there was no one else to address the pressing problem of how to keep the business afloat.

Troubled by the recent drop in customers, Claire frowned at the cash receipts and disbursements, unable to determine a cause from the numbers penciled into each column.

"Why has business been so bad?" she asked.

Louisa and Betsy paused in their cleaning.

"Perhaps the men are staying away because Maggie's been gone," Betsy offered.

Claire nodded. It was a distinct possibility. Her mama personally entertained a select clientele. But didn't such attention create loyalty? Apparently not.

"We compete in this town," Louisa said. "Someone else, they compete better."

Claire looked at her. "Southern Charm?"

Louisa shrugged. "Maybe. Maybe no."

Was Belle Mason taking advantage of Maggie's absence? It was common knowledge the two of them publicly feuded and intensely disliked one another. The exact reason why had never been clear, at least not to Claire. Her relationship with her mama had never been one of intimate secrets, or of trust. It was disheartening, her lack of confidence in her mama's intentions. A sudden yearning overtook Claire—she could simply leave. She'd already done it, when she'd gone to Texas with Molly, but it hadn't taken long for her conscience and strong sense of obligation to pull her back to Las Vegas. Her time with the Ryan's had given her a taste of life as a *normal* person, and now a small part of her longed for the simple things—a real home, respectability, a man to love. Unbidden, an image of Logan's handsome face came to mind.

She was already nineteen years old. The longer she stayed at the Dove, the more likely she'd soon be serving drinks and climbing the stairs to a room on the second floor.

Alice May entered from the kitchen, stopping abruptly when she saw Claire, surprise evident on her face. Dressed conservatively in a dark skirt and white blouse, it appeared she'd just returned from town.

"Is something wrong?" Claire asked.

Alice hesitated and flicked a glance to Louisa, who had halted her table cleaning once again.

In her mid-thirties, Alice was, as Claire had heard her called, a career girl—serious about moving on to bigger and better things. With a pretty face framed by strawberry-blonde curls and a figure more well-rounded than most of the other girls, Alice had made no secret that Las Vegas was just a stop on her way to Denver.

"Well," she said slowly. "I hope you won't take this the wrong way, Claire, but I've just come from a visit with Belle."

Claire had a feeling what was coming next. "She's made you an offer?"

Alice nodded. "I'm grateful to Maggie, but who knows when she's coming back. I can't turn my back on more money. And Belle's refurbished the Southern Charm. I hate to say it, but it's a step up."

At one time, the White Dove had simply been a brothel. To increase profits, Maggie had expanded it to a saloon, catering to men who wanted drinks and gambling as well as those who desired something more from the women who served them.

"Why do you think Maggie isn't returning soon?" Claire asked.

"Belle told me she's not been seen in Cimarron."

"But I thought that's where she took Jimmy. You yourself told me."

Alice threw her hands up in defense. "Don't blame me. That's what Maggie told us before she left. But if she's not in Cimarron, and she's not here, then where is she? Look, I know she wasn't herself after you disappeared, and since we all feared you were dead, I'm sure that's what she thought too. I don't blame her for trying to get away, but it seems to me more and more each day that she's abandoned the business but forgot to tell the rest of us. Maybe Ellie might step forward and buy it, but I'm not getting that tied down. I just need a few more months of consistent work then I'll be able to pack my bags and move on."

An uneasy suspicion settled over Claire. "Where have Griffin and Sandoval been seen lately?"

Alice sighed. "Well, Rusty Simmons told me the other day they've been in Cimarron. You think there's a connection?"

She did, but Claire had no desire to share her thoughts with Alice or any of the other girls. She hadn't told them Sandoval had been the one to attack her, and none of them had indicated any knowledge of what had happened, so Claire had concluded that Maggie hadn't told them. Obviously Maggie hadn't told anyone since Sandoval was a free man. Her mama must have had a reason for not bringing Raul Sandoval to justice for what he'd done; she had to believe that. The alternative made Claire's heart race with panic—that her mama simply didn't care.

"I don't know," Claire replied. "I was just curious."

"Maybe you shouldn't be hiding," Alice said. "Maybe if Maggie found out you were here, she'd return."

"Possibly." Claire wasn't sure what to think anymore. If her mama was involved with Griffin and Sandoval, then it probably wasn't good. In the end, Claire knew she couldn't influence Maggie Waters, but there was Jimmy to consider. Too young to decide the course of his life, it was up to Claire to look out for him because God knew Maggie had never done a great job at it.

Claire stood and collected the ledger. "I'll be in my room."

"There's one other thing." Alice wouldn't look her in the eye. "Belle wants Louisa, too."

Claire glanced at the sultry Mexican, but Louisa's face remained impassive. That's when Claire knew that Belle hadn't contacted the two women—they had taken an offer directly to Southern Charm.

"I understand." Claire moved past Alice, aware the business had just fallen apart. She went out the back door and crossed the yard to her cabin, feeling shock. Alice and Louisa were the only prostitutes currently working at the White Dove. Ellie was in no shape to resume her duties, and unless Betsy could suddenly be convinced to disrobe and spread her legs—Claire grimaced inwardly from the crude imagery. The only one left to maintain the business was Claire herself.

No.... No. She couldn't do it.

*Where the hell are you, Maggie?*

Once inside her cabin, she slammed the door shut in frustration.

---

"Are you from Texas, Señor?"

Logan glanced up from his plate of smoked ham, potatoes, and carrots to see an older Hispanic woman addressing him. "Yes, ma'am."

"I'm *Señora* Chavez."

Logan cleaned his fingers with a napkin and stood before taking the hand she extended in greeting. Dressed in a fine black gown with gold buttons reaching to her neck and black hair twisted into a neat bun atop her head, she smiled politely at him.

"Logan Ryan."

"I am sorry to interrupt your dinner, *Señor* Ryan, but I was speaking with my friend *Señora* Baca just down the street and she said that a gentleman had been around today asking about the Griffins."

"Yes, that's true. Please have a seat." He gestured for her to take the chair opposite him.

He'd spent the day searching for information about Dee and her brother but had turned up only the basics. They lived here most of the time but weren't in residence at the moment, Frank had several business ventures around town but was generally not held in high regard, and there was a sliver of sympathy for Dee since her husband had died suddenly after the Christmas holidays. Stopping at the Graaf City Bakery and Restaurant to eat, Logan was considering whether he really wanted to pursue Dee or not. Thoughts of Claire lingered in the back of his mind and the desire to see her again was strong, although he could think of no legitimate reason to return to the White Dove except to drink and gamble. Perhaps he'd do well to pick up a few vices.

"Are you a lawman?" *Señora* Chavez asked.

"Used to be. Now I help my pa raise cattle in Texas."

"Do you have business with *Señor* Griffin?"

"No. I'm an old friend of his sister's. I was hoping to say hello."

*Señora* Chavez nodded and drummed her fingers on the table. A young girl approached the table to take the woman's order but was promptly waved away.

"I was hoping you might be here to investigate him. I will be blunt—*Señor* Griffin ruined my husband financially. And Dee Luttrell, or Griffin, or whatever she calls herself these days, is no better than the harlots that work the saloons and disgusting bordellos in town."

Logan took note of the woman's disdain of the seamier side of town.

"You're saying Miz Griffin is a prostitute?" he asked carefully.

"Oh, I do not know. Probably no, she does seem to love her little boy. But she has no mind of her own. Is it not the same thing?"

Dee had a child? The knowledge that she'd moved on with her life, with never a backward glance, stung.

"Are you certain you do not hold any jurisdiction in these parts?" *Señora* Chavez continued, her earnest expression dragging Logan back to the conversation.

"Quite certain, ma'am. Didn't you take your concerns to the local officials?"

She glanced around before answering, her voice lowered. "*Señor* Griffin controls them, do not ask how, that I do not know. It was useless to go to the sheriff."

"What about Raul Sandoval? Is he involved somehow?"

A look of horror flashed in her eyes. "*¡Póngote las cruces!*" She crossed herself, then whispered, "*El maldito.*" Shaking her head, she added, "The devil."

"Do you know where Frank and Dee Griffin are right now?"

*Señora* Chavez shrugged, her shoulders sagging in defeat. "Cimarron, maybe. But I do not care what becomes of them. Perhaps you will consider what I have told you. Perhaps you can bring justice to those of us who are undeserving of our fate."

A tall order. *Tell your husband to stop trusting dishonest men*, he wanted to tell her. But he'd trusted Dee at one time. Misplaced faith could happen to anyone. "I'll keep it in mind, ma'am."

---

CLAIRE'S EYES skimmed the shelf above her bed as she sat in the one-room dwelling. During the past few years, she had collected several books on math and Latin after hearing talk that army doctors were tested on such things. Many a night she had read until her eyes ached and her head hurt trying to understand the many symbols and formulas that often frustrated her but which she eventually fathomed. For a moment, she considered muddling through a page of calculus, but her mind was hardly focused enough to make the effort worthwhile.

Her thoughts returned to Logan as she wondered if he'd already left town—her mind filled with images she had no business thinking. Never before had she been so drawn to a man, his presence unsettling her from the moment they'd met in Texas. In the darkness of his bedroom he'd startled her, naked from head to toe, triggering an automatic response in Claire to get away from him. But now, with so many endless nights to dwell on the encounter, her dreams had twisted the scene into one where she doesn't scramble for cover and demand he leave. Instead, she allows him to stay, and without words he obliges. In the shadowy scene she struggles to memorize every inch of him, her body's response both frightening and exciting. But always she awakens before he touches her....

She shook off the dream and reminded herself again of her

situation. She lived in a saloon. Her social standing equaled the droppings from a horse. Extending herself, even in friendship, would only bring heartache. And to engage in more was not something she could tolerate. She'd seen firsthand what sex, outside of marriage, could do to a woman.

Knowing this, however, didn't lessen the almost oppressive sadness she felt in knowing Logan was leaving town today. The man had succeeded in scattering her thoughts, and she wondered if they would ever be in order again.

There was also the more pressing problem of Maggie's whereabouts and the fact that beginning tomorrow morning Claire would be forced to close the White Dove, or at least run it without *entertainment*.

She thought of Jimmy. She'd mothered him as if he was her own child and not her brother. If nothing else, she needed to find him.

And to do that, it was becoming apparent she couldn't keep hiding.

At nightfall, she would leave for Cimarron.

---

DUSK SETTLED over the plaza as Logan leaned against a hitching post. He ran a thumb over the dove carving he held in his hand.

Why did the idea of leaving Claire behind bother him so much?

"You look like a man not certain where to go." One-Eyed Jack appeared beside him.

"Just thinking, that's all." Logan shook the man's hand.

"I've been known to do that, from time to time. Tia claims that's when I usually get a headache." Jack settled against the post and crossed his arms.

Together they watched the movement of men and women, freight wagons and buggies, horses and an occasional dog.

Enclosed on all sides by one and two-story commercial adobe

buildings, the plaza was the main thoroughfare for the Santa Fe Trail, which entered and exited via easterly and westerly outlets. The perimeter buildings comprised several merchants, two hotels, a hardware store, the Graaf City Bakery and Restaurant, and a bank. There was also a billiard saloon right next door, but only one saloon interested Logan in this town.

A large, odd-shaped windmill stood at the center of the plaza, comprised of two platforms, one above the other, which gave the structure an incredible height. Rumor was it had been used more than once to hang a man. Logan didn't find that too hard to believe— he'd come across a lynching or two in his time. Although in both cases he'd been too late to save the man at the end of the rope.

His gaze swept the plaza once more. Porticoes surrounded all the ground level storefront facades, as well as some on the second level. The columns that supported the porches were whitewashed which lent an endless unity among all the dwellings.

Logan glanced across the street and watched the crowd moving back and forth before the blackened remains of several buildings.

"Romero Building," Jack said. "The fire started there then burned the other two places. Happened a few weeks ago."

"Any injuries?" Logan caught sight of a man atop a horse, wrapped in a large Mexican blanket and wearing a wide, floppy sombrero.

"Thankfully, no."

*Not a man, a woman.*

"Sonofabitch."

"I think they'll rebuild," Jack said. "The Romero's have always done well in town."

"Is that Claire?" Logan asked. The horse was definitely old Reverend. He'd returned the animal to the saloon that morning.

Jack squinted in the same direction. "Now, why would you say that? Tia told me she was hiding until her ma returned. I was sworn to secrecy." Jack made a humming sound in his throat. "That hat seems a might too big."

"Where's she goin'?"

"That's the way out of town. The soldiers use it to and from Fort Union. It'll also take you up to Cimarron."

"She's leaving." Logan realized he might never see her again. He didn't like it.

"Hmm. Claire's a strong girl, I've always thought so." Jack looked at Logan. "But she's stubborn, too. All females are, really. Tia and me looked after her as much as we could, but we're getting old. If you've a mind to help out, we'd be much obliged."

"You think she's in trouble?"

Jack eyed the darkening sky. "I think night comes." His gaze met Logan's. "Go after her, son. You want to anyway. Would it help if I kicked you in the ass?"

Logan's mouth turned up at the corner. "Maybe."

"Stop talking and get out of here."

Logan adjusted his hat. "Yes, sir." He nodded toward Jack as he hurried to retrieve his gear from the hotel and Storm from the stables.

# CHAPTER 4

C laire knew the most logical course of action was to wait until morning to head out, but instead decided she needed the cover of night. Despite this, however, she still donned a new disguise.

The sky faded to black as she left the outskirts of town and headed north along the well-worn Santa Fe Trail. The path forged a noticeable rut, several wagons wide, across the open plains, yellow grama grass on either side. To the west, the distinct outline of the Sangre de Cristo Mountains marked the horizon. Unusual Hermit's Peak was also visible, a prominent landmark just outside the town. Jutting from the ground, the peak was a pale contrast of sheer rocky cliffs and flat expanse, slanting upward at an angle as if the earth had tried to shove it out of its interior in one huge geological burst. Serving as a visual beacon, it reminded Claire of the last fourteen years she'd spent living in this place, of memories good and bad, of dreams and hopes that had filled her head when reality became too much to bear.

Despite Maggie's dedication to the business, there were times when she would—out of the blue—take Claire, and Jimmy after he was born, into the wilderness. Her favorite spot was at the base of Hermit's Peak. If happy times existed in Claire's childhood most of them had occurred during these *breaks* from being the outcasts of society. She and her mama would build a fire, make a stew of rabbit and potatoes, and sleep under the stars. Only then had Maggie ever spoken of the life she'd led before Claire was born, of her own childhood in Charleston and the family that hadn't approved of her out-of-wedlock pregnancy.

"The sunsets are different back east," Maggie had said more than once. "Not like the ones here with all the orange and red flames in the sky. My pa used to take me into the mountains, and I remember those times at dusk when God would paint the world with lavender and violet."

Guilt washed over Claire. Her mama had endured a difficult life after leaving South Carolina alone, headed west, but had done her best to give Claire and Jimmy a roof over their heads and food to eat. It would be wrong of Claire to turn her back on everything Maggie had worked so hard to achieve. Whether she found her mama or not, Claire knew she needed to try and salvage the business at the White Dove upon her return from Cimarron.

She removed the heavy blanket and tied it behind her but found it difficult to keep the large hat on her head as the horse moved more quickly. Once she was far enough out of town, she removed the sombrero and let her blonde braid trail down her back.

Claire pushed Reverend as much as she thought he could handle, aware that, at any moment, he might refuse to go any farther. The older he got, the more obstinate his disposition had become. Cimarron was about fifty miles to the north, and although it was unlikely she'd get far tonight, she hoped to put a good distance between her and town before she made camp.

Diverging from the main trail, she moved closer to the foothills and better cover. Nightfall blanketed the land, and a smattering of stars filled the sky. Claire breathed deeply and realized how good it felt to leave the confinement of the saloon. Out here in the wilderness, alone save for the wind in the trees and the strong smell of pine, she felt settled in a way she hadn't for some time. A glance at the sky made her wonder if Logan was looking at the same patch of starry brightness, surely many miles from her, on a road back to Texas. She took another deep breath and tried to push him from her mind.

Maybe one of these days she would return to the SR to visit Molly. Logan would undoubtedly be married with a house full of children by then. The thought saddened her.

*It's not for you to have, Claire, so let it go.*

The approach of a rider sent a chill down her spine, making her realize how vulnerable she was, alone in the middle of nowhere. The man saw her, effectively cutting off the prospect of sidestepping him until he passed. With a pounding heart, Claire moved Reverend forward at a steady gait and hoped the encounter would pass without much fuss. As they neared each other, the rider turned his horse and forced her to stop.

"Whatcha doin' out here?"

Claire wished she hadn't removed the blanket and sombrero, feeling exposed without the buffer of a disguise. She wore trousers and a man's shirt she'd found in Maggie's room—the original owner's identity a mystery—but her hair was harder to hide.

The bearded face looked familiar. She could only trust he didn't recognize her from the saloon and would let her pass.

"I'm not looking for any trouble," she said in a quiet voice. "If you don't mind, I'll just be on my way."

"You travelin' alone, honey?"

"No, I'm meeting up with my husband at Ocate Crossing." She flinched inside at the lie. Ocate Crossing was still another twenty miles away, too far to scare the man with the threat of a husband that didn't exist.

"Well, that's a ways off, ain't it? What kinda man let's his wife ride alone at night?"

"Thank you for your concern, but I'll just be on my way." Claire guided her horse around the man. And that's when she remembered who he was—Harry Myers, one of Frank Griffin's men. Claire didn't like Griffin, despite her mama's long history with the man. Or, maybe because of it. Either way, she had no desire for Griffin to learn she was alive and back in town. He would likely tell Sandoval. A bone-deep fear surfaced at the thought of the cunning Mexican and the relentless beating that had almost killed her.

"I think maybe you should let me help you, miss," Harry said as he reached to grab her.

Claire tried to avoid his hand, but he had hold of her wrist and started pulling her toward him. "Let go of me." She yanked her arm out of his grasp.

Now that he was closer, he stared at her more intently. "You look a lot like that Water's woman. Ain't you her daughter?"

"I'm just passing through," Claire said and made to ride, but Harry grabbed her again. "Let go of me!"

He clutched her harder, and she slipped out of the saddle. Stunned by the fall, she bit her tongue, the metallic taste of blood coating her mouth. Rolling to her knees, she started to run as she heard him jump off his horse.

"Goddammit, c'mere!" He snatched her around the waist. Despite her struggle to stay upright, he pushed her to the ground. "Why you fightin' me so much? This don't have to hurt. I just wanna have some fun."

Claire landed on her back while the man loomed over her. She twisted her hand free and smacked him hard across the face—pain bolted from her fingers down to her elbow. In an instant, Sandoval's attack spilled into her mind and a frenzy of rage and terror overtook her.

Kicking, screaming, and clawing she went crazy against Myers, tears streaming down her face as she fought him with a fury that consumed her. Then the man was gone, and her arms and legs flailed against nothing. Ragged breathing filled her ears—it was her own. She sat upright and blinked frantically to focus. Maybe she was dreaming.

*Logan!*

She watched as he pushed his boot into Harry's back and forced the man's face to the ground, then bent one of Harry's arms painfully behind him. He pointed a gun at the man's head. "You worthless piece of shit," Logan said. "Do you always attack defenseless women?"

"I wasn't gonna hurt her," Harry gasped. "I thought she was lyin' about a husband."

"If I kill you now and dump your body in the hills, no one would find you for a long time."

"Jesus," Harry said in a rush. "This was jussa mistake."

With a jerk Logan dragged Harry to his feet. "I have a long memory."

Harry loped awkwardly to his horse, jumped atop him and rode off, leaving a cloud of dust in his wake.

Logan holstered his gun and walked to where Claire sat. He knelt down. "Are you all right?"

Claire nodded, still stunned. "What are you doing out here?" she whispered.

"I've been following you."

"Why?"

"Damned if I know." He helped her to stand. "But it's a good thing I did. Do you know him?"

Claire sniffed and wiped her face, feeling a bit self-conscious. "Yes, but not well. His name is Harry Myers. I don't think he recognized me. Well, no, he did guess who I was." She frowned. "Maybe he'll forget. You were very persuasive."

"Who're you hiding from? Sandoval?"

His accurate guess surprised her.

"It was Tia's guess," he said. "Let's make camp, and maybe you can tell me what's really going on."

"You should be halfway to Texas by now," Claire said, but was heartily glad he wasn't.

"Yeah, well, the scenery around here is starting to grow on me."

Tears sprang to her eyes once more. Before Logan could notice, she turned to her horse and pulled into the saddle. She knew she shouldn't involve Logan in her problems but was overcome by a strong impulse to throw herself into his arms. For once, she wanted to feel safe. For once, she wanted to trust someone. And for once, she wanted to believe that men were more than the ones who patronized the White Dove. A tall order, even for a man like Logan to fulfill.

"Let's get out of sight," he said from his own horse. For a moment he watched her, then said gently, "You should eat something. Flapjacks are my specialty."

"It's well past breakfast."

"Then I'll just have to cook for you twice."

He never failed to keep her slightly off-balance. "I don't think I've ever had a man cook for me."

"Then you're in for a real treat."

And she'd never had a man offer to *treat* her.

Claire followed him into the darkness.

---

THE FIRE CRACKLED BETWEEN THEM. Claire sat on a blanket on one side while Logan sat across from her. He quickly deduced she'd brought very little with her, so it was just as well he'd trailed her. He was accustomed to helping folks—his ma had told him often enough

45

it was his calling. And that was all he was doing with Claire, he told himself. Helping a woman in need.

She was clearly shaken from Myers' attack. The urge to shoot the son-of-a-bitch had pulsed unnaturally through Logan's veins, surprising him with its intensity. He wasn't the type of man to hold a grudge. But seeing Myers force himself on Claire hadn't sat well with Logan. Not at all. One thing saved Myers—Logan's deputy days still rang strong in his head. Killing a man in cold blood wasn't something he could stomach, although he definitely would've roughed Myers up a bit more if Claire hadn't been there.

Now that he'd gotten some food and water into her, she appeared calmer, and her color looked a damn sight better.

"Are you headed to Cimarron?" he asked.

She nodded.

"Any particular reason?"

"To find my mama." She sat with her legs crossed and held a tin cup of coffee between her hands.

Despite a slight chill in the air, sleeping outside wouldn't be uncomfortable. Still, Logan planned to grab his extra blanket and offer it to her.

"Is she in trouble?" he asked.

"You seem to think that's all I'm good for," she said with a sad laugh.

"Trouble? I'm just worried about your welfare, Claire, and I get the feeling you've never had anyone to look out for you. Where's your pa?"

Claire shrugged. "I don't know. I never knew him. Mama brought us here when I was five."

"And you've lived all this time at the White Dove?"

"For the most part."

"Tia told me you're not a prostitute."

Claire's head snapped up. "And does that fine distinction make a difference to you?"

46

"Doesn't it to you?"

"I still live on the wrong side of town. I still mix with the wrong kind of people."

"You could choose to leave," he said matter-of-factly.

"Yes, I've thought of that, many times. But it's not so simple."

Logan threw another piece of wood on the fire. "Actually, in my experience, most things are that simple. If you're dealt a hand you don't like, then shuffle the cards and start over. Why don't you tell me what's going on."

Claire swallowed more coffee and stared into the fire. "Several months ago, my brother Jimmy and I were on a stage headed to Albuquerque with my mama. The stage was ambushed."

"By who?"

"A group of men," she answered. "One I knew."

"Sandoval?"

She nodded.

"Did they rob you?"

A pained expression crossed Claire's face. "That's what my mama thought at first. She told us not to struggle, to give them what they wanted. But the raid was something more. I could see it in my mama's eyes, as soon as she saw Sandoval in the group."

"What happened?"

The color drained from Claire's face. "He took me and told me not to struggle. As long as I didn't fight him then Maggie and Jimmy wouldn't be hurt." Her voice broke. "He told me that."

Logan glanced up at the stars, a restlessness gripping him. "You don't have to say what he did to you." He could piece it together in his own mind, and any which way it wasn't pretty.

She paused for a long moment. "He beat me until I was certain I would die." Her hands gripped the tin cup tightly, the whites of her knuckles showing.

"And no one stopped him?" The image swirled in his mind, accompanied by the sharp crackle of the fire as it consumed the wood. The urge for retribution surged through him like a flash flood. In a perfect world, he'd take care of Myers and Sandoval in one night, without a doubt finding satisfaction in the deed. But the world wasn't perfect, and evil went hand-in-hand with the living. That was a truth from which there was no escape.

"No."

"And no one found you?"

She shook her head. "Not until Molly. The details aren't clear to me—how long I was out there, how long I'd been with Sandoval. Eventually, he left me in the desert." She took a deep breath. "I thought maybe Molly was my guardian angel when she rode up on her horse and found me."

"Why did you come to Texas? Why didn't you return to town and press charges against him?"

Claire shifted her legs and wouldn't meet his gaze. "A bit of cowardice and a bit of anger, I suppose. I had a feeling there was more to it, that somehow...." Her voice faltered. "That maybe my mama knew." She shook her head. "I just wanted to get away from it all, and Molly presented an opportunity, so I took it. Maybe I shouldn't have gone. You certainly wouldn't be here right now if I hadn't."

"No. I wouldn't." But he couldn't imagine being anywhere else, despite his brief indecision over whether to follow Claire or not. "Why do you think your ma knew that Sandoval was going to attack you?"

"No, I don't think she knew or planned it. But it seemed to me it wasn't a surprise when he showed his face. And why would he do that? I think he wanted her to know it was him." She set her cup down and rubbed her arms. "And he wanted me to know."

Logan stood and grabbed a blanket from his things. He shook it out and walked around the fire to place it on her shoulders, his hands lingering as he enjoyed the feel of her. When he realized he'd overstayed his welcome, he gave her a friendly pat on the arm and returned to his spot near the fire, frustrated from wanting more.

He didn't want to give her a friendly pat on the arm, he wanted to kiss her, and touching her only made the desire more urgent. But he sensed that a move from him might make Claire so skittish she would ask him to leave her alone.

"Why?" he asked.

Claire pulled the blanket around her. "He came after me once."

With effort Logan remained silent so she would continue, but a sharp longing surfaced—he wished he had known Claire earlier, before all this happened. Maybe he could have prevented it.

She glanced at him. "I tricked him, slipped a concoction into a glass of whiskey that made him sick and unable to function."

Logan blinked, uncertain he'd heard her correctly, then he nodded in comprehension. "Good for you."

"Maybe.... But I don't think he forgot. I was in a rush and gave him more than I should. He was in bad shape for days."

"Served him right." Logan considered the information. "So Sandoval attacked you as revenge?"

"Maybe. That was probably part of it. But my mama has been involved with Frank Griffin for years, and Sandoval is Frank's...." She struggled to find the word.

"Lap dog? He does Frank's dirty work?"

Silently Claire agreed.

"What's Maggie's relationship with Frank?"

"She met him in Denver when I was five years old and followed him here. She loves him—I guess you could call it love—but it's more like an obsession. She claims Jimmy is his son. Frank used to come around a lot, but not so much during the past year; that's when Mama started acting strange. Frank has a sister, her name is Dee I think, and her husband died around Christmas. I've thought a lot about it and it was around that time Mama became...nervous, even a little paranoid."

Logan let Claire's reference to Dee pass. Perhaps he should explain his connection to Frank's sister, but for whatever reason he didn't feel like dredging up his past. Claire was opening up to him, and he didn't want to stifle her impulse...and trust.

"You think there's a connection between that man dying and what Sandoval did to you?" Logan wondered also if Maggie Waters had been involved in the death of Teddy Luttrell, but, again, he didn't want to put Claire on the defensive, so he didn't voice his suspicion.

Claire shrugged. "I don't know, but finally Mama said we were taking a holiday to Albuquerque and piled Jimmy and me into the stage. It felt like she was running away from something, but as usual, she wouldn't talk about it."

"You're going to Cimarron to find her?"

She nodded. "The girls in the saloon said she traveled north with Jimmy. It would make sense she'd go to Cimarron. Frank and Sandoval have been seen there."

"So, you thought you'd waltz right in and check it out?"

"What else could I do?" Displeasure flashed in her eyes, and Logan caught a glimpse of the fiery woman Claire kept well-hidden.

"You realize how foolhardy this is, trying to find your ma and Jimmy alone?"

"Well, in case you hadn't noticed, there was no one around to accompany me." Claire's body became rigid, and anger filled the air between them.

"You could've asked for my help." Damn, he sounded resentful.

"No."

When she didn't elaborate further, he mentally added headstrong to her list of personality traits.

Frustrated, he said, "I'm here now, and in light of everything you've told me, you could use backup." He continued before she could interrupt. "You best get some sleep. We'll head out at first light."

She watched him. "Why are you doing this, Logan? Why are you here?"

*Because your eyes remind me of springtime in Montana, because your hair is as bright as the sun warming the Texas plains, because your presence makes me think of longing and release, of gentle breezes and endless possibilities.*

"To help you," he said simply.

# CHAPTER 5

S hortly after sunrise Claire changed into a blue cotton dress, wrinkled but still presentable, and she and Logan continued the trek to Cimarron. Having slept fitfully, she wondered again why he was with her. She felt the pull between them—it was hard not to —and honestly couldn't believe he would abandon his family responsibilities to make certain she was safe. But a part of her was so relieved to have him with her that she didn't care what his reasons might be.

As if in a dream she suddenly had a man by her side who, by all accounts, was fair-minded, kind and hard working. A man from a respectable ranching family, a man who shouldn't be dealing with the likes of her. While she had never sold herself, her reputation had been set at the age of five when her mother began servicing men from the small shack they occupied on the edge of town. It hadn't taken long for Claire to realize she was different, unable to go to the same schools as the other children, the same churches, or even the same social functions. In all her nineteen years, she'd never formed a close friendship with another girl.

Not until Molly.

During their time together, Claire came to see that her new

friend had also lived in the gray areas of life—Molly understood how survival bred hard choices and recognized the necessity of holding onto dreams of a better tomorrow. Claire did have aspirations for the future, but the harsh reality of her life often dragged those dreams back to the ground. So her longings remained unattainable goals— fantasies—not unlike the mythical tales of knights and princesses she would tell Jimmy at bedtime.

To envision a future with a man like Logan was surely the most whimsical wish she'd ever entertained. A woman could give her body easily—her mama had demonstrated that—but the heart was another matter. Claire would never give her body or heart, not unless she was absolutely certain of the outcome, and what man would hang around long enough for her to decide?

They rode hard until they passed Fort Union, the buildings and men noticeable in the distance, situated as it was in the middle of a flat, open plain. Near the shade of a tree they stopped and let the horses take a rest while Logan distributed water he had brought.

"Are you always so prepared?" Claire asked. She placed the large Mexican hat onto her head to shield the sun from her eyes.

"There's always a minimum you should carry. Water, rations, blankets." He looked her square in the eye. "Weapons."

It almost sounded as if he scolded her. "Are you trying to tell me something?"

Logan started to speak, then stopped and blew out a breath. Turning to face her, he planted hands casually on his lean hips and watched her. "Do you even know how to defend yourself?"

Claire squinted and pressed her lips together. "Well, there's a gun kept at the saloon. It's used to control unruly customers."

"You've handled it?"

"Mmm, no. We don't keep any bullets in it, but I've touched it once or twice." Claire realized how pathetic her statement sounded. "Mama always felt it was too dangerous to keep it loaded, one of the girls could be shot. And while business was usually good, she didn't want to waste money on a better firearm or ammunition. It was bad enough that the merchants overcharged her for liquor and food. And then there were the monthly fines when the girls were dragged to jail for solicitation. Not much rhyme or reason to it, but it always seemed worse when the more upstanding citizens in town complained too much."

"Would that include *Señora* Chavez?"

Surprised, Claire nodded. "Do you know her?"

"Briefly acquainted, yes."

*Señora* Chavez had always been a vocal opponent of all saloons, gambling establishments, and dance halls in town. Claire had wondered how it was possible for one woman to stick her nose into so many people's business and still have time to raise a family.

"The woman enjoys making trouble," Claire said. "Maggie always had high standards when it came to hiring the girls, but none of them were familiar with handling a gun. Men didn't come to the saloon looking for a woman who could shoot anyhow—their minds were elsewhere."

She instantly regretted the rush of words. Logan watched her, his gaze penetrating, unrelenting. Unreadable. His jaw flexed, and she had a wild thought that maybe he was thinking of her as a man would when his mind was *elsewhere*. The idea made her a little lightheaded.

"You should at least have a basic understanding. I'll teach you." He withdrew his gun and moved beside her. "This is a .44 Colt Army revolver, sometimes called a Peacemaker or M1873."

"What does the forty-four mean?" She eyed the long barrel.

"It's the size of the cartridge. I can use forty-fours in my Winchester rifle as well. Makes it a little easier, not having to carry two different types of bullets.

"There's a six-barrel cylinder," he continued. His fingers efficiently released a hinged gate on the side of the gun. "This is part of the recoil shield, but you have to move it aside to load the cartridges." He made fast work ejecting the bullets that were already in the gun. "There's a spring-loaded ejector rod that helps you remove unused cartridges or spent casings." Logan dropped the bullets into his shirt pocket. He flipped the gate back into place and handed the gun to Claire. "Let's lose the hat," he added softly, and tossed the large round contraption to the ground.

"Be careful with that." She tried to grab the sombrero from him. She also tried to ignore his proximity. "That was a gift."

"I'm relieved. I thought I might have to school you in the proper attire for a lady. You're too pretty to keep hiding behind all these disguises."

"I'm not a lady," she murmured.

"Could've fooled me." He grinned at her. For a moment, his eyes flashed with more than amusement. Or had she imagined it?

She concentrated on the heavy weapon in her hand before she got herself into trouble by saying something silly.

"Cock the hammer like this." His arms moved around her from behind and their fingers touched as his thumb pulled the hammer back, clicking it into place. "You sight your target by lining up the groove here." He ran a finger along the top, indicating the slot cut into the rear part of the gun. "Then match it with the sight here." He pointed to the raised notch at the tip of the barrel.

Claire tried her best to ignore the man and concentrate on the gun, but it proved difficult. The lingering odor of coffee and the morning cook fire mixed with the more appealing scent of the man himself. She paused to regain her composure.

Logan guided her other hand to the firearm and straightened her arms. "This gun is heavy so it's probably best if you use both hands. I'll get you something smaller next chance I get. Line up your sights, but if you're in a mad rush just aim for a man's chest. You'll likely hit something, slowing him down. Why don't you take some practice clicks." He stepped away from her and she immediately missed his touch, however impersonal it may have been.

After she did his exercise, he took the gun and inserted two bullets. "When it's loaded, it'll have a kick so be prepared. You're not that petite, so as long as you hold your ground you should be all right."

Claire wondered if he preferred petite women.

"Let's get away from the horses," he continued. "Mine won't spook, but I doubt yours is used to gunfire."

She followed behind as he led her about an eighth of a mile toward the foothills. He pointed at a pine tree with a wide trunk. "Let's use that one as a target."

She raised the gun and spread her legs as she cocked the hammer, trying to sight on the tree. When she pulled the trigger, the force of the discharge pushed her into the firmness of Logan's chest.

Surprisingly, he laughed, his hands coming to rest on her hips. "That wasn't bad. You held your ground pretty good. Let's try it again."

Logan let her shoot several rounds, and by the end she had hit the target seven times. "You've got a good eye," he said as they walked back toward camp. "You sure you've never shot a gun before?"

"You're my first." Appalled by what she'd just said, she struggled to hide her embarrassment. *This is what happens when you spend your life around fancy girls.*

"I'm not sure I remember my first."

Uncertain she heard him correctly, her voice was barely a squeak as she said, "Pardon?"

She caught the twinkle in his eye and realized he teased her. A slight smile tugged at her mouth.

"The first time I shot a gun," he said. "I suppose I was seven or eight."

"That seems terribly young." She lost her smile at the thought of giving Jimmy a gun.

"Not really. Boys'll be boys—guns, horses, fights. My pa figured it was better to teach us the right way than have us learn the wrong way on our own. Of course, he wasn't so forthcoming when it came to members of the opposite sex."

Claire gaped at him then snapped her mouth shut. The girls at the White Dove had often joked about a young kid coming in for his *first time.* Ellie claimed she'd done a fourteen-year-old once. The image had honestly turned Claire's stomach. What parent would let their child learn about sex at such a young age, and from a woman who was as old as his mother?

Despite the education Claire had received at the hands of the women who worked for her mama, she was still terribly naïve about what occurred between men and women, and what she saw only led her to believe that men needed sex and nothing more. Men could choose and women couldn't. It didn't seem right, it didn't seem fair, and Claire hadn't understood what was so compelling about it all.

A glance at Logan, however, gave her a clue.

"I think your pa was right to shelter you," she responded after sidestepping a patch of prickly pear.

Logan laughed. "Yeah, I suppose I'll feel that way about my offspring one day."

"Especially if they're girls," Claire said, mostly to herself. She was determined to give her children a life completely unlike her own. *If* she was ever blessed with any.

"Daughters," Logan said. "I never thought of that. I hope I'm up for it."

"I think you'll be a fine father one day."

He looked at her, an amused expression on his face. "Why Claire, I think you might actually like me."

"Because I just paid you a compliment? I'm just returning the favor."

"How's that?"

"You said I looked better as a blonde." Her face burned and she was certain she must be quite red in the cheeks. She would never forget his comment and now he knew it as well.

"You do. I always tell it like it is."

She stopped, and her eyes met his. "Always?"

"Yeah, always."

Looking into his blue-green gaze, the same enriching color as a blue spruce pine, Claire felt time fall away. She was caught in a web created by the two of them. The urge to go to him, to touch him in some way, even if only to hold his hand, pushed at her rigid control. The sheer intensity of the craving stunned her—she had never felt this way with any man. Every inch of her skin that had been exposed to Logan's hands when he'd taught her how to handle his gun felt inflamed. God, she wanted him to touch her again.

Her face betrayed her—she could see it in his eyes. Immediately his awareness of her was impossible to miss. Her body responded to his dark gaze, to the hungry desire she knew was all too physical, but a brief flash of shock in his expression brought her up short. Logan didn't want this any more than she did. It was a complication neither of them needed.

With effort, she broke the mood by shifting her focus to the ground and striding resolutely back to the horses.

They continued to ride north, slowly for a time so as not to tire the horses under the heat from a cloudless turquoise sky. The wind wafted off the mountains from their left, pushing past them onto the flat expanse.

"Have you always wanted to be a rancher?" She hoped small talk would ease the awkwardness of their unspoken attraction.

"No. I only just returned to Texas last year to help out my pa."

"Where were you before that?"

"I did odd jobs here and there. When I was nineteen I drove cattle in Montana, then worked as a scout for the army. After that, I moved freight in Kansas then lumberjacked outside of Denver. Once I got older and wiser, I became a deputy in Virginia City."

"You've seen so much, been so many places." Claire was more than a little envious.

"It's not all it's cracked up to be," he replied. "My ma thinks I wandered around too much. She's probably right."

"She's your mother. She's supposed to worry about you."

"I suppose. But now that Matt's gotten hitched, the old man is talkin' about dividing up the SR. He wants me to take a chunk."

"You're very fortunate. Your folks obviously worked hard to make that ranch successful."

Logan glanced at her. "What about you? You can't spend the rest of your life living in a saloon."

"No." She shifted the reins from one hand to the other. "But it's not that easy. I have no way to support myself."

"Isn't there something you'd like to do? Something you're good at?" His eyes met hers.

She rarely confided her dream to other people. It never seemed worth the effort. *Was Logan worth the trouble?* The thought came out of nowhere. Somewhere in the back of her mind a voice whispered yes.

"You don't want to tell me?" He smiled. "I'm not gonna bite you. I'm really a nice fella, when you get down to it. I've never once laughed at a woman's dreams."

She glared at him and shook her head. "Quit teasing me. You think life is simple? You're a man. Everything's easy for a man." She was unable to restrain the sharp edge in her voice.

He pretended to look for his gun. "Wait, let me make sure my gun's not loaded, or else you might shoot me. You learned faster than I thought you would anyhow."

She nailed him with an annoyed look, but he just laughed.

"Claire, you gotta lighten up. Tell me what you want to be when you grow up."

She turned her head away from him. The yellow grama grass swayed in the wind and she felt as important as an ant clinging to one of the wavering stalks. "If you must know, I want to be a doctor," she uttered quietly.

He whistled in response. "You can't be accused of shooting too low. You don't think this could happen?"

She looked at him like he hadn't the sense of a prairie dog. "I've no money, there's hardly a school in the country that takes women, and if you've already forgotten, I live in a whorehouse." She yelled the last part, her own frustrations bursting forth.

Logan raised an eyebrow. "I guess I must've forgot. Thanks for reminding me." His eyes still held that damn twinkle.

Discouraged, Claire kicked Reverend into a canter. She no longer wanted to talk about the state of her life. What pulled at her more than anything was that she'd end up selling herself eventually simply to survive. If that happened, she'd surely have to abandon any hope of something better.

They continued north, passing through Ocate Crossing and watering the horses at Rayado, a stagecoach stop with only a handful of buildings. The Sangre de Cristos flanked their progress, a protective barrier as the sun moved to a steady descent behind the hills. By late afternoon, they rode into Cimarron.

The town was located in the foothills, the mountains on the left a looming reminder of the mining hopes of the many men who ventured into the interior. Struck by the allure of the immense slopes, strongly outlined by the setting sun, Claire couldn't take her eyes off the promise of anonymity and peace the high country represented. Would losing herself in those hills give clarity to her life? Make all of the struggles disappear? It was an enticing thought, and an entirely unrealistic one, but she tucked the image away to revisit when needed.

They rode past the jail, the structure surrounded by a ten-foot-high stone wall, and guided their horses behind the Barlow, Sanderson & Company stage office. On the opposite side of the road

Claire noticed Schwenk's Hall and beyond was a three-story square building with a sign that read Aztec Grist Mill.

Glancing in the direction of Schwenk's again, Claire knew that soon women would start peddling their bodies to any man willing to pay for it. She wondered if her mama would be there. More than likely she was at the St. James—if she was here at all. She had frequently mentioned that saloon in the past.

They approached the Old National Hotel, situated across from a hardware and livery stable. Next to it sat a gazebo that covered a well. Having been here once before, Claire noted that not much had changed.

"I'm going to check the registry," she said and climbed down from Reverend, giving a tug on her skirt when it caught on the sombrero tied behind the saddle. "I'll be right back."

Logan nodded.

It didn't take long to learn that her mama's name wasn't in the hotel's logbook. She stewed over that while she returned to the porch and stared at several men to her right. One caught her eye—a tall Mexican with a splotchy, scarred face shaded by the brim of his hat. He walked toward them.

*Sandoval.*

Fear slammed through her. She struggled to breathe as her heart pounded at twice its speed.

Having tied the horses off, Logan climbed the porch to join her. Their eyes met and she closed the distance between them in one rapid movement. She brought her body into full contact with his and kissed him.

His lips were warm, but Claire was too tense to do anything other than stand there, her hands clutching his shoulders for dear life.

It was seldom life threw the unexpected at him, but Logan was surprised as hell by this woman suddenly all over him. It wasn't that the thought of kissing Claire had never crossed his mind or that her determined lip-lock undoubtedly had little to do with him, what astounded him most was her total lack of expertise in the task. As he broke the highly unromantic mating of their mouths, he said quietly, "I'm not a piece of wood, Claire."

He shifted so his body shielded her from anyone on the street and pushed her up against the hotel exterior. If it was a show she wanted, he'd teach her a thing or two about kissing a man while at it. Taking control of the situation, he brought his hands to the sides of her head and took her lips with his. She was a temptation he hadn't planned to indulge, but now he gave himself to the task with a focused tenacity. He would enjoy Claire like he'd wanted to since the first moment he laid eyes on her, months ago at the SR.

She hardly moved. And her eyes were wide open. "Relax," he murmured, and covered her mouth fully with his. Tentative, yes, but she wasn't completely unwilling. Slowly she yielded, her lips surrendering in small increments, teasing him with the promise of so much more.

Sweet and soft, he savored the intimate contact with her. He needed to touch her and now that he had, he wondered how long he could go before needing to again. He was a man who could control himself but damn if he wasn't close to tossing all that restraint to the wind. It'd been a long time since he felt this way about a woman.

"Are they gone yet?" he asked quietly. He still protected her with his body.

"What?" Her rapid breath and flushed face aroused him yet again, and he willed himself not to skim her curves with his hands. He took it as small comfort that she wasn't immune to him, no matter how hard she tried to pretend otherwise.

"I'm sorry I threw myself at you," she said in a frantic whisper. "I saw Sandoval and wanted to hide."

"You can hide behind me anytime." Logan allowed his thumb to caress her cheek before he turned around to scan the street. He wanted to get a good look at the bastard in question.

"He's gone," Claire said from behind him. "My mama's not at this hotel, but she could still be in town. I plan on staying the night. If you need to move on, I understand."

"No." He continued to scrutinize the street. "I'll be staying, too. I'll get us a room together."

"Pardon me?"

"There's no way in hell I'm leaving you alone if Sandoval is here. I'll sign us in as a married couple. Do you have a middle name?"

Claire appeared flustered and confused. Logan could certainly relate to that.

"Margaret," she replied. "Why?"

"Well, that won't do," he said. "I'll register us as Logan and Peggy Ryan."

She nodded uncertainly. "That kiss," she said, "you realize that I'm not going to...that I'm not going to entertain you, no matter how much you offer me."

Logan looked at her and enjoyed the appealing angles of her face, her small, straight nose, the green eyes that suddenly flashed with defiance. He supposed she wouldn't be worth the effort if she came to him easily. Not that he was pursuing her.

"I seem to recall you threw yourself at me, Claire, not the other way around. Your inexperience shows."

*Hell, that came out wrong.*

The flash of humiliation on her face confirmed it.

"Claire—" But she disappeared into the hotel before he could stop her.

*Nice going.*

He went inside and within ten minutes they were registered as

Mr. and Mrs. Ryan. In an uneasy silence they went to their room to get settled.

# CHAPTER 6

C laire sat in the tiny hotel room and waited for Logan to return. Despite the darkness of night, he still felt it too dangerous for her to be out in the open asking questions about Maggie Waters. Shortly after he brought her to the room, he left to see what he could learn on his own.

Getting to her feet, Claire began pacing. The room was small and simply furnished—a wooden chair and a narrow nightstand with a pitcher and basin atop it were placed near a broad window; an additional table stood against the wall opposite the bed, the white marble top perched on three spindly legs. A chamber pot sat discreetly in one corner. Then there was the modest double bed, covered by a faded blue quilt. It unwillingly drew her gaze again and again. A black, wrought iron frame marked the territory clearly, filling her mind with Logan, his mouth and his hands, *his presence*. The way he kissed her on the porch made her pulse quicken and her limbs feel weak, even in memory.

She wondered over and over why she'd pressed herself on him that way.

Fear.

Sandoval terrified her, and the sight of him had flooded panic in her. Vague images of her lying in a cactus-filled arroyo all those months ago clouded her thoughts—her face in the dirt, bloodied and beaten, her life slipping away. *Which desert animal would attack first and finish the job?*

This afternoon, her legs carried her to Logan, and instinct snagged his undivided attention as only a woman could. She'd wanted protection, and Logan would do the job. Obviously, she was desperate enough to get that protection in any way she could. She threw herself into his arms, then told him she wasn't available to him.

Claire closed her eyes and hung her head. A good prostitute would have at least followed through on the promise of payment. If her mama were here, she'd probably scold her for not using that most basic lesson of the business.

Everyone had a price. Even Claire.

She forced the thoughts aside. She would decide how to handle Logan later. Right now, she had family matters to consider.

It didn't make sense for her to stay put. Logan didn't know her mama or Jimmy, or what either of them looked like. In his haste to leave, she hadn't had the chance to tell him she'd brought along the wig.

She retrieved the black mop from her leather satchel as well as the black dress Louisa had loaned her. She debated whether to wear it, since she planned to check out the St. James Saloon. Would such a dress draw unnecessary attention, or would the simple cotton calico she'd also brought make her stand out more? For a few indecisive moments she wondered what to do, then quickly removed the trousers and oversized shirt she wore and wriggled into the saloon dress.

She'd forgotten the stockings, so she pulled the fancy black boots painfully over bare feet. She twisted her long hair into a bun and stuffed it beneath the wig as she positioned the black tresses around her shoulders, arranging it in, what she hoped, was a natural-looking display. A quick scan of herself in a small oval mirror on the wall above the nightstand showed a dreadful reflection—the wig did nothing for her complexion and the dress pushed her breasts together in an obscene display of skin. She grabbed the Mexican blanket and wrapped it around her shoulders like a shawl. A minor improvement.

Aware she couldn't just traipse out the front entrance of the hotel looking like this, she muttered thanks that their room was on the first floor and faced away from the street. She pushed the lacy curtains aside and groaned as her arms strained to push the window upward. She perched herself on the edge of the windowsill, swung her legs out, then leaned forward and fell to the ground in a muffled heap.

---

LOGAN PUFFED a cigar acquired at Schwenk's Hall as he crossed the street and headed toward the St. James. Folks in town were a bit skittish these days, if the talk he heard was any indication. Problems over the Maxwell Land Grant persisted—the investors who had taken it over in 1870 from Lucien Maxwell were trying to push squatters and settlers from their property, and if the rumors were correct, doing it in an underhanded way. Two years ago an outspoken Reverend Tolby, speaking against the false allegations directed at the townsfolk, was killed. It set off a chain of events that had left the local constable dead. More deaths had ensued, and people in town still distrusted the men who worked as official Grant Representatives. And the most interesting tidbit of all was that Luttrell had been one such representative.

Logan shook his head—two million acres of land. It was a damn powerful motivator, and he doubted Griffin and Sandoval had kept their hands clean of the mess.

So far, as he investigated various establishments around town, he'd found no sign of Maggie Waters or young Jimmy. He hoped to turn up something at the St. James. It was either that or return to the cramped hotel room, give Claire news she didn't want to hear, then attempt to keep his hands to himself. A few stiff drinks ought to cure that impulse.

*Like hell.*

He'd deal with sharing a room with Claire later.

He entered the saloon, scanned the crowded room, and headed to the bar at the back. He ordered bourbon and had no sooner taken his first sip, before a heavily perfumed and well-packaged young woman sauntered over to him and smiled.

"Evening," he said.

"It is now." She twisted her torso to make her ample bosom quite apparent to him.

She wore a breast-revealing deep red dress that made Logan think of Claire's saloon get-up.

"Haven't seen you around here before." She patted her thick red curls. "Would you like some company tonight?"

The answer to that last question was yes, but it was Claire's company he desired. Still, she might have useful information. "I'm in search of a blonde," he said, referring to Claire's description of her mama. She'd said the two of them looked almost like sisters.

The girl began to pout, which made her appear less attractive. "I may not be blonde, but I can still show you a good time." She lowered her voice and winked. "And I'm red everywhere. That's what everyone calls me...Red."

Logan laughed and swallowed his drink in one shot. He'd never figure out women, but they were damn interesting. "I'm lookin' for Maggie Waters. Seen her lately?"

"Maybe. Any particular reason?"

Logan shrugged. "What reason would a man need to look for a woman?"

The redhead scanned around the room then leaned close. "Just a bit of advice, handsome. Maggie Waters likes to stir up trouble. Why go chasin' after that? I'll take care of you." She stuck a finger into the open collar of his shirt and tickled his chest hair. "For as long as you like."

Logan removed her hand. Life had always slid around him rather easily, and rarely did it raise his shackles, but he didn't particularly care for Red's touch, as flattering as he supposed it was. But this wasn't flattery, Red was working. And his thoughts, and desire, were on a tightly wound woman who dreamt of becoming a doctor.

However, Red might know more than she was letting on, so he ordered another drink and settled in for a time.

---

CLAIRE STARED AT LOGAN AGAIN.

*The damned man isn't looking for my mama, he's looking for a good time.* The redhead was all over him, and he clearly enjoyed it. A sharp stab of disappointment and humiliation welled up in her. From experience she pushed it aside, but it wouldn't let her go. She'd grown up in a saloon, had seen men behave like this all the time. It was normal, it was expected, but watching Logan flirt with that woman cut Claire to the bone like nothing else ever had.

With tears in her eyes she ducked out of the saloon as quickly as she had entered and lost herself in the darkness behind the building. What should she do now?

"She cries for her boy at night. I'd watch your back."

Claire froze at the sound of that voice with a Mexican accent. *Sandoval.*

"I can take care of Didi, but this shit with Maggie is taking too long."

*Griffin!*

Quietly, she stepped farther into the shadows and peeked

around the corner of the building. Sandoval tied off his horse while Frank Griffin's tall frame stood in silhouette beside him. They disappeared into the saloon.

Claire's mind raced. Was her mama with them? Maybe they were holding her somewhere, against her will. And what about Jimmy? Her stomach clenched in protest, but she knew what she needed to do. And to do it, she would need her horse.

Quickly she ran to the next street and spotted the stable where she and Logan had left the animals before settling at the hotel. As she entered the structure, the scent of hay and manure overwhelmed her senses, causing her to pause and catch her breath. A young boy jumped to his feet from where he'd been dozing on a stool.

"I'd like to take my horse, please," Claire said. "Would you mind saddling that one?" She pointed to Reverend, who slumbered in a corner stall. She made a silent apology to her old friend for disturbing him.

"Yes, ma'am," the boy replied. He rubbed his eyes and squinted at her. "And who would you be?"

"Clai-" she stopped abruptly. "Mrs. Ryan."

The boy nodded. "That sounds 'bout right."

After what seemed an excruciatingly long wait, the boy saddled Reverend and brought the horse to her.

"Thank you." Claire moved swiftly out of the stable and led Reverend back to the St. James.

With relief, she saw that the two horses Sandoval and Griffin had tethered to the rail hadn't moved, indicating the two men remained inside the saloon. All she had to do was bide her time until they came back out, then follow them. She wiped her palms on the frilly skirt of her dress and waited nervously, several times reconsidering her plan, but ultimately deciding it was the best course of action.

THANKS to the redhead Logan learned that the two men who entered the saloon were Frank Griffin and Raul Sandoval. *Jackpot!* He half-listened to Red as he watched them.

Tall and lanky, Sandoval pushed back his shoulder-length black hair from his pockmarked face in greasy strands. Even if Logan hadn't known what the man had done to Claire, he would never have made the mistake of turning his back on him. Sandoval looked the type to betray his own mother if he thought it would save his hide. Logan knew Claire couldn't have stood a chance against this bastard.

But Logan would. Expectation thrummed in his veins as he anticipated a confrontation.

The men walked past where he sat, and Frank Griffin resembled Dee too much to leave any doubt that they were brother and sister. They shared the same brown hair—although Frank's had thinned— and the same enigmatic eyes, deep-set and compelling. On Dee the look had been seductive, on Frank it was simply shrewd and dangerous.

Griffin and Sandoval took seats at a table on the far side of the room where they ordered drinks and ogled an occasional saloon girl, but mostly they talked. And drank sparingly. Smart men. Then, suddenly, they were on their feet, headed for the door.

"Wouldn't you say?" the redhead was asking Logan.

"Yeah, sure." Logan threw a glance her way and pushed away from the bar. "Thanks for the conversation, Red, but it's time I was on my way."

"Hold on." She pulled on his arm. "I've spent a good hour with you. Aren't you gonna make it worth my while?"

"And here I thought you fancied my good looks." He turned, but through the window could still see Griffin and Sandoval headed around the side of the building. "It was your choice to chat with me."

"Are you daft? I don't want to chat with you. I'm trying to make a living here."

"It's always a crapshoot, darlin'." Logan shrugged. "I thought I made it clear, I have a thing for blondes." *One blonde in particular.* His mouth twitched slightly at the string of names Red called him, but he left without a backward glance.

He moved swiftly to the stable that housed Storm and immediately noticed that Reverend was missing. A slight shake to the stable boy woke him up.

"Where's the other horse I brought in earlier?" Logan asked.

"What?" the boy asked, blinking rapidly. "Oh, the lady came and took him."

"What lady?" Logan got a bad feeling. He seemed to have a lot of those lately since he'd found Claire.

"Mrs. Ryan."

"What did she look like?"

"Well, she was a right fine-lookin' lady, although she must've been headed for one of the saloons."

"Why?"

"Considerin' the way she was dressed." The boy scratched his mussed brown hair. "You two havin' marital problems?"

"You're too young to talk like that. What color was her hair?" he asked, a gnawing suspicion taking root in his gut.

"Black," the boy answered. "Almost didn't look real."

"No shit," Logan muttered. He should've known she wouldn't do what he told her. And it'd never occurred to him to rifle through her belongings, but in hindsight he probably should have. "Any idea where she went?"

"No, sir." The boy shook his head.

Logan pulled a coin from his pocket and gave it to the boy. "Saddle my horse and make it fast."

"Yes, sir." The boy hustled to the task.

CLAIRE DID her best to stay far enough behind Griffin and Sandoval as they rode through town so they wouldn't notice her, but twice she almost lost them. She pulled the Mexican blanket around her, yet still elicited unwanted attention from men as she rode by the other few establishments in town. Unfortunately, the blanket didn't cover her exposed legs and they seemed to be a beacon to any male within a quarter mile.

Claire had been to Cimarron once before, accompanying her mama to interview new girls for the saloon. Maggie hadn't felt well but refused to delay the journey, so Claire had insisted on coming to watch over her. She'd spent most of the time, however, at the hotel where she and Logan now resided, taking care of Jimmy. When they'd returned to Las Vegas, her mama had only acquired one girl—Louisa Pérez.

Griffin and Sandoval headed toward the mountains and away from the cluster of buildings in town. The main road was part of the Santa Fe Trail—the very lifeblood of the community—which wound its way through the center of town. But there had to be more to this place than Trail business, Claire thought, as she moved into unfamiliar terrain.

She lagged farther behind, afraid her horse might be heard. Luckily, there was a clearly marked path so she followed it and hoped she wouldn't lose them, hoped also they wouldn't see her.

*What am I doing out here?*

Trying to find out what happened to Mama and Jimmy, she reminded herself. She would head back to the hotel as soon as she made certain the two of them weren't wherever it was Griffin and Sandoval were going. She needed to keep her mind on that goal. Hopefully Logan would be none the wiser.

An image of him and the redhead flashed to mind. If she caught him in their room, with that woman...the man would certainly have more sense than that. *Damn him.* It was nothing short of stupid, forming an attachment to him.

As she rounded a bend, she noticed in the distance the dark outline of a house. Light glowed from the windows and smoke swirled from the chimney. Claire stopped Reverend and dismounted—grateful she didn't fall this time—and led the horse into the underbrush.

She secured Reverend out of sight and draped the colorful blanket over the saddle. Then, she crept closer to the structure. Griffin and Sandoval's animals were nowhere to be seen. They must have put them in the back and gone inside. Claire stayed where she was for a time, nervous about moving closer, but she wanted to make certain she didn't miss anything important. No movement was visible inside the house and there was no indication as to who or where the occupants might be.

She decided to approach the right side of the house. The front porch didn't seem like a good idea and the back most definitely didn't—the horses were probably there and might signal her presence. When she reached the dwelling, the window was too high for her peek through. She considered retrieving her horse—atop him she would be tall enough—but doubted he would be quiet. Her eyes scanned for a rock or piece of wood to stand on, but she didn't see anything large enough.

Her stomach clenched with anxiety. Taking a deep breath, she crept to the front of the house then slowly up the steps onto the porch. To the left of the doorway a large window revealed the interior of the cabin, shielded by partially open curtains. She crouched and peeked inside. Griffin sat on the far side of the room at a wooden table. He appeared to be cleaning a gun. A woman entered and Claire strained to see her more clearly. She was pretty and young, with dark hair. Claire thought it might be Griffin's sister Dee, her memory of the woman somewhat foggy, having exchanged words with her only once or twice in the last few years.

"Looky here." The voice rose from the darkness behind her.

Claire froze as boots sounded on the steps, moving closer.

Sandoval's voice was unmistakable.

She stood, instinct pushing her to run, but pain lanced her spine as he pushed a gun between her exposed shoulder blades, the barrel cold against her skin.

With the black wig covering her blonde hair, maybe Sandoval wouldn't recognize her. She held tightly to that thought as she raised her hands, still faced away from him. "I'm looking for Maggie Waters. She told me to come to Cimarron for work."

"That right?" he said from behind her. "You always slink around at night?"

"Isn't that what a working girl does?" She could only hope her whispered question didn't sound as desperate as she felt.

Sandoval rammed the gun into her back and shoved her forward. She gasped, but squeezed her eyes shut in an effort not to cry out.

"You're spying," he said. "For who?"

"I don't know what you're talking about." With her face pushed up against the rough board siding of the house she knew her chances of escape dwindled with each passing moment. Sandoval jerked her arm and spun her around. His fingers wrapped around her neck with a painful grip as he pushed the gun barrel against the side of her head.

"Who are you?" he asked, his face so close that she smelled the distinct aroma of the tobacco he smoked. She swayed, remembering the last time he had been this close to her. *He doesn't recognize me.* She tried to hold onto that, to quiet the frantic bone-deep fear she had of this man.

"Peggy Ryan." She whispered the lie but knew it didn't matter anymore. Sandoval might not recognize her, but odds were he would kill her anyway. "I work for Maggie."

"Bullshit." He trailed a finger over her bare shoulder. She

pressed closer to the wooden exterior of the house to escape the touch.

"I've done every girl at the White Dove," he continued. "I know I haven't done you, so you lie."

She fought back a wave of panic as the pounding of her heart pulsated in her ears. He would blow the trigger, any second now, and her life would be over. God, how she hated him. How she hated the helplessness and the terror.

Tears rolled down her cheeks and she struggled to pray as a sob escaped her mouth. She'd learned of God from Tia.

*His wings lift you up. The dove flies with His breath.*

She sent her mind to the clearing in the woods—to the place she'd sat when she was a girl. A dove as white as snow had come to her, as though it had known she was there, waiting.

*The dove.*

A dark blur charged out of nowhere and twisted Sandoval's arm. Claire winced from the deafening sound as a gun discharged. She screamed. Her hands flew to cover her ears and she fell to her knees while splinters sprayed her face. Another ragged cry escaped her as a large person knocked Sandoval unconscious.

"Are you all right?"

All she could see was the dark outline of a man. Through the tears and the loud ringing in her ears she felt cut off from the world. Was she dreaming? It was Logan! She reached out and felt the solid strength of his hand as it grasped hers. The flesh was warm, alive— that must mean she still lived. He pulled her up to him and into his arms.

The click of a weapon startled her. Logan spun around and shielded her body with his, aiming a gun she hadn't even noticed at Sandoval's motionless body. Frank Griffin stood on the porch across from them, a shotgun leveled in their direction.

"You're on private property, asshole," Griffin said. "Drop it, or I'll shoot your whore and call it self-defense."

"Then I'll kill him." Logan's voice was quiet, calm.

Claire worked hard to steady her breathing.

"Who the hell are you?" Griffin asked.

Sandoval moved. Before Claire could think to warn Logan, he shoved her to the porch floor, exchanging gunfire with the Mexican, then yanked her arm and dragged her back down the stairs behind him. "Stay low," he warned. He pulled another gun and continued to shoot as they moved to the side of the house. Pausing, he reloaded both guns, his swiftness astounding her.

"Make for the trees." He nodded to the cover about fifteen feet away. She moved, he fired, and soon they ran rapidly around cactus, pine trees, and prickly bushes that repeatedly scratched and burned Claire's arms and legs. Her side ached and she thought a branch must have really scraped her good.

She stumbled, but Logan hauled her back to her feet and continued to drag her along. She had no idea where they were and completely relied on him to find the way. When it became clear they weren't being pursued, Logan stopped to let them catch their breath.

The burning pierced Claire's ribcage. Instinctively she put a hand on her right side and stared in shock when she felt moisture and it came away covered in something dark. *Blood.* The scratch must be worse than she thought. She raised her eyes to Logan's and saw wildness reflected at her. His rage frightened her as he closed the distance between them.

"Sonofabitch, Claire. You've been shot!"

She wanted to say something, but the darkness narrowed her vision. And then, there was nothing.

# CHAPTER 7

Logan caught Claire in his arms as she swooned, his mind screaming in denial. He wasn't going to lose her. No way in hell. He lay her against his lap and yanked off his shirt, buttons flying into the dirt. He reached down between his knees and tugged a knife from his boot. Carefully, he slit the side of the black dress she wore, then cut the blood-soaked chemise underneath.

In the darkness he tried to examine her wound. Despite the poor visibility, her ribcage appeared to be only grazed. He couldn't locate a bullet or large wound that would indicate it had entered her body. He relaxed, but only slightly. She was losing too much blood. He took his shirt and cut several patches off the bottom then pressed them against her ribs and tied them tightly in place with the remainder of the cloth.

He took a steadying breath, suddenly aware of the impropriety of his behavior, literally tearing Claire's dress from her. But as he held her inert body, fear welled inside him, and a primal urge took root. He wanted much more than to claim her flesh, he wanted *her*— the spirit and essence that only she embodied—and he needed more time to explore the possibility of what lay between them. He wouldn't let a damned bullet steal that chance from him.

Stroking her forehead, he said quietly, "Claire, wake up."

She stirred slightly.

"We need to get back to my horse. We'll never make it to town otherwise. Sweetheart, can you hear me?"

She opened her eyes. "What's happened?"

"You've been shot, but it's a shallow wound—you'll be fine. But we need to get out of here. If I help, can you walk?"

"Yes," she replied, her voice a scratchy whisper. "I'll try."

She stood unsteadily and glanced down at the makeshift bandage, then attempted to cover her semi-nakedness with her arms. Shirtless, Logan regretted that he had nothing left to offer. The black silk gown still covered the important areas and Logan hadn't seen anything he shouldn't. It hadn't crossed his mind to look—he'd been too concerned about her injury.

"Don't be embarrassed," he said. "I only cut the side of the dress, near the wound."

She recovered quickly. "You've stopped the bleeding?"

"For the moment." He put an arm around her waist and held her good side against him. He moved slowly at first. A quick scan of the stars and terrain gave him their general location. He just hoped Griffin, or the person who'd fired the initial shot, wouldn't find his horse hidden behind a clump of juniper trees a good quarter mile from the ranch house.

"I have medical supplies back at the hotel, so don't call for a doctor," she said, her breathing labored.

"Why?"

"No reason to call more attention to ourselves. Promise me, all right?"

"I won't make any promises like that. Let's just get to the hotel, then we'll see what needs to be done."

When Claire's breathing became too strained Logan lifted her, careful not to touch the wound.

"You'll get too tired," she said, but her head rolled against his shoulder.

With relief he found Storm right where he'd left her. Carefully, he lifted Claire into the saddle then settled behind her.

"What about Reverend?" she asked.

"He'll be fine. I'll come back for him tomorrow."

Logan watched their back trail as he let Storm pick her way through the wilderness. He avoided the roadway, and briefly considered not returning to the hotel, but they weren't being followed, as of yet, so he would risk it for tonight. He needed to tend to Claire as soon as possible.

Once they were at the hotel, Logan tied Storm off behind the establishment and quickly carried Claire around the front and entered through the lobby. Thankfully it was deserted at such a late hour. With long strides, he moved down the hallway, awkwardly retrieving the key from his shirt pocket, then unlocking the door and slipping into the room. As he laid Claire on the bed, she winced and closed her eyes. He grabbed a blanket and covered her, then quickly removed her fancy boots. She had several nasty blisters on the heels of her feet. She obviously wasn't accustomed to wearing shoes like these.

"In my bag, you'll find a pouch full of sugar." She rubbed her forehead.

Logan rummaged through her saddlebags. "This?" He held up a small rawhide sack. She nodded, her face pale.

"You'll need water...and more cloth," she said, her voice ragged.

He grabbed the water pitcher on the dresser—relieved it was full —and another one of his shirts. He wished now he'd thought to bring back a bottle of whiskey from the St. James, but at the time it would've only appeared he wanted to get Claire drunk and have his way with her. He was trying his damnedest to be on his best behavior with this woman. *The hell with it.* Decorum wasn't keeping her safe, she'd seen to that.

Carefully, he folded the blanket down from her shoulders and started to untie the bandage he'd put on her earlier. She glanced down at his handiwork.

"Just cut it off me," she said. "The dress, too."

"I don't want you to accuse me of trying to get you out of your clothes." He grabbed his knife and made quick work of the bandage. Then, he moved to what was left of her dress.

"Louisa's going to kill me," she said.

"The owner?"

She nodded. He crouched between the bed and the window and slit the silky material down her right side, all the while attempting to preserve her modesty.

"I'm sure you've seen a naked woman before. Just get it off," she said in irritation.

"You picked a hell of a time to flirt with me," he muttered, a little unnerved. He'd never stripped a woman down, except for the most obvious reasons.

"I'm not flirting." She pressed her lips together and stared at the ceiling. "I saw you without clothes in Texas, obviously we're past that stage."

Logan hesitated. He *had* been naked during their first meeting, but he thought Claire hadn't noticed beyond making certain he stayed away from her. Her memory of the incident unfurled a warmth in his belly, igniting hope that the incident was burned into her mind as much as it was in his—as much as the kiss in front of the hotel.

He pulled her gown and chemise to her slender hips, catching a glimpse of her rose tipped breasts before he covered her with the blanket. He had never thought himself the type of man to take advantage of a woman but here he was, doing just that. His hands froze as he debated whether to remove more of the dress and her undergarments.

"I know you prefer redheads."

The jealousy in her voice, slight though it was, caught him off-guard. Somehow, Claire had seen him with Red. Logan's pulse kicked up a notch—he sure as hell couldn't remove anymore of her clothing now, and it had nothing to do with preserving her modesty.

Stifling the impulse to press his advantage and seduce her, Logan tucked the blanket around her shoulders and tried to maintain focus on what was important. Her life. "I was just fishin' for information. I don't particularly care for redheads." He ripped several strips from his other shirt and dipped the white cloth into the basin of water behind him on the broad windowsill. Moving the blanket just enough to view where the bullet grazed her, he made a conscious effort to keep her breast out of sight. "Can you raise your arm?"

She did, but her face twisted with the effort. For several minutes he wiped at the caked blood until finally he saw where the skin was split, moist and bleeding anew.

"Sprinkle the opening with the sugar," she said.

"I've never heard of this remedy." But he opened the bag and did as she said.

"It'll dry the wound and help it heal faster."

"I still think I ought to get some whiskey, so it doesn't get infected," he said.

"The sugar will help with that, too."

"I should probably stitch you up."

Claire shook her head. "No. The location of the injury isn't worth the effort."

"You might have a nasty scar."

"I'd rather leave it open to help it heal. Can you replace the dressing?"

Forced to remove the blanket to tie a new bandage around her ribs, he came to appreciate a kind of suffering he'd never before experienced. Claire's pale skin, narrow waist and full breasts triggered a hunger so sharp, Logan felt like a boy who'd just caught his first glimpse of a female. But he was no boy, and he was hard-pressed to believe that Claire was a woman he couldn't live without.

"What about the pain?" he asked, his voice edged with frustration and anger. "Do you have something you can take?" He put the blanket atop her then moved away from the bed—away from her, away from temptation.

Her breathing rattled and echoed through the small room. "Not really. I didn't bring all my medicines."

"Will you be all right for a few minutes?"

"Why?"

"I need to take care of Storm before she's noticed, and I'll get you something to dull the pain."

She nodded.

He leaned over and kissed her forehead, shocked by his own behavior. The last thing he should do is touch her, but he couldn't help himself. "I'll be right back."

The wig was history, lost somewhere during their escape, and while he was glad it was gone, he knew it needed to be retrieved. If found, Claire's identity would be jeopardized.

"Be careful," she whispered.

Their eyes locked, then he left the room before he decided it would be better to stay. He made swift time getting what he needed.

---

CLAIRE AWOKE. She gasped from the throbbing and burning sensation that shot down her side. Moving slightly, she bit her lip from the excruciating pain. Logan dozed on the chair, his shoulder propped against the wall and his legs stretched out to the end of the bed. He cradled a rifle in his arms.

*He should have just slept with me. It wasn't as if he found me irresistible. I was completely naked, and it didn't affect him at all.*

Her disappointment served a purpose, which was to distract her from the agony of her body. In a rush of determination, she pushed herself upright, her teeth clenched as she fought back groans. The bottle of whiskey Logan had brought back last night sat perched on the nightstand next to the bed. She snatched it and took several swigs before leaning her head against the iron bed frame. The liquid burned, making her cough. A wave of nausea assaulted her. She really didn't like to drink but being somewhat tipsy kept the pain from holding tight to her mind, a meager blessing but certainly one to embrace.

Logan stirred. "How're you doing?" He stood and looked out the window then moved toward the bed, resting the rifle against the wall.

"Never thought I'd be drinking first thing in the morning," she said, her eyes drawn to his unbuttoned shirt. Her gaze skimmed a nice view of his chest—covered with a patch of brown hair—and his stomach, which flexed as he moved around the bed. Warmth filled her belly. *It has to be the liquor.*

"Yeah, it doesn't give you anything to look forward to later." He grinned. "You really slept hard and look better."

"I don't feel much better. What time is it?"

"A bit after noon."

"Oh!" Her eyes widened as she thought about the gunfight in the woods. "We shouldn't stay here."

"I was thinking the same thing."

A soft tap at the door interrupted them. Logan pulled one of his six-shooters from the holster where it lay in a heap on the floor, alongside a smaller handgun nestled in a black harness. Claire frowned at all the firepower Logan packed. "Who is it?" she whispered.

He cracked the door and peered out before opening it further. "It's Red."

Astounded, Claire watched as the floozy from the St. James

entered the room. Great, she thought. She'd get to view her climb all over Logan firsthand.

The woman stared at Claire, then nervously looked back at Logan as he closed the door. "I guess you got your blonde after all," she said, disappointment and confusion evident.

"How'd you know where to find me?" Logan asked.

"I followed you last night, after you came back for a bottle of whiskey and shot out like your pants were on fire." She shifted her eyes to Claire. "Guess I can see why. You sure do look like Maggie Waters."

"You know her?" Claire asked.

A downward flick of Red's eyes the only indication of a yes.

"Do you know where she is?" Claire pressed.

Red hesitated. "No, I don't. There's another reason I've come." She nodded toward Logan. "Your fella here came around last night and was asking about Maggie. I thought to come and warn him. But seein' as how you were the blonde he was holdin' out for, well, maybe I ought to warn you both."

"About what?" Claire asked.

"Have you ever heard of a man named Teddy Luttrell?"

Claire nodded.

"He was killed last year. You knew that, right?"

Again, Claire nodded.

Red looked behind her as if someone might be standing there, but Logan had shut the door. They were alone.

In a whisper Red said, "I think Maggie murdered Luttrell herself."

"What?" Claire struggled to sit upright, belatedly aware of her nakedness. She struggled to maintain the sheet across her chest, grimacing as a spasm of pain crossed her ribs. "Why would you say that?"

"You got any proof of this?" Logan asked, his voice rough.

Red's eyes darted to him then back to Claire. "Look, I've

probably already said too much. I can't say more. I came here because...well, you caught my eye." She fixed her gaze on Logan again. "It's not often a man turns me down. Got me to thinking, about things I probably shouldn't. I just didn't want you getting mixed up with Maggie. She's not worth the trouble."

Red turned to leave, then paused. "There's another reason, too. My brother—his name's Shorty McClaren—got himself mixed up with Maggie some time ago. And I ain't seen him since." She looked directly at Claire.

"I remember him," Claire said. Several months back Shorty had been around the White Dove quite a bit. Then Sandoval had attacked her. "I'm afraid I haven't seen him."

"You Maggie's sister?" Red asked.

"No. I'm her daughter."

A flash of surprise crossed Red's face. "Well.... Maybe I'm wrong about her."

"Does Frank Griffin know where she is?" Logan asked.

"No, but he's hell bent on finding her. I sure wouldn't go lookin' to cross paths with him if you don't have to. I'd better go."

"Wait," Claire said. "Have you heard anything about Jimmy Waters? He's my brother—a towhead, a tall boy, eight years old. He was with Maggie when she came here."

Red shook her head. "Sorry. Can't say as I have." She opened the door and peeked into the hallway. She glanced over her shoulder at Logan, then said to Claire, "You best keep him happy. The good ones don't come along too often." She closed the door behind her.

Logan grabbed up his holster from the floor, buckled it around his waist and placed his six-shooter in the sheath. He sat down on the edge of the bed and the hinges squeaked under his weight. One of his large hands pulled a blanket up to where Claire clutched the sheet against her bare breasts.

"We need to get you dressed," he said.

His touch was impersonal, but Claire trembled all the same.

"What was your mother's relationship with Luttrell?"

"I don't know. Men came and went. I never paid it much attention." She looked at him. "I guess I should have."

"You're not safe here."

"I'm probably not safe anywhere. Sooner or later, Griffin and Sandoval will know I'm alive. Then they'll be after me, if only to make me lead them to Maggie."

"Then let's not give them a chance to get you. I like you better alive." His blue-green eyes watched her.

"I just pray Jimmy's alive."

"Chances are good he is. Griffin and Sandoval don't have Maggie, so I think it's safe to assume that wherever she is then so is Jimmy. Despite everything that happened last night, I think you should be hopeful."

Logan's optimism encouraged her.

"Did you really turn down that redhead last night?" she asked before she could think better of it.

Logan's gaze grew hot. "I seem to have it bad for a woman with black hair named Peggy."

Claire's body burned and she knew a blush extended from her face clear down to her feet. Her breasts reacted as if he'd touched them, and an urge to push aside the sheet filled her.

She wanted Logan.

Claire had never understood why women sacrificed their own wants, their own desires, for any man who happened along. But Logan wasn't any man. She wanted him in a way she knew she shouldn't, in a way that should be easy enough to resist. Unfortunately, it wasn't.

She reached for him.

He caught her hand. "Red didn't tempt me, but you do. If we start this, I'll be wantin' to finish it, and you're in no shape for it."

When he kissed her palm, his lips warm and soft, the warmth in her belly definitely wasn't the result of whiskey.

He placed her hand on her lap then let it go. "I've a mind to find the sheriff and fill him in on what happened."

"But...."

"But," he interrupted gently, "I know what you're thinking, and you may be right. Involving the law at this point may do more harm than good. I'd like to get you back to Las Vegas."

"But we might be able to learn more here."

"Maybe. Maybe not. Either way, you need to rest."

"Then I shouldn't be traveling."

"I agree, but I suspect we'll have a hard time hiding here. Cimarron's a small town." Logan stood and buttoned his shirt. "I'll take care of things. Can you be ready to go by nightfall?"

Claire nodded. The sheet shifted, caressing her bare skin. How would it feel to have Logan touch her? His own breath sliding across her...The longing, hand in hand with the disappointment of him moving away from her, sat heavy on her mind and in her heart.

One thing was plain—Logan got past her defenses like few people had.

It should bother her.

God help her, it didn't.

# CHAPTER 8

Reverend followed behind Storm as they slowed and entered a wooded area south of Cimarron. Logan had retrieved Claire's horse early that morning. She was grateful they hadn't had to leave the animal behind. Although she doubted Sandoval would have linked Reverend to her, he might have connected the horse to the White Dove.

Until now, they'd kept the animals at a canter along the road in the dark, Logan never saying a word, but he must have sensed that Claire's horse couldn't keep going at such a brisk pace for much longer. And neither could Claire, for that matter, if the stinging in her side was any indication. She clenched her teeth and shifted in the saddle. Her dress pulled on the bandage, and she felt the urge to strip off the skirt and petticoat but refused to complain—Logan was surely quiet for a reason.

The moon, nearly full through the trees, illuminated their path. A breeze blew down the secluded valley they occupied, jostling the limbs of the cottonwoods that sheltered them. The sound of a stream could be heard in the distance. It was the perfect location to build a home, and on the heels of that thought a building came into view, light visible through the windows and smoke idling up from the chimney.

Logan slowed them to a walk as they skirted the homestead. Then they continued on, maintaining a path along the foothills of the mountains. They avoided the open prairie to their left.

Stifling a groan, Claire pulled the whiskey bottle from a pouch and swallowed another swig. Had she become a drunk? She couldn't say for certain, but her side burned and she didn't know when Logan would choose to stop for the night. She wasn't sure how much farther she could go.

As they came around a large outcrop of rocks and trees, Logan grabbed her horse's bridle and guided the animal behind a cluster of pines. He put a gloved finger to his lips to silence her and leaned over, his lips tantalizingly close to her ear. "We're being followed." Her skin tingled from the warmth of his breath.

She nodded as he retrieved his rifle, dismounted, and disappeared on foot the way they had come.

Uncertain what to do or how she might help, Claire came off Reverend with a contorted face while she struggled to keep from moaning as her wound throbbed. She took off the big sombrero and found the gun that Logan had bought for her earlier in her saddlebag. The Colt revolver was smaller than his Peacemaker, with a five-cartridge cylinder. As Claire moved to the top of the outcropping, she repeated the number in her head. *Five.* She would have five chances to defend herself if someone tried to attack. Hopefully, five would be all she'd need.

The horses snorted and danced nervously. Claire looked over her shoulder into the shadowy forest.

She smelled tobacco.

Fear gripped her and she nervously searched her surroundings, praying it wasn't Sandoval.

*Where are you, Logan?*

Moving might reveal her position but she couldn't stay put while

Sandoval, or whoever was out there, possibly put a bullet into Logan.

Ignoring her own discomfort, she eased off the rocks and into the woods then she picked her way through the darkness. Pine needles crunched beneath her boots, permeating the silence. She stopped and gripped the revolver more tightly, knowing she needed to be quieter.

"*Puta.*"

She froze. The voice chuckled from behind her, and the odor of tobacco filled the air. Sandoval was the only one who'd openly labeled her *whore*. He knew it was her.

"There was something odd about the stranger in town," he continued, his voice a burr against her skin, making her want to move away from him. "But I never would have guessed he would lead me to you. We all thought you dead."

Claire moved her right hand slightly and placed the gun before her, inside one of the folds of her skirt. Hopefully, it was enough to conceal it, but her mind raced to what could possibly be done since she was no match against Sandoval's shooting skills. She didn't doubt his pistol was pointed directly at her.

"Do not think that *desperado* will help you. I took care of him."

Panic rolled through her. He could be lying—he *had* to be.

*Five shots.*

"Your disguise was convincing. I wonder how long you've been back, fooling everyone," Sandoval said quietly in his clipped accent. He laughed again. "I spook you, don't I?"

He stepped closer, and she flinched when his finger traced a path between her shoulder blades. The barrier of her blouse didn't lessen her revulsion at being touched by him again within the span of a few days.

He was close enough that he might see the gun. She had to do something.

"I never forgot what you did to me," he said.

She knew he meant her drugging him when he attempted to rape her.

*Move fast.*

She cocked the hammer and spun around, but Sandoval grabbed her wrist as she fired. The bullet ripped upward into a tree. A scream tore from her throat, piercing the solitude of the forest, and she struggled against him. Bringing her hands together she readied the revolver again. It discharged loudly into his shoulder and she fell back, Sandoval's grip on her loosening. She scrambled to her feet but lost the gun. Frantically, she searched for it.

*No. Run.*

Her legs moved quickly and she didn't look back, running through the trees with a burst of energy fed by fear. The night air chilled her cheeks, her braid bouncing along her shoulders.

She ran hard, her legs and arms pumping in a cadence all their own. Claire had never known this—escape and freedom. She'd barely gotten away from Sandoval the previous night and hadn't evaded him at all three months ago. But she'd be rid of him tonight. She would keep running and he'd never be able to catch her.

And maybe—for once—she'd have control over a life she'd rarely felt her own.

A creek blocked her path, forcing Claire to stop; her loud gasps for air thundered in her ears. She examined her surroundings and tried to breathe through her nose to hear if anyone followed. Pain pierced her right side and she struggled to ignore it. She was alone, her only companion the water that trickled softly in the stream.

*Where is Logan?*

She had to find him. What if Sandoval *had* harmed him?

In the stillness of the forest Claire felt as if her identity had been stripped away. If she fled into the mountains, no one would ever have to know. She could start over—follow a different path.

Shocked by her thoughts, she shook them off. *Crazy. Irrational.* She'd fled once already—to Texas with Molly. That had brought

Logan into her life, and now he was here, possibly in trouble. All because of her. She had to help him.

She began to retrace her steps—back toward Sandoval. Conscious of no longer having her gun, she crept forward to the area where she thought he'd cornered her. She paused and watched for movement but saw none. It seemed unlikely that Sandoval had fled. She circled the location but there was no sign of the Mexican, no smell of tobacco.

A hand snaked out and covered her mouth—she strained against it and blew out a muffled scream. Her assailant yanked her back against the hard wall of his chest. Terror shot straight to her feet like a bolt of lightning.

"No, Claire, it's Logan," came a whisper.

She stopped resisting and sagged against him in relief. When he released his hold on her she spun into his embrace. "Thank God you're all right." She hugged him.

His arms closed around her, and the feel of his body was like a beacon in a storm. She ignored the sharp ache across her rib as he held her, surrendering to her need to touch him.

"I heard gunfire," he said. "Are you hurt?"

"No." She buried her face into his neck. "It was Sandoval. I think I shot him...Are you hurt?"

"It'll pass."

That caught her attention. She leaned back and saw a large welt over his left eye. "Did he knock you out?"

"I was damn stupid. I want you to hide while I scout the area."

"Are you crazy? I—"

He kissed her, his mouth demanding and thorough. Abruptly, it ended.

"Hide," he whispered, his hands firmly on the sides of her face.

She nodded, stunned by the intensity of his touch and all it implied. He left her, and she crouched in the anonymity of the darkness. After a long while, he returned.

"There're horse tracks leading back to Cimarron. And blood. You did shoot him."

Claire stood. "It all happened so fast."

"It was enough to make him turn tail and run. Just promise me something."

All she could make out was Logan's large silhouette, radiating anger and protectiveness and point-blank sexuality, and it was focused solely on her. A sharp yearning exploded inside, and she swayed from the impact. An image crossed her mind, of stripping her clothes off and giving herself to him, of touching him, joining her body to his. Reeling from her own desperate feelings, she knew she was in trouble. "What?"

"In the future, no more gunfights with that bastard. The image doesn't sit well with me."

She nodded. "Do you want me to have a look at that bruise?" She reached out and pushed his hair away from the welt, trying to get the lustful thoughts from her mind. A wave of pain from her own wound helped.

Logan flinched. "Yeah. Let's set up camp first. No fire."

Reluctantly, her hand fell away.

Logan brought the horses around and they rode south before stopping. Claire sat beside Logan on the one bedroll they possessed and examined his head injury as best she could in the starlight. There appeared to be no external bleeding, which was good. No chance of infection.

Her body still hummed with desire, and she wondered what Logan would do if she kissed him like a woman who was ready to take a man inside her. Not that she knew, but her jumbled senses told her she could figure it out real quick for his sake.

No, for *her* sake. Driven by an urge she couldn't seem to control, tears burned her eyes from the intensity of wanting him.

The yip of a distant coyote distracted her train of thought, briefly breaking the spell.

Logan's hand came to her forehead. "You're burning up. Why didn't you tell me you were feverish?"

Was she? A new wave of desire slammed into her. She leaned into him and kissed his neck, his cheek, anywhere her lips could find some part of him.

"Claire." His voice held concern, but that's not what she wanted. She brought her mouth to his and he pulled her to him, matching the hunger she couldn't hold back anymore, grinding his lips into hers. She climbed onto his lap, frantic for more.

"Sweetheart." He pushed her back. "You're not well enough for this." He grazed his thumb across her lips.

She closed her eyes, a shudder rippling through her body. Logan gently lowered her onto the bedroll, and she couldn't hold back the tears any longer.

"Shhh." He stroked her hair. "Try to sleep."

He lay down beside her, and she sobbed into his shirt. In a haze of fatigue, she realized she was worse than she'd thought. She hoped the fever would fight off the threat of infection, but what would fight off the sexual awareness of her own body? Gripped with madness, she couldn't think, only *feel*, and the sheer force of it frightened her.

She rolled onto her left side, needing distance from Logan.

"Claire, you could go back to Texas and stay with my folks," he said from behind her. "Let me find your ma and Jimmy."

The offer was tempting in her defeated state.

"No." Her voice cracked, and she wiped the wetness from her cheeks.

"Are you always so stubborn?" Logan's hand rested on her hip.

The flame in her abdomen ignited again, swirling, reaching lower. If Logan would satisfy this need then maybe the fever would lessen and she could rest, maybe she would find the peace she had long sought in her life. Her lips trembled as she struggled to breathe. "Mama always said it would be my downfall."

His touch burned and her skin tingled, despite the barrier of her clothes. She squeezed her eyes shut to resist the impulse to beg him.

All her life she had held tight to her internal code of morality, and she'd been strict and unforgiving when it came to herself. She needed to remember those rules now before she did something she might regret.

"Stubborn females tend to survive," he said. "But don't be afraid to lean on me."

"You shouldn't be here," she replied in a rush.

"Maybe not, but I've been known to be stubborn, too." He moved closer to her backside and pressed against her shoulder blades. "Stay with me, darlin'," he said with conviction. "You fight this."

She wasn't sure if he spoke of the fever, or her overpowering attraction to him.

"I'll try."

# CHAPTER 9

By late afternoon the next day, Claire rode into Las Vegas with Logan at her side. Her fever had broken by mid-morning, so she insisted they push to get back to town. Her fatigue faded as they entered the plaza and several people threw furtive glances at her, too numerous to chalk up to chance. Without a disguise for the first time since she'd returned to the White Dove three weeks ago, she was bound to stir up gossip. The thought made her distinctly uncomfortable.

She caught a glimpse of Maria Chavez and the middle-aged woman stared at her. *Señora* Chavez strongly objected to all forms of prostitution and never hesitated to make her opinion known. When Claire was ten years old, she had attempted to attend one of the fandangos around town—a gathering full of food and dancing and socializing—but Maria Chavez had been so vocal about a local whore's daughter being present that Claire had quickly left in embarrassment. She wouldn't even have gone at all if it hadn't been for Sarah Brightman, a girl near her age who had begged Claire to attend one of the festivals she had heard so much about.

Sarah's father was an officer at Fort Union, and she had befriended Claire one afternoon while in town. It didn't take long before Colonel Brightman realized Claire's situation and forbade his daughter to have anything to do with her. Maria Chavez had uttered under her breath one day in passing that she would pray for Claire's soul at *Nuestra Señora de los Dolores*, the local Catholic Church at the time, but she was sure it wouldn't make any difference.

As they brought their horses to the White Dove, Claire dismounted with a grimace, favoring her right side. A sign hung in the window: CLOSED INDEFINITELY.

Logan came to stand beside her. "Problems?"

"Some of the girls defected before I left. I was forced to close." She tried the door, but it was locked. Logan followed her as she went around the building and entered through the kitchen.

"Ellie? Betsy?" Claire's voice didn't carry far as they walked into the empty saloon. She took the stairs slowly.

"Take it easy," he said from behind. "You ought to get some rest. It was a long night."

His remark about what had passed between them the previous evening made her face burn with embarrassment. They hadn't spoken of it and Claire, unsure how to address her desperate attempt to seduce him while ill, had simply avoided the topic. With her mind and impulses under better control, she considered that Logan hadn't wanted to bed her after all and instead tried to let her down easy.

Claire was grateful he had refused her. Wasn't she?

Betsy appeared in the hallway at the top of the stairs. "Claire, thank goodness. We weren't sure what happened to you." The woman's eyes settled on Logan.

"Betsy, this is Mr. Ryan." Claire paused to catch her breath. She had changed the dressing on the bullet wound herself that morning, its appearance puffy and swollen, so she knew she needed to take care the next few days until it healed properly. "Logan, this is Betsy Williams."

"Miss Williams."

"How's Ellie?" Claire asked.

"Doing much better, but still in bed. Did you find Maggie?"

Claire shook her head.

Betsy hesitated. "We need supplies."

"I'll take care of it," Logan said. "Make me a list. Claire, I'm gonna tend to the horses."

Claire dared to look back at him. "Where can I find you? At the Wagner Hotel?"

"Not while you're here."

She dared not read more into the statement, not after losing her self-control the previous night.

"You're not safe alone," he added.

Betsy gasped. "What's going on?"

"Nothing," Claire said quickly. "Mr. Ryan is just being overprotective."

"I'll be staying here." Logan's voice was decisive.

Betsy wrung her hands together. "Well, we do have extra rooms."

"Sounds good," he said. "I'll pay for it."

"I can make your meals for you," Betsy offered. "And I've some skill with sewing. I could mend and launder your clothes. And for additional money I could, well..." The woman looked nervously at Claire. "That's what we do here."

Claire stared at Betsy in shock. When had the young woman decided to expand her job duties? And why the hell would she choose to start her new career path with Logan? A sharp possessiveness gripped Claire.

"That's not necessary," Logan said. "I seem to have a weakness for women with black hair."

Surprise crossed Betsy's face, and Claire cheeks grew hot.

"I'm sure you want to see Ellie." He winked at her, his mouth turning up slightly. "I'll be out back."

Claire watched him leave, stunned. With just a look and a half-grin he successfully re-ignited the fire in her belly she'd tried all day to extinguish.

———

LOGAN ATE a generous helping of *posole*—a chili dish flavored with pork and hominy—and followed it with a bread pudding Betsy called *sopa*, sweetening it with a thick homemade syrup known as *melado*. Considering they were local dishes, the girl's cooking skills impressed Logan. Claire sat beside him at the wobbly and nicked saloon table, doing a somewhat adequate job on the meal. He was glad she ate—she needed to keep her strength up as she recovered from the gunshot wound. It worried him she would have another setback.

It also concerned him that he might not be able to resist Claire the next time she decided to ply her innocent and explosive sexuality on him. Not that he expected her to let loose any time soon —he knew her well enough to recognize her behavior during the night was unlike her. It was the reason he'd pushed her away, but it had taken more willpower than he ever thought he possessed.

He'd wanted her.

He still wanted her.

But he wasn't certain Claire understood what would happen if they gave in to their attraction. He was more experienced—he needed to be the voice of reason.

Claire had cleaned up and now wore a white blouse and colorful skirt that wrapped around her slender hips, making her much too easy on the eyes.

*The voice of reason.*

A knock on the door startled all of them from their mealtime silence. As Betsy rose and approached the door, Logan moved a hand to the gun strapped to his waist. Claire noticed and concern crossed her face. She stood to join Betsy who had retreated to admit their visitor, One-Eyed Jack.

"Many thanks, Betsy," he said. He took one look at Claire and with a heartfelt expression embraced her but frowned when she winced and held her side. "It is good to see you, *Palomita*. Are you hurt?"

Claire smiled. "It's nothing. I'm glad to see you, Jack. Would you like something to eat?"

"You know I never turn down food."

"I'll get it." Betsy left for the kitchen.

Claire introduced the old Indian to Logan.

"We've met," Logan said. "Good to see you again." He stood and shook Jack's hand.

"Well, I feel a little better, what with the talk around town." Jack sat in the chair Logan offered.

"What talk is that?" Claire carefully lowered herself onto her seat.

Betsy returned and placed a bowl of *posole*, a bowl of *sopa*, and a large glass of milk before Jack then resumed her spot at the table.

"Talk about you," he replied. "Everyone knows you're alive, everyone knows you're back. I was worried, but I feel better knowing Mr. Ryan is here."

"We all do," Betsy said with a high degree of enthusiasm. Her face turned crimson when everyone glanced at her.

Logan hoped he could do justice to the blind faith on the girl's face. The welt above his eye was still swollen from Sandoval's surprise attack the previous night.

"Hit a door, or somethin'?" Jack asked, indicating Logan's injury.

"Or somethin'," Logan replied.

Jack wisely let the matter drop.

"Any word about Maggie?" Claire asked.

Around a mouthful of food, the Indian shook his head. "No,

ma'am. Tia and I sure would've tried to help if we knew where she was."

"I know."

After Jack finished his food, he withdrew the Bible from his coat pocket. He squinted to read as he held the tattered black book in front of his face. "'Whatever is has already been, and what will be, has been before; and God will call the past to account'."

"You're almost half-way through that," Claire said. "You're making good progress."

"Yep. Can't say I always understand it all, but this Christian God certainly is interesting." He focused on the page, running a finger across the print. "But here's what I wanted to read to you. 'God will bring to judgment both the righteous and the wicked, for there will be a time for every activity, a time for every deed.'"

"Ecclesiastes," Logan said.

Jack stretched his lips into a smile.

"You know the Bible?" Claire asked.

"My ma made both Matt and I read it when we were boys."

"Your folks had a nice selection of books. Your ma was kind enough to let me borrow a few while I was there."

So that's where Claire had disappeared to night after night. Logan had never tried so hard to make it home for supper after working the ranch all day as when Claire had been a guest at the SR. Her presence had been a definite draw. He had even gone out of his way to clean up more than usual before mealtime.

He was smart enough not to be done in by a pretty face, but that didn't mean he wasn't susceptible to the picture she presented—restraint and allure, contentment matched with irresistible temptation. Odd as it sounded, he felt very comfortable with her, like they'd known each other far longer than a few months.

Another knock. Logan intercepted Claire before she managed to get to the door. Did the woman have no caution when it came to her safety? Standing in front of her, he ignored the look of annoyance she shot him as he cracked open the door.

"Excuse me." A Mexican woman stood on the other side. "Is *Señorita* Claire here?"

"It's sure busy around here, considering you're closed," he murmured. The scent of lavender filled his senses and the heat of Claire's body mixed with his own as she nudged him aside. He couldn't deny he liked it when she touched him.

"Juanita, what is it?" Claire asked.

"We are so glad you are back. Can you come, *por favor?* It is Mary Beth, she not so well."

"*Sí*. Wait while I get my bag."

Logan stalled Claire's movement with a hand on her shoulder and stepped between her and the stairs. "Where do you think you're going?" As she came to an abrupt halt, his arm brushed against her breasts and the look on her face told him she was aware his casual touch was anything but casual, but beyond that he couldn't read her reaction to him.

"Down the street to Southern Charm. I'll be fine. I've been there many times."

"But not after being shot."

"Thank you for your concern, but I think I can manage. Then I'll come back and rest. I promise."

"You know I'm going with you, don't you?"

She studied him, then nodded. "All right." Her green eyes showed a hint of gratitude and weariness.

"Claire, you don't have to do this," he said. "You don't always have to put yourself on the line for other people."

"I know." But her voice held a tone of resignation.

He released his grip on her shoulder. "And you can't live like this, always watching your back."

"This is my life and believe it or not, I'm used to it." She headed to the stairs, but not before he saw the bleakness in her eyes.

CLAIRE SAT in a side room off the main saloon of Southern Charm, examining her patient. The young woman sat listlessly on a chair. Evening had settled over the town and men crowded the drinking establishments. With regret, Claire knew the White Dove could have absorbed some of the traffic.

The room was filled with most of Southern Charm's girls despite boisterous calls for them from the outer room. Claire suspected they were curious to see her, but it was equally apparent they were also interested in the man who accompanied her. Although glad Logan had come with her—there was no telling when Sandoval might show his face again—she had to admit she didn't like how the other girls eyed him. Behind this low-key jealousy and her concern for Mary Beth lurked a desire for a long sleep in a decent bed. She might even indulge her pain and take a dose of laudanum; the ceaseless throbbing on her rib cage was draining away her aversion to taking the highly addictive drug.

Belle Mason, owner of the saloon, stood to one side. Dressed in a deep yellow gown with tassels that rustled along the edges of the black petticoats underneath, Claire thought she appeared terribly overdressed for the likes of this town—they were hardly in Denver after all. The square neckline, outlined by a black border, accentuated her bosom but she was no longer in the bloom of her youth, her gray-streaked brown hair curled and piled atop her head. The girls at the White Dove, as well as her mother, had never dressed so extravagantly. Out of the corner of her eye she noticed Louisa and Alice and wondered if they were happy with their new boss.

Claire felt behind Mary Beth's ears. There was slight swelling. "Does it hurt to swallow?"

The young woman nodded. The girls got younger and younger, Claire thought in disgust.

"I haven't felt well for more than three days now," Mary Beth said.

Claire didn't say it aloud, but her color didn't look good and in general she appeared exhausted. Moving her hand to the girl's forehead, she confirmed that Mary Beth was feverish. "Open your mouth." Claire peered inside—it was as red as an apple.

Carefully, Claire searched through her satchel and found a bottle of honey mixed with raw garlic. "Take one teaspoonful four times a day." She handed the mixture to the girl. "It will help with the pain and inflammation." In addition, she retrieved a bag marked Purple Coneflower. "Brew a tea with this and drink one cup every two hours. You should feel better in a day or two, but I'll come back to check on you tomorrow."

"Thank you." The girl smiled. "I appreciate it."

"You'll be fine," Claire said. "Get some rest and drink a lot of water to help with the fever." Quietly, she added, "And no customers for a few days."

Mary Beth acknowledged the last bit with a flash of relief. Two of the other girls helped her out the side door and to the stairs that led to Mary Beth's room.

"Everyone get back to work," Belle said, clapping her hands.

The room cleared as Claire repacked her bag.

"Wait," Belle said. "I have someone else I need you to see."

"You gonna pay her?" Logan said.

"I beg your pardon?"

"Do you expect Claire to do this for free?"

"She always has."

"It's all right, Logan." Claire stood. "Is the girl too ill to come down here?"

"It's not a girl. Follow me."

Claire didn't need to look at Logan to know he was annoyed. He didn't understand how things worked, how Claire had developed a relationship with the girls in this part of town. Belle might take advantage of her, but the truth was Claire felt sorry for all of them. Maybe she shouldn't—some undoubtedly were quite happy about their position and the occupation they practiced—but Claire still saw a void in their spirits and for some inexplicable reason it drew her to them.

Even Maggie hadn't understood.

Belle led them through the bar area and up a stairwell against the far wall. Logan silently took Claire's bag and carried it for her, and she took several deep breaths to control the pain from her ribcage. Soon they would be back at the White Dove and she could rest.

At the end of the hallway, Belle softly knocked on the door before she entered. "Rosa, it's me."

Claire knew Rosa Brown and nodded to the girl. Not more than twelve or thirteen years old, Claire wondered if her folks, Hyman and Pablita, knew she was here. She'd have to look into that later. The Browns were good people—Hyman had often brought medical books on his supply wagons from Kansas City for Claire to read.

Once in the room, Belle's countenance changed as she knelt beside the bed and smiled at the young boy lying there. "How's he doing?"

"He's sleepy."

"This is Dylan," Belle said to Claire. "He's about eighteen months old."

"Is he yours?" Claire asked, surprised that Belle Mason harbored a child in her saloon. In and of itself it didn't shock her— she and Jimmy had grown up in such an environment—but savvy and self-centered Belle had never struck Claire as the maternal type. Perhaps she and Maggie had more in common than their ongoing feud.

"No. He's just staying with me for a time."

"What's wrong with him?" Claire moved beside Belle, aware of

Logan behind them. Out of the corner of her eye, she saw him cross his arms to wait.

"He's had a rash on his arms and legs that's been getting worse." Belle pulled the covers down to show Claire.

Dylan's large brown eyes watched her with caution and dark hair framed his face in a tousled mess.

"Hi there," she said. "My name's Claire." Gently she examined the red, flaky patches on the inside of his arms. "Do you like peppermint sticks?" She pushed the blanket farther down to inspect his legs. Some of the patches were cracked, exposing raw skin. Claire thought quickly about a treatment.

Dylan nodded at her question.

"I think I might have one in my bag," she responded. Although she rarely treated children, she did keep a few sweets on hand to bribe Jimmy.

She handed him the candy, then began to clean his legs with soap and water—working quickly when he squirmed and tried to push her away. Once that was completed, she rubbed a mixture of petroleum jelly and boric acid gently over the red splotches. She'd learned of this method when she overheard the town doctor speak of it one day while in the mercantile.

"All better now." She smoothed the hair from his forehead, trying to calm him. "Try not to scratch it no matter how much you want to."

Dylan didn't speak as he sucked on the peppermint stick. Claire smiled at the sweetness of him, wishing she could hold that part of Jimmy's childhood in her hands once more.

"Will he be all right?" Belle asked as they moved to the door.

"Yes." Claire gave her the tin with the jelly in it. "Use this two or three times a day. Keep the cracked areas clean and don't let him play outside until the skin is healed, otherwise he'll risk infection. Don't let anyone else who is sick come around until the sores are scabbed over. I'll try to come by tomorrow and see how he's doing." Claire wiped her hands on the cloth Belle offered.

Logan loomed close and Claire caught the wink he gave Dylan. The boy held his hand out and Claire sensed Logan's uncertainty before he grasped the tiny fingers within his considerably larger ones.

"Shriff?" Dylan asked, startling them all with the question. Claire wondered how much the boy usually spoke.

Logan's confusion was plain to see.

"Sheriff," she whispered.

Understanding lit Logan's face. He turned back to the boy. "No. Just a friend."

Dylan watched with unwavering eyes while Logan gently released his hand.

"You take it easy, partner." Logan gently pinched his cheek and grinned, then followed Claire out of the room.

The image of him with the boy stayed with her. She liked it, the idea of Logan one day becoming a father. Unbidden an image struck her of holding a babe—a precious blend of herself and the man behind her.

In no time they were out on the street and headed back to the White Dove. Logan took her hand, and together they went toward the only home Claire had ever known.

# CHAPTER 10

W hen Claire entered the White Dove, Betsy was nowhere to be seen and Jack must have returned to wherever it was that Jack went, Claire had never been sure. Logan steadied the swinging doors then shut the main door and locked it. He struck a match and lit an oil lamp on one of the tables.

"Do you trust Belle Mason?" he asked.

Claire set her bag on the bar as the soft, flickering light chased away the shadows, but not all. "No, of course not."

"Then why in the hell do you run up there anytime her girls are sick?"

One-Eyed Jack's voice bounced in her head, his obsession with the Bible coating his words. *Do not announce your intentions to the world, Claire. Do what you must because it is right. It is just. Your reward is in God's hands, not that of men.* Claire hesitated. She sensed this wasn't the answer Logan wanted to hear and wondered if he would even understand—most of the time she certainly didn't.

She reminded herself that Jack frequently spoke with his head in the clouds, never with his feet firmly planted on the ground. But maybe that explained her fondness for him.

She had never really told anyone how much she enjoyed helping people, how obligated she felt to do *something* to ease their discomforts. She wanted to be a doctor and was realistic enough to know that the attention given to the prostitutes in town might be her only chance to make a difference. They needed someone to help them. Who better than her?

"I can't stand by and do nothing," she said. "Life isn't as simple as you would have it."

"Haven't you ever wanted more than this?" He watched her, his gaze demanding, and it banished her fatigue with a jolt. She felt both uncomfortable and exhilarated.

"You seem awfully determined to change my life, Logan. It doesn't need changing." But the statement didn't ring true. Her life was already altered, Logan's presence the irrefutable proof.

He closed the distance between them and placed his hands against the bar behind her, boxing her in. "I'm not good watchin' from the sidelines."

His heat surrounded her, and she remembered the previous night, filled with feverish need and the memory of Logan's mouth on hers. "This isn't going to work," she whispered.

"So you see into the future now?" His mouth hovered inches from hers.

"I don't expect you to understand my life." Cornered, a part of her rebelled, while the other part urged her to give in to temptation. What did it matter anymore? Claire almost laughed out loud, but fear welled up inside her. Logan's nearness soothed and hurt at the same time. Her heart, her body, felt too much for him and an instinct, long employed throughout childhood, took over—self-protection.

"You're going to leave," she said. "Eventually."

Logan stared at her mouth. "Probably. But I'm here now, and I can't stop thinking about you."

Anticipation thrummed through Claire. Logan represented a side of the world unknown to her, a world filled with excitement and longing and possibilities, all packaged in an irresistible combination. His lips came to hers, and she didn't push him away.

LOGAN SAVORED the texture of Claire's mouth despite her less than overwhelming response. He needed to touch her. He knew she was tired, he knew she needed to rest, but for a brief moment he wanted to feel her close. She didn't deny him, so he deepened the kiss, careful to keep his desire under control. He concentrated his attention on her lips, her cheeks, and the feel of her neck. When his resolve began to slip, he pulled back.

With a hand buried in her hair, he brought his forehead to hers and took a steadying breath. What he wanted was pretty simple really—he wanted to make love to her. He wanted to forget all the reasons they shouldn't, all the reasons *he* shouldn't, because he knew if he pushed the yearning between them, he'd have her flat on her back in no time.

He inhaled her scent, putting him in mind of the forests, the mountains and the streams that stretched across the West—the essence of freedom in the palm of his hand. He remembered something his ma had told him about the smell of a baby and how potent it was to the mother, how it bonded them. It had been a long time since he'd wanted a woman so much, a long time since the wanting had turned into a bond that tugged at more than just a craving to touch Claire and satisfy the physical arousal of his body.

He wanted more than that from her. Much more. His stomach tensed at the thought.

He wasn't ready to desire a woman as much as he had Dee. He wasn't ready to serve his heart up on a platter, to be roasted and sliced at the whim of fate and Claire's own reluctance toward what lay between them.

He backed away. "You'd better get some rest."

Her eyes clouded with confusion.

"Do you need help with your bandage?" he asked.

"No. I'll change it in the morning." A pensive expression crossed her face. She paused as if to say something then moved around him.

He let her go.

"Goodnight," she said softly as she walked toward the kitchen.

"'Night," he murmured and stared at the bar.

CLAIRE ENTERED the one room cabin she occupied behind the saloon, lit a lamp then bolted the door. Her quick glance took in the disarray of the room, and to occupy her mind with something other than Logan she grabbed a rag from a wooden cabinet in the corner and wiped down the table and two wooden chairs that sat near the window. Stiff from her injury, she carefully closed the curtains and felt, at last, truly alone.

Tears blurred her vision as she opened a chest and withdrew a nightgown. Carefully, she folded down the covers on her bed, the white sheets threadbare and the comforter never sufficient to keep her warm during the winter.

She looked at the smaller bed on the far wall, near the door, where Jimmy had slept. There was a good wool coverlet on it, hand knitted by Claire herself. She hadn't liked knitting, and proof of her lack of skill was in the many mistakes present, but Jimmy had needed to stay warm, so Claire had painstakingly suffered through the endeavor. With a swipe at her wet cheeks, she took the blanket off his bed and held it close, as if the material itself was her little brother, then sank onto her bed.

What if she never found her ma or Jimmy? In truth, the thought had never occurred to her. What would she do? As much as she had wished for a different life, a respectable life, she could never consciously wish away the only family she had. Maggie Waters had many faults, but she was still her mama. And Jimmy...

Claire squeezed her eyes shut as the tears pressed forth. She couldn't bear it if she never saw her brother again, with his blond mop of hair so like her own, his impish smile and amazing adaptability to the circumstances in which he lived. She loved him more than her own life.

He was the only one.

Claire loved her mama but had always struggled to measure up to whatever standard Maggie held in her head regarding her children.

Startled by the revealing thought, Claire realized she'd always wanted to make her mama proud of her ability to heal the ills and everyday maladies of the prostitutes in town. Didn't it in some way validate that these women were worthy of something? Didn't it in some way validate that her mama was worthy? The pride and shame had warred inside Claire for years. And beneath it all, she craved the approval of her mama. She'd craved it desperately all her life.

Maggie had done nothing when Sandoval attacked Claire months ago, the incident slicing Claire's life into two parts. Before, she had believed that, despite everything, Maggie loved her children and would do whatever she could to protect them. Now, Claire didn't hang onto such fanciful notions. Closing the curtains earlier had hidden her in a cocoon of her own making, but only now did she comprehend she was truly without any foundation.

Why hadn't she become a soiled dove? Why hadn't she given in to the mindless survival mode that drove the other women to exist in this lifestyle? Claire didn't know. Somehow, she'd been determined to hold onto herself in spite of the many influences around her. Claire didn't like selling out.

But was she so different from her mama? There were parts of

Maggie she would never know, parts of her that were a part of Claire. Was she prostituting herself by giving away her medical services for free? By standing in the background and mopping up the disarray that Maggie left behind?

When she stood to lay Jimmy's blanket onto her bed, her thoughts wandered to Logan.

She never saw the world so clearly as when he kissed her—an existence full of prospects and magic. The magic of hope. Was it foolish to harbor such a notion?

As she sat on her bed, a soft tap at the door made her jump. She unbolted the door and opened it a crack.

Ellie Hicks.

She'd wanted it to be Logan.

LOGAN LEANED against the windowsill in the darkened room and stared at the building where Claire lived. He occupied Maggie's old room above the saloon, with a frilly white quilt on the bed and one wall papered with a pattern of roses. She had a love of feminine décor and a love for her children—the proof lay in the proximity of her room to their small cabin. Perhaps there was more to Maggie than seemed obvious. For Claire's sake, Logan sincerely hoped so.

Claire hovered in his mind, ever-present, and he wasn't sure what to do about his burning attraction to her.

Rubbing his eyes, he glanced out the window again. Immediately his senses shifted when he saw a figure move toward Claire's door. The person knocked, then went inside. Logan grabbed his revolver and headed downstairs.

"Ellie, what are you doing here?" Claire asked. "Please, come inside." She stepped aside to let the older woman enter. "Are you feeling better?"

Ellie removed the many-colored shawl she had draped over her head. Her grayish-red hair was combed and pulled back, and Claire was glad to see some color had returned not only to the woman's cheeks but also to her eyes. Some, but not much.

"I seem to be recoverin' fine, missy." Ellie's lips spread into a forced smile. "I never got to thank you proper-like for what you did. I'm thinkin' you saved my life."

Claire felt the sadness in the woman and she wanted to cry. "I'm sorry I couldn't have saved more."

Ellie waved that off, but her eyes glistened and it broke Claire's heart. "That child was a mistake." But her words came out in barely a whisper. Ellie leaned her head down and covered her face with one hand, then took a deep breath. "No, it weren't no mistake." She looked at Claire again. "I wanted the babe. And I'm realizin' that I can't do this no more. I never thought I'd want to get out, I never thought I was good enough to get out, but I just can't do this no more."

Claire silently agreed. Ellie had always been the strongest of any of the women her mama employed. Strong in mind, strong in spirit, and strong in attitude when she dealt with the customers. Watching her now, broken and spent, Claire felt keenly the sacrifice Ellie had made all these years. It was painfully obvious it had been too much.

"I hate to do this to you, missy, 'specially now," Ellie said. "I figure you're hopin' to reopen once I can work but...I just can't work no more. I'm sorry. I know this is a hard time, what with Mags gone. If there's anything else I can do, I'll surely try."

While Ellie's admission pushed the White Dove further into the ground, it also restored Claire's faith in the human spirit. *The will fights back, even in the depths of despair.* That was something Jack would say.

"I understand," Claire replied. "I'll manage, somehow. You can stay here, for now, but I honestly don't know how long that will be possible. I'm not sure what I'm going to do yet."

"Mags did everythin' wrong in raisin' you, and you turned out so right." Ellie smiled. "I've never been much of a God-fearin' woman, but he musta sent you to us, a dove from the heavens."

Ellie turned and left. Claire stood rooted in place, staring at the shut door, moved and surprised by the woman's assessment of her. She had never really thought of herself as the salvation of the White Dove girls.

A knock at the door startled her for a second time. It was a good thing she hadn't climbed into bed yet. "Who is it?" she asked.

"Logan."

She opened the door. "What are you doing here?" Anticipation engulfed her.

"Worrying about you." His eyes glittered. His unbuttoned shirt hung open around the waist and Claire caught a glimpse of the black harness he wore underneath, as well as the larger gun in his hand. Altogether he appeared dangerous and far too appealing.

He entered, and she closed the door behind him.

"What was that all about?" he asked.

Logan had been watching her. She was strangely comforted by it.

"It was Ellie."

"Problem?"

"No. A ray of hope, actually. She's decided to leave the business."

"That doesn't sound good for the White Dove." He holstered his gun. With his shirt open he looked like a renegade who would carry her off into the wild. Claire gave herself a mental shake and wondered why her imagination was so active when it came to this man. The kiss earlier in the evening wasn't helping matters either.

"Maybe not," she said. "But it'll be good for her. That's the important thing."

Silence ensued, and Claire became acutely aware of their close proximity and Logan's minimal clothing. She tried not to look at the hair curling down his chest, but her eyes had other ideas.

Logan's gaze shifted to the single shelf above her bed. "Are those your books?"

Claire glanced over her shoulder and nodded.

He reached past her, took down one and scanned a page. "I sure never learned this in school." His eyes held amusement when he glanced at her.

"Doctors are expected to know Latin." She wondered how he did that, how he entranced her with just a look.

Extending his arm past her again, he pulled down Gray's *Anatomy*. Claire steeled herself as disappointment hit her—she had thought he might reach for her.

Logan flipped through the book and something fell from it, clanking to the floor. Claire leaned down and picked up a key.

"Is that yours?" he asked.

Claire shook her head. "No." Taking the book from him, she sat on the edge of her bed and flipped through it again. She found a small piece of paper with the words written: BOX 23.

"I think it could be my mama's handwriting."

Logan sat down beside her and his long fingers took the key from her hand. "Might be for a safety deposit box. How many banks are in town?"

Claire shrugged. "Two or three. I'm not sure."

"Might be worth checking out tomorrow." He glanced at her door. "Make sure you bolt that, all right?"

She chided herself for wishing he would stay.

"I'll keep the key." He stood.

His suggestion surprised Claire—it flowed too easily from his mouth—and sent warning bells off in her head. Did he know something she didn't? Or did he hope there was something of value in the box?

"I think I should keep it," she said and reached for the key. His warm hand stopped her, and she looked into his blue-green eyes.

"I'm not stealing it," he said. "I'll check it out alone, tomorrow."

"But—"

"Claire, it's unlikely the bank would let either of us have access to the box."

He paused, and as she stared at him understanding dawned. "You're going to break in?"

Logan frowned. "Well, I can't quite do that. I'm a retired lawman and that wouldn't be right." He leaned forward, his mouth inches from hers. "Trust me. I'll work it out."

*Trust.* Could she believe in him? What would it cost her if she did?

"I'll return as soon as I know something," he vowed.

He kissed her, his mouth gentle, his touch full of sweet promise.

Claire suddenly remembered the bank clerk who had spent some time in the saloon, as well as time in Maggie's room.

*Trust.*

She gripped Logan's forearm. "There's a man, his name's Tannenhill I think, and he works at First National Bank. Maggie entertained him frequently awhile back. Maybe the key will work there and he can help you. I could try to talk to him."

"I'd just as soon leave you out of it." He took both her hands in his. "You need to rest. If I have any problems, I'll come and get you." He let her go. "Lock the door."

He exited the cabin and she bolted the door, hoping she had done the right thing. Perhaps Maggie had placed money in the safety deposit box and Claire could use it to get the White Dove up and running again. Or perhaps she had left some clue as to her and Jimmy's whereabouts. Or maybe it was full of useless trinkets

Maggie had collected over the years from men grateful for the favors she bestowed behind closed doors.

*Men grateful for favors...*

What did Logan want from Claire?

As hard as it was, she had to consider he had a reason for helping her, for staying with her. For romancing her.

What was his price? And was she willing to pay it?

# CHAPTER 11

Logan inserted the key into the long rectangular box and was rewarded when the lid released, giving access to the interior and its contents. It had taken a bit of convincing to get Mr. Tannenhill to relax normal bank procedure—bypassing the standard signatures and identification protocols—to allow Logan entry into the rear of the bank where the safety deposit boxes were kept. Ultimately, Logan had appealed to the older gentleman's business sense, stating the great need Maggie's daughter had for additional funds to pay the outstanding saloon bills and the hope that whatever Maggie had stashed away would help the White Dove through its current rough spot.

Tannenhill's gaze, rimmed with sagging skin but still clear with intelligence, continuously darted to the welt above Logan's eye and the man's wariness was obvious. Oddly enough, however, he silently agreed to the request. Logan could only guess that the early morning hour helped—there were few people about and the bank was empty except for the two of them. But he also sensed the bank clerk had a weakness for the White Dove, or Maggie Waters, or maybe both.

Dressed in a conservative brown wool suit and with dark hair slicked back—emphasizing the prominent jowls below his chin—

Tannenhill was likely not a great success with the ladies. Perhaps Maggie had lavished extra attention on him during his visits to the White Dove and in doing so instilled a loyalty that was about to pay off for Logan.

He lifted the lid and found a piece of paper inside which he hastily scanned. Trying to understand the implications, he read it several times before returning it to the box and securing the contraption.

Did Claire know about this? And if she did, why hadn't she told him?

And why the hell would Luttrell do this?

He passed Tannenhill on his way out.

"Find what you were looking for?" the banker asked.

"Unfortunately, no." He shook Tannenhill's hand. "But I appreciate your help all the same."

As Logan walked out of the bank, he caught sight of dark smoke billowing upward several streets away.

A quick deduction sent a shot of adrenaline through him. *The White Dove.*

---

CLAIRE STUMBLED ABOUT, her legs tripping over the hem of her nightgown. She flung an arm across her nose and mouth to block the smoke that filled the second floor of the saloon and was forced to close her burning eyes. She couldn't stay here much longer.

She'd already made her way to Ellie's room and found no one—she prayed Betsy had gotten her out. But Logan was nowhere to be seen, and Claire feared the worst. Heat from the flames rolled against her, and the wood that comprised most of the saloon snapped and crackled loudly as it was consumed. She ran down the hallway and used a hand to feel along the wall for the doorways, counting as she went. Her bare feet stepped on a hot spot, she shifted rapidly from foot to foot, and opened a door. *Please let this be the right one.*

"Logan!" She covered her face and struggled for breath, her lungs trying to consume air that wasn't there. *Where is he?*

Falling to her knees, she crawled toward the bed. *What if he's unconscious?* She had to reach him, even though she couldn't see past her nose and her breathing came in short gasps. She wouldn't leave him.

In that instant, she knew she wouldn't be leaving, either.

---

TWO WOMEN SAT in the dirt outside the White Dove when Logan rushed to the saloon. He recognized Betsy and assumed the other was Ellie. Groups of men shouted and brought buckets of water from somewhere, while smoke poured from shattered windows on the second floor. He quickly scanned the crowd but saw no sign of Claire. Panic squeezed his chest, propelling him around the building to the cabin that Claire occupied.

Empty.

Frantically, he headed inside, his gut guiding him upstairs. He knew Claire would have worried about Betsy and Ellie, would have come back in to help them. The heat blasted him, pushing him backwards, and the smoke made it impossible to see anything. He used his arm as a mask and stumbled to the second floor, then fell to his knees and crawled on all fours. Holding his breath, he prayed he would find her. He couldn't remain much longer.

The last place he dragged himself was his room, a location he thought to avoid altogether. Surprise flooded him when he bumped into Claire's soft form on the floor. He would have shouted his relief, but no breath remained.

With sheer willpower, he scooped her into his arms and

struggled down the smoke-filled hallway and stairs. His eyes stung and he stumbled, hitting the wall. *Have to get out...Move.*

Finally, the first floor. He staggered to the door, kicked it open, and was thrown off the porch as one of the interior walls collapsed, shattering his ears and shaking the other buildings. Glass rained down on his back as he covered Claire's body with his. Amid the screams of women, hands grabbed his arms and dragged him farther away from the burning building. For a moment all he could do was breath, his lungs hungry for air like an almost-starved calf desperate for milk from its dead mother. *Just breathe.* He coughed and gasped, his chest heaving. Black soot covered him.

*Where's Claire?*

He opened his eyes and saw her nearby on the ground, surrounded by Ellie, Betsy, and some of the girls from Southern Charm. He edged over to them and nudged the women aside more forcefully than he should have so he could reach her. He felt Claire's forehead, then moved the same hand under her shoulder blades as he brought her torso upright. She began coughing.

"Easy," he murmured. "You're all right."

She continued to cough and wheeze as she gulped air. His hand tightened on her shoulder and he buried his lips into her hair, mindless of the layer of grime that had dulled the blonde tresses and coated her like coal dust.

"Logan," she whispered. She leaned into him and grasped his shirt.

He held her close and blinked back the moisture in his eyes. *She could have died.* He'd wasted so much time looking in other rooms—he hadn't even planned to look in the one he had occupied for only one night. Why the hell would she risk her life for him? He'd barely gotten her out in time. By all accounts, she should be dead.

He would never understand the whys and wherefores of women, and he would never understand the reason Claire had gone in there to save him, but it stripped something fundamental from his core, from his belief system about the nature of women as they related to him. With Claire in his arms, he watched the final destruction of the White Dove Saloon.

---

CLAIRE SAT in the room Logan had rented at the Wagner Hotel. Dazed by the turn of events, she stared numbly at her hands. The saloon was gone and with it everything her mama had worked so long to achieve. Supplies, bedding, dry goods, pictures, mementos—all burned to nothing. Any business papers and the ledger were gone. Money? It was dust now unless some coins survived the blaze. Maybe tomorrow she would go back and sift through the ashes.

Claire closed her eyes and tried not to think of what she'd lost in the cabin, also destroyed. Her clothes, the wooden train Jack had given to Jimmy on his sixth birthday, all her medical books. Her dreams. Her life had been stripped bare—all she had was the torn and filthy nightgown she still wore.

Ellie survived, as did Betsy. *Thank God.* Someone had released Reverend and Storm from the makeshift stable in the rear of the building before it burned too.

Claire glanced across the room at the man standing at the window. *And Logan is alive.* It had terrified her when she realized she might lose him. Truly, the rest of it hadn't mattered....

The thought shamed her. When had Logan become more important than everything else in her life?

"In the safety deposit box is a land deed," Logan said, watching the street below. Still covered with black soot, he appeared menacing. "Do you know anything about that?"

Claire gave a slight shake of her head. "There wasn't anything else?" Her lungs felt as if they were full of ash and the wound on her ribs throbbed steadily.

"No."

"What is the deed for?" She swallowed against the dryness in her throat.

"Teddy Luttrell has left you a present."

"Me?" Claire frowned. "What are you talking about?"

"Two hundred thousand acres near Cimarron. The document was dated December of last year."

"Two hundred...." Claire's voice trailed off. "The land is mine?" she asked in disbelief.

"Mostly. Luttrell did put in a stipulation that only your husband possessed the right to manage or sell the property."

"Are you sure it was me and not Maggie?"

"I'm certain. I left the deed at the bank for safekeeping, but we can go look at it if you don't believe me."

"It's not that. I just don't understand. Why me?"

"Claire, exactly what was your relationship with Luttrell?"

Taken aback by Logan's frosty tone, she saw the truth in a flash. "I barely knew the man. I had little contact with him."

"Are you married?"

Logan's accusatory tone made her spine stiffen.

"No! Don't you think I would have told you if I were?"

"Then why would he leave the land to you and a husband that doesn't exist?"

"How should I know? You said that deed was dated in December. That was six months ago, and this is the first I've heard of it. The man died...." Panic slammed into her. "Do you think people might think I had something to do with it?"

Logan watched her, his eyes darkened with anger and lacking the warmth he'd shown her during the previous days. "Did you?"

"No!" The accusation rattled her.

"Was your mama involved with Luttrell?"

"I don't know. Maybe.... It's possible." Was Maggie behind all of this?

A knock on the door interrupted them. Logan accepted a note from a hotel employee and brought it to Claire.

"It's for you," he said.

Unfolding the paper, she scanned the contents. "It's from Betsy." The young woman had taken Ellie to Belle's place, thereby making the defection of the White Dove girls final. Claire honestly couldn't blame them—they literally had nothing and nowhere to go —but she still wished there had been something she could have done for them.

"Is anything wrong?" Logan asked.

She glanced at the note. Betsy had also written that a man was searching for Claire. "It seems Shorty McClaren wants to meet with me."

"Red's brother?"

Claire flinched at the reminder of the woman Logan had flirted with at the St. James.

"What do you know about him?" he asked.

"Not much. He hung around the White Dove a lot—seemed to be Mama's friend. Outwardly he's a part of Griffin's circle, so he may know something. He wants to meet at six o'clock."

"I'll go with you."

Claire took a steadying breath, uncertain whether Logan's presence would be an asset or a liability. He still appeared edgy, distant, and annoyed. She glanced down at her nightgown and shook her head.

"I need to ask a favor," she said, refusing to look at him. "I don't have any money or clothes."

"You don't have to look so disgusted asking for help."

"I'll pay you back, somehow."

He stood his ground by the window then grabbed his hat. "I'll have the hotel send up a tub and water. Don't leave until I get back."

Hardly. She wasn't about to hit the town naked.

When Logan was gone, Claire closed her eyes and let her shoulders sag in defeat.

———

BETSY'S NOTE told Claire to meet Shorty in the stables behind the Wagner Hotel. She touched the snouts of Storm and Reverend as she walked past their stalls, Logan trailing behind her. He murmured softly to the animals.

The earthy smells of hay, dirt and horse droppings filled Claire's nose, and she wondered again why Shorty wanted to see her. The wound on her side smarted and her breathing was still labored from the smoke—all in all she wasn't in good shape. She felt weary of this game her mama played, especially when she didn't know the rules. A brief thought of leaving town swept through her, but it was gone as quickly as it had come. She couldn't abandon Jimmy. But for the first time in her life she thought that maybe...maybe she *could* leave her mama.

They passed a youth who tended the place and continued on until she saw Shorty standing at the far end of the stalls. The three of them came together, alone and isolated from the people and wagons outside.

The young man pushed away from the wall as they approached and watched them closely. Red-haired and tall, his wiry frame hinted at barely contained energy. He swallowed hard and wiped his hands on his trousers. Claire took note of his nervousness. The few times she'd seen him around town with Griffin he'd been brash and confident, always interested in saying hello to her mama. And he had always played a lot of cards at the White Dove.

"Miss Claire." He nodded and removed his hat. His eyes darted to Logan then back again. "It's good to see you. I wasn't sure you'd meet me."

"Let's hope there won't be any trouble," she said as a warning.

After the last few days, she couldn't assume anything anymore. "This is Mr. Ryan," she added.

Shorty nodded, his gaze flicking from one to the other. He leaned forward and said, "It might be better if we speak in private."

"I prefer to stay," Logan said.

Claire considered everything Logan had bought her—several dresses, a handful of undergarments, a hairbrush and two pairs of new shoes. It was too much, but she was grateful and certainly in no situation to refuse his generosity. Layers of petticoats brushed against her legs beneath the dark gingham dress she wore, and the flat, black boots covered her feet with a snug tightness. Logan had dressed her as a respectable woman—asking him to leave was out of the question.

"Why did you want to see me?" she asked Shorty.

"Well," he said and cleared his throat. "I'm not quite sure where to start exactly."

"Do you know where my mama is?" she asked abruptly.

His gaze darkened with concern. "No. Do you?"

Claire shook her head. She had no reason to *distrust* Shorty, but she certainly had no reason *to* trust him.

"This is a lot more awkward than I thought it'd be," he said. "Your ma and me were close. Do you know about the land?"

"What do *you* know?" Logan asked.

Shorty nodded several times in succession and scratched the side of his nose. "Well, Maggie explained it all to me, and she asked if I would help her. Help you," he added quickly.

"How?" Claire asked.

"You'll be needing a husband to gain control of the land. That's why I'm here." He looked expectantly at her.

"You're here for what?" she asked.

"I'm here to marry you."

Claire's mouth dropped open. She'd expected Shorty to threaten her, or coerce her, or tell her something terrible might have happened to her mama, but she never, ever expected this.

---

LOGAN STEPPED FORWARD, and his chest brushed Claire's shoulder blades.

"You're here to marry Claire?" he asked, stunned by the presumption of the man. Shorty looked barely twenty.

McClaren nodded again in what was fast becoming an annoying habit.

"Why would you do that?" Logan asked.

"Maggie had trouble with the deed to the land, and she was worried Griffin would somehow get his hands on it. Giving it to Claire's husband seemed the best way to have access to it but still make it harder for Griffin to get it."

"But you work for Griffin," Claire accused.

"Yeah, but I'm in love with Maggie."

"What?" Claire asked.

"I know it sounds crazy, but she and I have an arrangement."

Logan could imagine what kind. Maggie Waters probably had arrangements with many men.

"So you know where she is?" Claire demanded.

"No," Shorty replied, stricken. "I haven't seen her in several weeks. But we'd discussed the deed and what to do beforehand, and when I learned you were in town, I came straightaway to see you."

"If you're in love with Maggie, why do you want to marry Claire?" Logan asked.

His eyes widened. "It won't be a real marriage, just a paper one. I'll take control of the land and give it to Maggie. I'm hoping she'll come back once she catches wind of it."

"What about Griffin?" Logan asked. He hitched an arm on a stall gate and remained close to Claire. All this talk of marriage was pissing him off. "Aren't you the least bit concerned about how he'll react to all of this?"

"Sure. I'm prepared to protect Claire. That was part of the deal."

Logan decided he'd heard enough. One thing was plain, the boy was in over his head. And Logan sure as hell wasn't going to pin Claire's safety on his questionable ability to safeguard her.

"How did Maggie get the land?" Claire asked.

Shorty shrugged. "I dunno. She's a smart lady though."

"Luttrell was killed last year," Claire said. "This implicates her. This implicates *me*."

Shorty stared at her. "Maggie didn't kill him."

"That's not what your sister says," Claire shot back.

"Paulina?" Shorty asked. "She's got no right spoutin' off. I know Maggie wouldn't have done it. And you didn't know about the land, did you? So you wouldn't have killed him neither."

"And you?" Logan asked.

"I didn't kill him." Shorty shifted from foot to foot, his gaze a little wild-eyed. "I'm just here to help Maggie like I promised her."

"I'm not going to marry you," Claire said.

"Why not?"

"Because this whole plan is ridiculous." She threw her hands up.

"Maggie was certain this was the best way, and she said you'd agree to anything."

"Why would she say that?"

Logan stood close enough to Claire that he felt her shallow breathing against his rib cage.

"Because the land was meant to give you money for school. She said somethin' about you wantin' to be a doctor."

Logan sensed the change in Claire's body instantly. Stillness filled her and he feared she'd stopped breathing. If Claire was tricking him about Luttrell then he was a fool because he was beginning to believe she hadn't known anything about the land. It had rubbed him the wrong way, how Luttrell had taken Dee from him, and now was taking Claire too.

He placed a hand on her shoulder, trying to let her know he understood about her shock. She never expected her own mother to pay such attention to her dreams. Despite everything, Logan's opinion of Maggie Waters grudgingly went up a notch.

"Claire can't marry you," Logan said to Shorty.

The young man frowned and replaced his hat. "Why's that?"

"Because she's gonna marry me." And with that, Logan solved his dilemma of what to do with Claire and his burgeoning feelings for her. He wouldn't let her slip from his hands as Dee had.

But first, he'd have to convince her.

# CHAPTER 12

L ogan married Claire the following afternoon before a Justice of the Peace at the town courthouse. It was a simple ceremony well attended by the prostitutes in town, who seemed happy to be in a place of law for a reason other than answering to solicitation offenses.

Claire appeared distracted throughout the brief exchange of vows, and her back couldn't have been more straight and rigid. Logan placed a hand just above the flare of her hips to help her relax. She wore one of the cotton calico dresses he'd bought her the day before, her blonde tresses loose and swept away from her face, and he felt both relief and concern for the future. As her husband, he could take control of the land and protect her from inexperienced upstarts like Shorty McClaren, as well as more serious threats from Frank Griffin and Raul Sandoval. Her new inheritance would undoubtedly make her a target. Logan had to believe she hadn't known about it, had to believe she'd had nothing to do with Teddy Luttrell.

If Luttrell hadn't already been dead, Logan would've enjoyed an encounter with the man.

As Logan knew she would, Claire had argued against the

marriage. She didn't believe he should make this sacrifice for her, couldn't understand why he would do it. Not entirely certain himself, all he'd had to do was look into Claire's green eyes to catch a glimpse of a future that for whatever reason made sense to him. He wanted her—maybe more than he'd ever wanted Dee—so took the opportunity presented him and stacked the cards in his favor as much as possible.

Claire hadn't stood a chance once he made up his mind. In an uneasy truce, they'd shared the hotel room last night—he on the floor, she on the bed—and came to the ceremony in an awkward silence.

"I now pronounce you man and wife," the Justice said.

Logan lightly kissed Claire while she watched him, her eyes haunted with distress.

"Smile," he said. "It's your wedding day."

An uncertain flick of her gaze was the only response he received.

Logan grinned. Despite everything, it was a mighty fine day to get married. The sun was shining, and Claire looked damn pretty. She had told him she worried the disarray of her life would burden him, but he felt quite the opposite. It made him feel more confident that together they would resolve the mystery of Maggie's disappearance, and then move on with their lives. Logan was generally an optimistic fellow and having Claire at his side made him...well, it made him happy. A mighty fine day indeed.

His thoughts turned briefly to Texas. Eventually he'd take *his wife* home. The thought swept through him with a rush of possession. He wouldn't let her go, he wouldn't let her slip away from him as Dee had.

"Congratulations, Claire," Betsy said and hugged her. "Congratulations to you also, Mr. Ryan."

"Thank you," Claire replied woodenly.

"You take care of this little lass," Ellie said. "She's a catch and don't you ever forget it."

"No, ma'am, I won't." Logan held tight to Claire's hand as other women came to wish them well. Some of them he recognized from Southern Charm.

Louisa whispered something into Claire's ear and a blush crept across his wife's face, reminding Logan of her innocence. But he took heart that she responded to him in small ways. With a little charm and patience, he'd be able to nudge her into his bed, and as her husband he now had every right to the lushness of her body. Marriage, he hoped, would affect her willingness to open up to him, to let him get close to her.

The crowd dispersed.

Tia and One-Eyed Jack, who served as their witnesses, came forward. Logan knew their presence would mean a lot to Claire and he refused to take no from the Indian couple, despite their protests that Claire might want someone else to stand at her side.

"We go now," Tia said.

"Thank you for coming." Claire bent to hug the Indian woman.

"Jack." Logan shook the man's hand.

"Watch out for our Claire," Jack said, then turned to embrace her. Logan watched as a genuine smile crossed her face.

"No," Tia said. "They will watch out for each other." She took Logan's hand and tugged at it until he leaned closer to her face. "The truth flies beyond our grasp. Remember, your heart will always tell you the way to go."

"Where did you hear that?" Jack asked. "Have you been reading my Bible?"

Tia shook her head and waved him off. "I no read that book. And I do not know why you spend so much time with your nose in it." She grinned at Logan and Claire, then moved to leave.

"Has it occurred to you that all these Christians running around might be on to something?"

"Jack, you cannot even read."

"I do read...." Their voices trailed off.

Logan ushered Claire toward the outer door.

"Who's that?" she asked, looking at the gentleman across the room.

Logan almost forgot. "He's from the *Las Vegas Optic*." He stepped back so she could precede him outside. "He's going to include our wedding in the paper tomorrow."

"Why?" Claire asked, her alarm apparent.

They stopped on the front steps as Logan placed his hat on his head. "Because everyone in town should know."

Claire stared at him and began to fidget. "What about Sandoval?"

"He already knows you're alive. I'd venture to say most folks do. The burning of the White Dove was front page news today. Now everyone will know that to get to you, they'll have to go through me first. I'm just your typical thickheaded cattle rancher, Claire. I protect what's mine."

He watched, somewhat amused, as she tried to think of something to say.

"It'd be my pleasure to buy you dinner, Mrs. Ryan." He offered her his arm.

She yielded and put her hand in the crook of his elbow.

---

CLAIRE FELT MORE than a little uncomfortable about this marriage. She would be the first to admit she had no idea what she was doing or where to go from here. Her dress and petticoats rustled around her feet as they walked around the corner toward the plaza, Logan's tall frame moving easily beside her. She wanted—needed—his presence but couldn't believe this marriage was what he wanted, what *he* needed. Their shared kisses and compelling attraction aside, she had the sense Logan wasn't the kind of man to be tied down.

And now he planned to announce their nuptials in the newspaper. Such public scrutiny troubled her. Claire was accustomed to hiding—her thoughts, her dreams, herself.

Would it make her more respectable in the eyes of the townsfolk? Or would suspicion be cast on her in Luttrell's death when knowledge of the land grant became public? Would her mama finally come forward if she learned her one and only daughter had gotten married?

"You look worried," Logan said as they crossed onto Pacific Street.

"Just a little."

"Can we talk about it? I'm a good listener."

Claire looked into his blue-green eyes and it suddenly struck her —*Logan is my husband*. Life had just taken a profound and startling turn, and here she was, standing beside the man of her dreams. Yes, Logan was everything she could have ever wanted in a man, in a husband. Tomorrow anything might happen, and Claire was hard-pressed to believe it would be for the good. But here they stood, together.

Live for the here and now, Tia had told her often enough, but Claire had never really understood it. Until now.

"I've never been married," she blurted out.

"I know, Claire."

They'd settled that the previous night when Logan had accused her of being more than friendly with Luttrell. A thought struck from out of the blue. "Have you?"

"Almost...once. It didn't work out."

That was a distracting image, but Claire pushed it aside.

"We'll work this out," he added. "Somehow." His gaze darkened and he said in a low voice, "There's no pressure for anything else, but you should know...I want this to be a real marriage."

Exhilaration rippled through her. Her weakness for this man was thorough and complete. If this was his price, then he'd hooked her because she wanted everything he offered—marriage, security, himself. Everyone had a price, and Logan was hers.

"Yes." The promise of having Logan brought her to this—uttering as bold a declaration as she was ever likely to make. She took satisfaction that she briefly rendered him speechless.

Logan took her hand and led her off the street into the semi-privacy of shaded area near a mercantile shop. He urged her back against the wooden exterior and propped a hand near her head.

"You sure?" But his voice was a caress, an enticement.

A shiver ran down her spine. "Yes."

"Then it must be my birthday."

"Why?"

He leaned close. "All my wishes are coming true."

Their lips met, barely making contact. Claire closed her eyes, closed out the sounds of horses and wagons on the street beyond, closed out the chatter of men and women moving about. Logan's mouth was warm and sweet and gentle. His smooth face smelled of soap, attesting to his efforts to look his best for their wedding, and Claire's mind swirled with what was to come.

*Don't think.*

Her arms came around his neck and his mouth molded to hers. Excitement exploded in her belly and Claire felt an overwhelming greed for more. She kissed him with abandonment, aware for the first time how much her body hungered for this—for him—and liberated by the fact that finally she would have the satisfaction she craved, the satisfaction that could only be found at his hands.

Logan wrapped her into himself and she gave herself to the sharp physical pleasure of his touch, her injury but a minor flinch, easily ignored. No thought occupied her mind except to hold him and kiss him like a woman who knew of such things. She didn't know, not firsthand at least, but Logan didn't seem to care. And neither did Claire.

She kissed his cheeks and ran her fingers into the hair at the nape of his neck, inhaling his potently familiar scent. It wasn't enough. Logan devoured her mouth, his tongue sliding against hers, and a jolt of restlessness shot through her body.

"Claire," Logan rasped as his hands framed her face. Her hair fell free from the pins she'd used to make herself look presentable for her wedding. Not just presentable—she'd had a strong urge to look pretty. And she'd wanted Logan to notice.

"Let's skip dinner." She nipped at his mouth with her teeth.

He exhaled a ragged breath. "Fine with me, sweetheart."

He ran a thumb across her lower lip and grinned, the action igniting a fire in her abdomen. He looked toward the street, took her hand again, and guided her back to the dusty thoroughfare. Claire struggled to keep pace with Logan's long strides as they crossed the open plaza. Upon reaching the Wagner Hotel they moved quickly through the lobby, up the stairs, and Logan unlocked their hotel room door so swiftly Claire wondered if he hadn't left it unlocked. As soon as they were inside the darkened room, Logan pinned her against the now-closed door and kissed her with an intensity that made her tremble. She decided she'd forgotten how to breathe.

In the cocoon of anonymity the hotel created, she pushed her inhibitions aside and let her body act purely on instinct. She rarely released the rigid control by which she lived her life day in and day out, rarely took the risk of opening herself to another human being. But with Logan, she burned to consume him, her passion obliterating all else.

Never had she thought it would be like this—shaking from his touch, wanting to be a part of him so completely that reasonable thought slipped from her mind.

As they kissed and their lips exchanged breath and heat and need, Claire pushed off Logan's hat and jacket. Both fell to the floor with a muffled thud. His hands moved to the front of her dress, quickly unbuttoning it and pushing it from her shoulders.

He yanked off his tie and she pulled his shirt from his trousers. Next came her camisole, which he peeled down to her waist. Her breasts reacted to the exposure, tightening, tingling as he touched her more intimately than anyone ever had. His lips moved down her neck. He knelt and his mouth covered first one nipple, then the other. Claire inhaled sharply as the sensation nearly undid her.

"Logan," she gasped.

"I'll be careful." His hand gently skimmed the bandages on her ribcage.

"Not that." She could barely speak the words.

"I know, sweetheart." His voice sounded desperate, almost strangled. Like hers. "I can't wait, either."

He pulled her into his arms and his mouth ground onto hers. He steered her toward the bed. When Claire felt the mattress against the back of her knees, she gratefully sat down on the edge—her legs had outlived their usefulness anyhow. Logan unbuttoned his shirt and trousers and removed his boots.

Then he shed all of his clothes.

The haze of their lovemaking lifted for a moment and Claire wondered what she was doing. In the darkness, Logan loomed large and otherworldly, a man not of this place, a man who wanted her and with that wanting changed her life. She swallowed against the dryness in her mouth, against the uncertainty pounding in her heart.

He came forward and with fingers that left a trail of fire on her skin steadfastly removed the dress and petticoats from her hips.

The vulnerability of a woman in this position became starkly apparent to her.

"Spread your legs." His deep voice vibrated at the very center of her body.

How could a woman do this without trust?

Did she trust Logan?

It was too late if she didn't.

She ignored another sudden burst of anxiety that hovered on the outskirts of what was left of her rational mind and slowly spread her legs. Logan watched her face as he reached down and touched her with his hand. Her hips jerked as he pushed a finger inside her. She gasped, clutching the bedspread in an effort to keep from flying off the bed.

"Jesus, you're ready," he said to her. "But you're so tight. Hang onto me."

Claire didn't understand. He brought his arms against each side of her head to support himself and pushed forward with one thrust, completely entering her. The sensation was unexpectedly thorough, unexpectedly personal. Her fingers dug into his shoulders as she grimaced and strained to suppress her moans.

He paused, bending his head, and took several steadying breaths. Sweat coated her hands as she grasped the muscles of his arms. Then he kissed her with a tenderness that seemed at odds with his rigidly held body.

It hurt as he came into her, but she feared if she told him he would leave. And now, as her body began to accept the fullness of him, she didn't want him to withdraw. He began to move inside her and she felt the tension build again, felt his chest move against her breasts, felt her senses heightened, aware of only him, of wanting him, of needing him.

Logan's hands brought her legs around his hips. He moved in and out of her with unrelenting precision, wrapping his arms behind her backside and pressing even closer. Claire hung onto him, overwhelmed by it all, tears trailing a wet path to her ears.

Her climax slammed through her without warning, and she clawed at Logan's back, every muscle in her body tightening around him. He tensed in response as Claire rode the intense wave, sliding back from the pleasure in a complete daze.

Logan shifted slightly from her bandaged side. He kissed her and rubbed his nose on her cheek. Claire closed her eyes as he rested his forehead on her shoulder. She could still feel him inside her. It was a wicked and satisfying dream, everything her body had needed, and more.

After a time, he rolled away, left the bed, and returned with a towel. He gently cleaned her then drew the covers over the both of them, gathering her into his arms. Too exhausted to speak, Claire drifted off as Logan's hand did lazy circles lower and lower along her back.

---

LOGAN THOUGHT of the woman in his arms, the steady rise and fall of her chest signaling the onset of sleep.

She made love as if her life depended on it.

And something in the back of his mind echoed the sentiment.

He didn't remember it being like this with Dee.

# CHAPTER 13

C laire awoke during the night. The covers had fallen away, and she was completely naked. It should have embarrassed her, but it didn't. She carefully propped herself on one arm and looked over to where Logan slept on his back. Moonlight filtered through the window, allowing her to view him in a white glow. A mat of dark hair covered his chest and his lean, well-muscled shoulders made her itch to be in his arms again. Her gaze trailed along his stomach to the patch of hair farther down. The mere sight of him made her body react.

He was her husband now. There was nothing wrong with what they'd done, and there was nothing wrong with the fact that she wanted to do it again. She lay down beside him, the tip of one breast grazing his arm. It surprised her that sex would appeal so much, that she would so willingly enjoy the act—so willingly give herself over to it. Perhaps it was the biggest mistake she would ever make, but it was hardly something she wanted to think about at the moment.

She needed Logan to touch her again, to make her feel frantic and mad and half-wild. She kissed his cheek then nuzzled his neck, and soon he began to stir. She felt bolder and moved to his chest, kissing and rubbing her nose through the hairs. His hands came to her head and pulled her toward his face, bringing their mouths together. She moved on top of him, the full brunt of his arousal pushing against her abdomen.

His tongue thrust in and out of her mouth as his hands firmly gripped the sides of her head. He came up for air and whispered, "Are you sure? I don't want you to be sore."

She didn't doubt she'd be tender, but that by no means discouraged her. She nibbled his ear and relaxed against him. "I'm sure."

He rolled her over and ran a hand over one breast and down to her hips, then stopped to gaze at her bared to him, body and soul. Logan compelled her and aroused her. With instincts newly discovered, she sensed the power and beauty she possessed and the way she aroused *him*. Sex was intoxicating. The sweetest medicine for any ailment.

Logan lightly ran a finger between her breasts as he kissed her collarbone then moved lower and placed his mouth over a nipple. As his tongue and lips circled and tugged, Claire arched back and her breath hissed, and her fingers became tangled in the sheets. Logan's left hand moved between her legs, caressing her, stroking her. She moaned, the sensitivity of her body stringing her as tight as a rope.

With his mouth on her breast and his finger inside her, he brought her close to completion. Logan removed his hand and Claire whimpered, nearly begging him not to leave her. With a sigh of anticipation, she waited for him to finish what he'd started, startled when he sat up and drew her to him.

She straddled him and hung tight while he pushed into her. Leaning her head on his shoulder, her body shuddered in response. As he shifted her closer, she wrapped her legs around him and with one hand braced behind her head he kissed her, uniting their mouths in the same way their bodies merged together.

She clung to him, her hair hanging down her back and tickling her exposed bottom. He lifted her slightly to move in and out, but

Claire's body succumbed quickly. Logan held her steady as he thrust into her with short, rhythmic bursts, and if his own shudders were any indication, he achieved his release at the same time.

Claire's body shook and tears once again ran down her face. Logan kissed her. "Shhh," he said against her mouth. "Darlin', don't cry."

She squeezed her eyes shut and buried her face into Logan's neck. He held her close as they sat on the bed. "I'm fine," she insisted, flustered by the show of emotion, wondering what caused it.

Logan gathered her closer, their naked bodies touching in the intimate darkness. The scent of their lovemaking surrounded her, not an unpleasant smell, and it made her feel connected to him—not as an acquaintance, not as a friend, but as a lover. The union made her body vibrate with longing for him, even now, buried as he was still inside her.

"I've thought of you like this," he murmured. "Ever since that night I found you in my bed all those months ago."

She sniffed then laughed, a sigh quickly following on the same breath. Her mind and her heart were a mass of confusion. Bewildered by her need for him, she nipped and tasted the skin below his ear, the contact sweet and desperate.

"I had no idea," she said. She couldn't deny she'd been interested in him after their initial meeting, but she never would have guessed at the hunger that consumed them tonight. She never would have guessed this had lain dormant between them. "You kept it to yourself very well."

"Maybe if I hadn't, you would've stayed on at the SR." He leaned back and faced her.

"I had to come back," she said quietly.

He kissed her, lips parted, wisps of her hair catching between their mouths. "Then it's a good thing I followed you, or else you'd be with Shorty right now." His tongue pushed open her mouth and entered forcefully as his hands braced the back of her head for his assault.

Dazzled from the kiss, her defenses down, she responded truthfully. "I'm glad I'm with you instead."

"Then we're off to a good start."

And to her amazement, Logan made love to her again.

CLAIRE AWOKE WITH A START. Logan stood at the open hotel-room door, dressed only in trousers, and let someone in. "Louisa!" she blurted with surprise. She sat up and clutched the sheets to cover her nudity. "What are you doing here?"

The sultry Mexican beauty wore an oversized duster and a hat with a wide brim, and when Claire's gaze dropped to the woman's feet and saw the heavy boots covering them, she knew something was wrong. "What's happened?"

Louisa shut the door quickly behind her. "I sorry to interrupt. I no have much time. The owner, he will awake soon." She indicated the clothing she wore. Gone was her beguiling nature and in its place was an earnestness Claire had never before seen from her.

"I hear Belle, at first not on purpose, but then *sí*, on purpose. She talk to Harry Myers. He ride north to find Frank Griffin. He speak of Maggie as if he know where she is. He say she go to the mountains, and he brag he know how to find her."

"How?" Claire asked.

"Harry and Luttrell were *compadres*, you know? Harry say Luttrell leave a treasure in the hills. He say Maggie know where it is. She go to the Cristos to find."

"If Harry and Teddy were so tight, why doesn't Harry just lead Griffin there himself?" Logan asked, folding his arms across his naked torso and drawing a speculative glance from Louisa.

Even in the woman's panicked state she still couldn't keep her eyes off Logan, irritating Claire. If she hadn't been completely unclothed, Claire would have crossed the room and stood between them.

Louisa shook her head. "I know not. But most *importante*, Myers say he and Griffin will do away with Maggie when they find her."

Claire's heart stopped. Her only glimmer of hope was that Maggie had yet to be found by anyone. Maybe Myers wouldn't locate her mother either. He'd never struck Claire as overflowing with intellect.

"I go now," Louisa said. "If I hear more, I bring it to you. I no want anything to happen to Maggie, she always good to us." She turned to Logan. "Will you check hall? I no wish to be seen."

Logan helped Louisa depart then locked the door. Silence filled the room.

"I can guess what you're thinking," he finally said from across the room. "And let me tell you right now—no."

"What?"

"You're not going after Myers."

"Somebody has to," Claire said loudly.

"I'll go. I want you to stay with Tia. Get out of town, and don't let anyone know where you are."

Claire bent her knees and leaned forward against them, the sheet still covering what Logan had already seen. She shook her head. "No. I want to come with you."

"I don't agree. This could be dangerous."

"You have no obligation to do this. You don't know my mama, or Myers, or Griffin. You're not in the middle of this. Why would you go?"

"You're wrong," he replied. "I am in the middle. You're my wife."

The statement hit her square between the eyes, and all she could do was stare at him. Logan would ride off, guns blazing, to help her, and while it was noble and flattering and something she'd never expected from a man, she also hated it. If Logan ended up dead, it would be all her fault.

"Since I am your wife," she said slowly, "then I want to come with you. I can't—I won't—let you do this alone."

Logan scratched his mussed hair and looked at the floor, but he wouldn't come to the bed—to her. Claire wanted him to touch her as he had all night long. She also wanted to make certain any images that lingered of Louisa—unattractive attire aside—were erased from his mind.

"We don't have much time," she said, her voice husky, her intentions clear. Women had long used their bodies to get what they wanted, why should she be any different? Besides, she wanted it too. "Come back to bed." She moved the sheet away from her.

The desire was plain to see on his face, and elsewhere, despite his trousers. He crossed the room and stood beside the bed. His eyes ran the length of her, and the excitement of what was to come spread like wildfire through her body.

"You realize, of course, that when our marriage hits the papers today, Griffin and Myers will most likely come looking for you."

"Then we don't have much time."

His gaze bore into her, his frustration evident.

"You stay close to me and do everything I say." He removed his trousers but didn't touch her.

Claire knew he talked not only about Myers, but also about making love to her. "All right," she agreed.

He brought her legs over the edge of the bed, and only when he was fully inside her did he lean over and kiss her. In a mad frenzy, their coupling didn't take long.

# CHAPTER 14

When they left town that morning, Claire rode a horse Logan purchased because he felt Reverend could use a rest. They headed north toward Cimarron and followed the same path from several days before when Claire had pretended she had a husband. Now, it was a reality.

Logan appeared to have some idea of where he was going, of what he was doing. Claire fell into a contemplative silence and wondered if chasing after Harry Myers would prove fruitful or a complete waste of time. Would they find her mama before it was too late? Would they find Jimmy? She sincerely hoped so.

With the sun shining bright and the open plains beckoning them forward, she had trouble getting hold of the thought that she and Logan were married. It had been only one week since he showed up on the steps of the White Dove. As if caught in a storm, she felt her head spinning, everything moving fast and furious, and last night was no exception. Logan had overpowered her, consumed her, had made every one of her desires come true—as well as a few she hadn't known about—all under the respectful guise of marriage.

They headed west of Fort Union, riding farther into the tree line this time, pine and cedar crowding around them, grand sentinels of the forest. Their progress was slow.

Were they behind Myers? There'd been no sign of the men in town before she and Logan had departed, for which she was grateful, but that didn't necessarily mean the man had left town at all. Perhaps this would help her and Logan gain a head start and locate Maggie and Jimmy first. The thought filled her with hope.

"Do you have any idea where we're going?"

"Some." His eyes flashed as he glanced at her, their horses side by side.

The heat in her belly kicked up a notch. What was wrong with her? They'd spent a long night together. Why did she wonder when he might touch her next? Not hold her hand or kiss her cheek but remove her clothes and make her body clench with need.

"I don't mean to be rude, but how in the world will we find Myers or Griffin?" she asked. "Are we going all the way back to Cimarron?"

Logan's dark gaze rested on her again. "We're following Sandoval."

"We are?" Alarm and dread both filled her at once. She was so stupid. Of course, Sandoval would be involved in whatever was going down with Griffin. "I didn't even know he was back in town."

"He kept a low profile. Seems you did nick him in the shoulder when you shot at him the other night. Louisa told me when I went out to buy your horse."

The casual mention of the sultry Mexican prostitute brought Claire up short. "I see."

"Sandoval has a bad habit of dumping the contents of his smoking pipe."

Claire looked on the ground around them. "You've seen it?"

Logan nodded.

"You've got a better eye than I do." She wondered if his *eye* had looked more than once at Louisa. She wasn't sure which was worse

—fearing for her life from Sandoval, or fearing the loss of Logan's attentions to another woman. "How do you know he smokes a pipe?" she asked distractedly.

"I smelled it on him the other night. It's a very distinct combination of tobacco and other ingredients, sometimes called *kinnikinnic*."

"I've never heard of it."

"It's an Indian mix. The tobacco is combined with willow bark or sumac leaves or somethin' else."

"Do you think he knows where my mama is?"

"Hard to say, but he's definitely moving with determination. I'm betting he's to meet up with Myers or Griffin. So, we'll just hang back awhile."

"All right," she replied reluctantly. Given a choice, she wouldn't follow in the footsteps of Raul Sandoval. Logan's apparent lack of concern eased her discomfort, but only a little. She knew he would never deliberately put her in danger. If anything did happen, it would be by her own hand since she insisted on coming. She should trust him. "If I hadn't been shot in Cimarron, we might not have left. Maybe we would have found her."

"But we wouldn't have found the key or the land title." He pushed his hat back a bit.

"My mama could be anywhere in these hills," Claire said, daunted by the task of searching for her.

"We'll get a bead on Myers and Griffin, let them lead the way, then slide in behind and get to her first."

Claire nodded. She just hoped when they did, it wouldn't be too late. And she prayed that Jimmy would be safe and sound.

---

NIGHTFALL APPROACHED as they rode into Cimarron once again. Logan wondered if Sandoval would stop first at the house outside of town where Griffin had been holed up—the same homestead where Claire had been shot. Not comfortable to leave her in town, he hid her in the wilderness while he checked out the spread, but it was deserted. The fresh tracks of three horses snaked away from the dwelling, and he concluded that Sandoval had met up with Griffin and Myers. After picking up the trail northwest of town, Logan retrieved Claire before heading into the mountains.

Complete darkness finally forced him to stop and set up camp with his wife. He liked the sound of that. While he'd been reluctant to commit his heart to another woman, he knew Claire was the only one worthy of the effort. And although he would've liked more time to ease them both into such a permanent commitment, he suspected they'd never have had that luxury considering the circumstances.

Life was a gamble, Logan had always believed that, and he knew he'd just taken a big risk. But there was no choice really—he wanted Claire too much to let her slip away from him.

He pitched a tent, then tended to the horses while Claire unpacked their gear. He told her no fire and she quietly agreed. He hobbled the horses as a breeze blew through the surrounding pine boughs, and for a moment he paused to savor the solitude. With Claire at his side, Logan found it difficult to view the future as an unknown void.

He sat across from where Claire perched on a low rock and offered her bread and cheese.

"It still seems strange to me," she said. "Being married." She stared at the food in her hands.

Logan removed his hat. "Regrets?"

"No, not exactly. But I'm sure you didn't plan to saddle yourself with a wife when you came to Las Vegas to make sure I wasn't sick."

"No, can't say as I did." He took a swig of water from his canteen.

"I never really saw myself getting married."

"Because of your ma?"

She nodded.

"That would make for a lonely life, don't you think?" he asked.

Claire tore off a piece of bread and ate it. "Maybe. But the girls at the saloon...they have an odd sort of freedom."

"How's that?"

"The ability to come and go as they will. There was a woman who worked at The Dove some time ago—she called herself Bronco Betty. She was quite a character and told the most fascinating stories of places she'd been, things she'd seen."

"You have a bit of wanderlust in you, Claire."

A wistful smile crossed her face. "I've always wanted to travel, to see what else the world has to offer. So many places, so many people. I've read of things in books that must be truly amazing to see in person."

"You're a romantic," he said.

"No." But she shook her head too quickly. "Just naturally curious, I suppose."

"You don't have to sell yourself like Bronco Betty to see the world."

"You're right. There was certainly nothing romantic about what the White Dove women endured night after night, but the rest of the time they did as they pleased. They didn't walk around town worried about what other people thought, because everyone already thought the worst."

"Sounds as if you admire them."

Claire slowly chewed a piece of cheese. "I guess you could say they were my role models, and they were far from women with black hearts. Survivors might be a better way to describe them."

"So, it bothers you that you're married." Logan wondered why he hadn't noticed it sooner. Claire valued her freedom.

"It doesn't bother you?"

If any part of it did, he wasn't about to dwell on it. As he saw it, the good outweighed the bad.

"No, not really," he replied. "I can't explain what brought us to this point, but I'm an honest fellow, and I'll try to do right by you."

"You've sacrificed a lot."

"I don't believe in sacrifice."

"How can you say that? What about going back to Texas to help your folks."

"That wasn't a hardship, I was ready to go home." Logan examined the cloudless, night sky. "*You've* forfeited a lot, putting up with all life had to offer because of your ma. You should follow your heart now."

"Have you?"

Logan hesitated. For the last few years his heart had been in limbo. Going home to his family's ranch had given him time to rest, to recoup his hurt over Dee's betrayal. He answered as honestly as he could. "You're a fire in my blood, Claire. I'd like to make this work."

Claire watched him in silence and Logan imagined her as a child, when a dove had come to her in a forest much like this one, and Tia had witnessed an extraordinary moment. Claire gave everything of herself—to her mama, her brother, the women in the saloons she tried to help—but at the same time she shielded her very essence from those around her. He suspected it had been a rare moment when the dove had been drawn to a young girl who had let her guard down.

"What will happen when this is all over?" she asked quietly.

He moved closer and lightly touched her face. "I was thinking I'd take you back to Texas. I was thinking that maybe we'd figure out a way for you to become a doctor."

"Then you *would* make a sacrifice. For me?"

"No. I'd call it a compromise."

"What do you expect in return?"

He brought his face to hers. "A babe, or two. A life—together."

He kissed her before a protest could pour out of her lovely lips.

"Maybe you don't realize what's going on here." He moved his lips down her neck then brought his face directly before hers, enjoying the slight tremble of her body. "But this magic we generate isn't the normal course between men and women."

"Like most men," Claire said in rapid whisper, "you place far too much importance on sex."

"I've had sex, darlin'," he said. "I'd rather have this." He took her lips with his and thoroughly kissed her. Barely touching her, he was already close to the brink, desperate to be inside her, desperate to touch her in the only way he knew.

Swiftly he stood, located a few blankets and, ignoring the tent, tossed them on the ground. He wanted her now, under the stars, with the scent of pine trees filling the air and urgency burning in his veins.

Claire didn't speak as she went to him. He brought his mouth to hers and tugged her against the length of his body. She matched his need with her own, moving a hand behind his head and deepening the kiss. Logan lowered her to the ground, knelt before her and unbuttoned the barriers that blocked his assault, his patience all but gone.

Baring her breasts, he moved his hands and mouth to them together. Claire released a sharp intake of breath as he eased her to the ground, slid off her skirt and undergarments, and moved over her, pausing just short of penetration.

"You seem to think this will make everything all right," she said, her voice ragged. "This only makes it harder."

"You think too much."

She lifted her head and kissed him, her hands cupping the sides of his face. He settled more fully onto her and enjoyed the pressure of her breasts and thighs against him. His body thrust into hers and she closed around him, taking him fully, and he lost himself to the pleasure of touching her, the intimacy shattering in its rawness.

Logan gripped her buttocks with one hand and her hair with the other, unable to stop the release that slammed into him. With every thrust he consumed and filled her, fighting for air, exhaling her name on the barest of breath. He grasped and struggled to get closer, to make it last longer.

He hadn't told her he loved her. He never said anything he didn't mean. But God knew she was an inferno in his blood, a blaze that burned through every nook and cranny of his mind and his heart. Resting his head against her shoulder, he was gripped with the fear of losing her.

He inhaled the scent of her—sex and woman—and ran his tongue between her breasts, tasting the salt of her sweat. He looked to the dark cleft where they were still joined, and an aftershock of release rolled through him. His mouth consumed one taut nipple and he began an aggressive assault with his tongue as her fingers dug into his scalp.

Gathering her close beneath him, he shielded her body from the cool night air. A primal urge overtook him—he wanted a babe in her belly, an irrevocable link that would bind her to him for all the years to come. He ruthlessly pushed aside the thought she might not stay with him. Buried deep inside her, he wondered if she had any idea of the rashness that overpowered him. In a haze of sex and lust and need, he convinced himself he had every right to stake a claim on her body in the most basic way a man could.

He had every right to stake a claim on her heart.

# CHAPTER 15

In the pre-dawn mist, Claire climbed up the hill to be alone, having left the warmth of Logan's body as he slept. She willed her mind to focus on the steady rhythm of the upward hike, but stray thoughts filtered past her resolve and her mind replayed the previous night's activities over and over.

Logan had made love to her with an intensity that frightened her, overwhelmed her, and left her wanting him even now. If she were completely honest, she'd gone to him with an equal amount of fervor—desperate to have him inside her, desperate for the madness whenever he touched her.

The woods were quiet, the stillness deafening. A white haze from the respiring trees wove in and out of the tall pine trunks. Claire stopped, closed her eyes, and inhaled deeply. Logan had woven his way into her life much the way the morning fog permeated every corner of the forest. But, it was her own desires that had led her to this point.

Logan thought he'd done right by marrying her, but she would have gone to him anyway. With her strong convictions faltering, the marriage had occurred at an opportune time, with the tension between the two of them hovering near a breaking point. Her helplessness and inability to think straight when he was near both frustrated and bewildered her. It seemed inevitable that the marriage and this whole dream existence would eventually come crashing down around her. All the more reason to embrace what she had and leave the worrying till tomorrow.

She opened her eyes and continued the uphill climb into a forest dense with fir, pine, and spruce. The exertion helped take her mind off the man she was fairly certain she could love—if she didn't already.

She came to a trickle of water cascading down a rocky slope and splashed cool liquid onto her face. A voice startled her, as it uttered a squeal of surprise followed by a muffled grunt. It sounded like a child. Looking around, she tried to locate the source as she methodically circled the area. From the corner of her eye, she glimpsed a small leg vanish behind a boulder.

"Jimmy?" The name escaped her lips in a breathless plea.

She dodged between trees and wondered why she couldn't see the youngster. She wasn't that far behind him. Distantly, Claire acknowledged her growing disorientation—Logan would wonder where she'd gone—but a fierce need to catch the child gripped her and she raced with the sole focus of reaching him before he disappeared for good.

"Wait!" she yelled, confused and curious.

She sprinted under a branch and veered around a tree trunk, the single braid flopping against her back and stray wisps of hair clinging to her mouth. The wound on her ribs began to hurt, but she didn't give in to the impulse to check for blood seepage from the healing laceration.

Her hair snagged on something—a tree branch?—and jerked her head back painfully. She twisted and fell to the ground, breaking her fall with her hands. Scuffed boots filled her vision, and the sweet smell of tobacco assaulted her nose, prompting waves of nausea and panic.

Sandoval gripped her arms and hauled her upright onto wobbly feet. His grin exposed brown-stained teeth and his eyes glittered with malice. "I have what you look for." He spun her around and dragged her behind a cluster of trees.

"Lemme go!" a young boy screamed, struggling against the rope that tied his hands around a skinny pine tree.

*Jimmy!*

"You lemme go, you hear me?" He shrieked like an animal caught in a hunter's trap.

Claire yanked free of Sandoval and ran to her brother, his blond hair dirty and his brown eyes wild with fear as he looked at her. Tears blurred her vision.

"Jimmy, it's me. It's Claire."

He gazed up at her as she tentatively reached out for him.

He flinched. "You're not Claire. My sister's dead."

She saw a half-crazed creature before her—torn shirt, filthy trousers, threadbare moccasins, and struggled to find any resemblance to the little boy who had enjoyed the bedtime stories she would create of far-off places and heroes with hearts of gold.

"I'm not dead," she said quietly, aware that Sandoval stood less than ten feet from them. "I've come back for you."

Jimmy's eyes flicked to Sandoval then back to her. He'd lost weight and he appeared taller. When she again reached a palm to his cheek he didn't move away.

"I'd never abandon you," she whispered. "I've been waiting in Las Vegas for you and Mama to return, but when you didn't, I tried to find you myself. What are you doing up here?"

His wide-eyed gaze bore into hers with equal amounts of fervor and terror. "Mama's lookin' for the color," he replied, his voice barely audible.

Claire didn't understand.

The click of a gun ended any further discussion.

"No secrets," Sandoval said.

Claire faced the Mexican, blocking his view of her brother.

"I'm not tellin' you nothin', you stupid bastard!" Jimmy grunted as he battled again with the rope that tied him to the tree.

Claire remained impassive despite her shock over her brother's outburst.

"Maggie's up here somewhere," Sandoval said. "I mean to find her." He looked directly at Jimmy. "Tell me where you left her, *cadajón*."

"You're a pile of horse shit, too!" Jimmy spit back. "And she's as crazy as you are. You'll both be struck down by the curse." His boyish voice rang with accusation.

"The foolish work of an *ambularia*," Sandoval muttered. "Luttrell does not scare me from his cold grave."

"You weren't there." Jimmy tugged hard against his ropes. "You weren't there when the spiders came!"

"What are you talking about?" Claire asked, alarmed by the image.

"Ma's lookin' for Luttrell's treasure. He told her he hid it somewhere up here, but when he got sick he had a witch put a curse on it. We're all gonna die up here." His face twisted as he struggled against the ropes, nearly pulling his arms from their sockets. "I think we were close 'cause there were big black hairy spiders everywhere. I ran as fast as I could, but that was yesterday. I don't know where Ma is," he said to her. He looked at Sandoval. "I don't know where I went or how I got here. I can't lead you back to her."

He paused and gulped for air, and his eight-year-old-self surfaced. "She probably didn't make it," he whispered.

Anger and horror sliced through Claire. Damn her mama for all of this. Maybe it would serve her right to be mutilated in some ghastly fashion, but on the heels of that thought shame hit Claire hard. *Let her be all right.* But God only knew what could have happened to Jimmy, running around alone up here. And they were still in trouble.

Sandoval stood across from them, his gun leveled in their direction.

"You'll just have to make an effort on my part, *cadajón*," Sandoval said. "What about you, *puta*? Any idea where is *tu madre*?"

Claire thought of Logan, knowing he would look for her. She nurtured that thought as she tried to devise a plan of getting away from the Mexican. "My husband and I were following you," she said.

Sandoval laughed. "Only a *maleficio* would get you a husband."

Claire winced at the reference she had cast an evil spell over Logan.

"Did you show him all your *medicinas* so he can protect his cock from your bad temper?"

"Don't speak that way in front of Jimmy."

Sandoval raised his arm and pointed the gun in her face. Claire stopped breathing.

"Don't mess with me, *señora*," he hissed. "I'll blow your lovely brains out and make your brother eat them for dinner. I owe you that for what you did to my shoulder."

Fear consumed Claire. Her heart squeezed her chest as she fought the urge to whimper. If he shot her in the face, she wouldn't survive—she wouldn't *want* to survive.

"Please, Raul." The sound of her voice surprised her, its calmness almost bordering on sweet. "Let us go back to Las Vegas. We don't care about the money, or gold, or whatever it is. Jimmy's just a little boy. For once in your life, show some mercy."

Sandoval's dark eyes narrowed. "Mercy?" He sneered and kept the gun pointed at her. "Where was mercy when *mi padre* beat me for no other reason than the sun was up and I crossed my eyes wrong? You have not suffered." He snorted. "You keep your body from men, but you have not learned—that is all you are good for."

He shoved the barrel of the gun onto her forehead, and she stumbled into Jimmy.

"You are nothing, *ramera*. You fancy yourself too much."

The trembling began in her shoulders and traveled quickly to her arms and legs. No matter how hard she willed her body not to betray her, her lungs rattled every time she sucked in air.

He sniffed close to her hair. "I can smell your fear." His low voice didn't keep the words from Jimmy. A mockery of a smile spread across his face, and his smell repulsed her. "It makes me think of *chapete*."

She knew his meaning, and tears sprung into her eyes. Her mind would snap if he raped her. Every hope she'd ever clung to, every dream of a world where good triumphed over evil, shattered in that instant. Everyone said she was strong, but she wasn't. She couldn't protect Jimmy, or herself.

"I'll take you to where my ma is," Jimmy blurted out. "I'll try to remember. I'll do my best, but only if you stay away from my sister."

Satisfaction showed in Sandoval's eyes. "*Cadajón* saves the day." He stepped back. "But only today. You will pay for all your sins, *vagamunda*. Vengeance is due the wronged, and I never forget. I'll take every one of your nine lives."

"The wicked will burn in hell," she whispered, tears rolling down her cheeks.

Sandoval let out a bark of contempt. "Hell?" he boomed. "We all burn in *this* life." He watched her with undisguised hatred. "And some more than others."

Numb, Claire knew Sandoval wouldn't kill them. He would do far worse. At whatever cost, she had to find a way to get Jimmy free.

Sandoval forced her and Jimmy onto a horse. Claire sat behind her brother, their hands tied to the saddle pommel. Sandoval held the reins as he rode ahead of them.

"Do you know where Mama is?" Claire whispered into Jimmy's ear.

Jimmy shook his head and glanced over his shoulder at her, clearly upset by not knowing. "It's so confusing. Everything looks the same."

Sandoval heard them. "The problem will be solved as soon as Maggie notices her kittens are with me."

Claire didn't know about that. Her biggest concern was how she might get Jimmy free. She wondered where Logan was, if he realized yet whether something had happened to her. Was he trailing them even now?

---

AT FIRST LOGAN WAS ANNOYED, then panic seized him. Claire's early morning disappearance was more than an effort for privacy. While he refused to believe she had willingly left him—her horse remained—he couldn't be one hundred percent certain. Last night had bound the two of them more tightly together, but maybe it was too much for Claire. He had to consider that perhaps he was pressing too hard to engage her heart.

He circled his horse around their camp, continually increasing his distance as he looked for a sign of where Claire had gone. In his distraction, he didn't hear the horses until he nearly ran into another party. With disbelief, his gaze took in Frank Griffin's suspicious frown, Harry Myer's stunned recognition of the man who'd threatened him, and Dee's pale features as she faced the lover she'd dumped nearly two years ago.

"I can't believe...." Dee's voice faltered. "How on earth did you find me?"

"I stopped lookin' for you months ago."

She wore a dark brown riding habit with a hat hanging from stampede strings down her back. Her dark hair and fair complexion were still as lovely as ever, but Logan couldn't help but notice the shadows clouding her gaze.

The strangeness of seeing Dee—after wondering at a reunion for so long—put Logan at a loss to say all the words that had hounded him for so long. He reminded himself again that her welfare was no longer his concern.

"Well, it's nice to see you after the shootout in Cimarron," Griffin said, the sarcasm in his voice hard to miss. "And how would you know my sister?"

"This is Logan Ryan," Dee said.

"That deputy you were shackled to in Virginia City?"

She nodded. "What are you doing out here?" she asked Logan, her voice edged with concern.

"I'm lookin' for Claire. She's my wife." Logan looked at the three riders opposite him and realized he'd been wrong about the third set of tracks belonging to Sandoval. Clamping down on the fear that gripped him, he forced his expression to remain impassive. Did the Mexican have Claire?

Griffin laughed. "Don't tell me you're talking about Claire Waters."

"Your wife," Dee repeated softly. "When did that happen?"

"It's recent," Logan replied.

"And where is your lovely wife now, Mr. Ryan?" Griffin asked. "Run off somewhere? You should've consulted me before marrying her. I could've told you—Waters women are slippery snakes. Most whores are."

"So that's your half-ass explanation for neglecting your son?" Logan asked.

Frank cursed under his breath. "I don't neglect the runt. I married his mother."

"What?" Dee asked. "You and Maggie are married?"

"She doesn't exactly inspire wedded bliss," Frank said. "But she has her uses."

The news fell into Logan's head like a puzzle no longer broken into pieces. If Luttrell had deeded his land to Maggie, then Frank would've eventually had his hands on it. So she'd hatched a plan to marry Shorty to Claire, and somehow manipulate the both of them to do her will. While he certainly didn't care for her tactics, he couldn't deny her ability to go after what she wanted in any way possible. Claire possessed a bit of that stubbornness as well.

As Logan thought of his wife, he realized the future wasn't set. Not by a long shot.

"One big happy family," Logan muttered, uneasiness settling around him.

"Maybe Claire knows where Maggie is," Dee said. "Maybe that's why she ran off."

"Well, anything might be better than following you, Myers," Griffin said, his gaze flicking to Harry.

"I know where I'm goin'," Myers replied. He squinted and picked at his teeth with a dirty fingernail. "At least, I'm pretty sure, but I can't control the women runnin' around."

"Why are you so hell-bent on finding Maggie?" Logan asked Griffin. "Doesn't sound like you plan to take her home and set up house."

"She's taken what's rightfully ours.... Rightfully Dee's."

The color drained from Dee's face as she sunk into her saddle, and Logan wondered at it. During their time together in Virginia City she'd been full of life and vitality. She had never cowered from what a new day brought forth.

"Do you trust Claire?" Dee asked him.

"Why?"

"There's a lot at stake, and I'd hate to think she's using you. Maggie's twisted. Sure as hell she twisted her daughter, too."

Logan didn't want to believe that.

"Watch yourself, Ryan," Griffin said. "Just because you did my sister years ago don't mean shit in my book. She's damaged goods anyhow—couldn't keep Luttrell satisfied and that's the entire reason we're in this mess to begin with. You interfere and I'll kill you, and

I'll kill slippery Claire, too. Maggie always hid that girl away, and she thinks far too much of herself now. Just so we're clear—don't go messin' with me."

"Then I guess you don't understand the situation as well I thought you did."

"And what's that supposed to mean?"

"Luttrell deeded everything to Claire and as her husband, you're officially on my land. Anything you find here belongs to me."

"Bullshit!" Griffin replied. He pulled his gun, but Logan had already drawn. They faced each other from atop their horses, evenly matched.

"You can bet your balls none of this'll stick," Griffin said. "I'll make damn sure of it."

"I'll shoot trespassers and ask questions later. Just so we're clear," Logan added.

"This is the last time Maggie fucks with me." Griffin lowered his gun and released the hammer. He laughed, but the sound held no humor. "Better sleep with one eye open. Seems to me that if Claire were suddenly widowed then ol' Harry here could fill your less than noble shoes."

"Too many witnesses," Logan said.

"Like I said, just because you've done my sister don't mean shit. Right Dee?" Griffin smiled.

Out of the corner of his eye, Logan saw Dee nod weakly and gaze downward.

"There ain't no witnesses out here," Griffin confirmed.

A bad feeling settled in Logan's gut. It was going to be damn hard to protect Claire from both Raul Sandoval and Frank Griffin, all the while watching his own back. And where was Claire, anyway? Sandoval could already have her...could already.... The thought chilled him to his very core.

"If you don't mind, I'll escort you while you're on my land,"

Logan said, aware his best chance of finding Sandoval—and Claire—undoubtedly lay with Griffin.

"Suit yourself. You're in the lead, Myers."

The malice in Griffin's gaze undermined the man's apparent willingness. Undoubtedly, he thought he could use Logan to locate Claire, and ultimately Maggie.

Harry headed north, while Griffin waited to bring up the rear. Logan didn't like the line-up but fell in beside Dee as they moved farther into the forest, Claire's horse trailing his.

They rode in silence for a time, an occasional aspen, with yellow leaves and a white trunk, breaking up the green of the pine trees.

"I guess congratulations are in order," Dee finally said, her voice low. "Do you still live in Virginia City?"

"No. I'm back in Texas with my folks."

"You're not a deputy anymore?"

"No."

"That strikes me as odd," she murmured. "You were so dedicated to it."

She looked away, but not before he saw her narrowed eyes. Anger flashed through him.

"And what were you dedicated to?" he asked harshly.

"You have no idea what I've been through." Her lips pressed tightly together.

"You never even said goodbye. Don't you think I deserved an explanation at least?"

They rode through a flat area, having crested the hill where Logan had made camp the previous night with Claire. It was midday, hotter than Hades, and Logan felt frustration pushing at his boundaries. He'd never been a man riled by the comings and goings of others, but Dee's disappearance from his life had shaken the earth beneath his boots. Claire's appearance, likewise, had done much the same. He was at a loss to understand what it all meant.

"There wasn't time," Dee replied. "I'm sorry. Maybe we could've worked it out."

"Regretting Luttrell?"

Dee gazed forward. "I regret many things."

"Yeah, so do I," he answered honestly.

Dee dabbed a night-blue scarf to her forehead. "I have to admit, I'm curious how you and Claire became acquainted. She disappeared without a word a few months back and talk around town wasn't good. Did you have something to do with that?"

Logan looked at her, stunned by the implication of her words. Apprehension played across her face, a face he'd known quite well at one time. He was caught unaware by a pang of one of those regrets they'd just spoken of.

"No," he said. "But I plan to kill the bastard who *was* responsible."

Surrounded by dangerous men and an ex-fiancée that still sparked his anger and resentment, Logan feared the worst of all possible scenarios—losing Claire. Determined to drag her out of these mountains at any cost, he prayed she was still alive. Because if she wasn't, Logan would damn his deputy days and take care of these men in any way possible.

# CHAPTER 16

S andoval pushed hard, moving them deeper into the mountains. Unsure of their location, Claire could only hope Jimmy would soon recognize something in the landscape, although it wasn't difficult to see why he hadn't yet found their mama. The Sangre de Cristo Mountains were a refuge of forest-filled, repetitive terrain. If she and Jimmy could escape, which direction would lead them to safety? Defeat hovered on the fringe of her exhausted mind.

For a day and a half, they traveled with little food and water. Jimmy told her Maggie had taken to the hills with gold on her mind, searching land that belonged to Luttrell, land he'd acquired as a representative of the Maxwell Land Grant. Jimmy whispered this to her during the night under the stars, and she marveled at the maturity in his voice, the scope of his knowledge. He was only eight years old, but the little boy he'd been was gone. She had already seen his newfound reckless aggression, and it scared her. It could get him hurt. Maybe even killed.

Jimmy told her he'd been with their mama for days, maybe weeks—he couldn't remember. Then the crazy incident with the spiders and he'd run away, only to get lost in the hills. And there he'd been, day after day—although he reassured her it hadn't been long—until Sandoval caught him. "And then your ghost walked through the trees," he'd said to her.

Claire hugged him close. For all his boastful might, Jimmy was still young, superstitious, and easily impressed by the good and the bad in the world.

To Claire, it was increasingly clear that Sandoval had no intention of meeting up with Frank Griffin or Harry Myers. The treasure must be great indeed if he didn't plan to share it. He stayed away from her and Jimmy, but Claire was hardly grateful, knowing his attention could change at any moment. He hardly fed them, and kept their hands and legs tied when they were on horseback. Soon, her energy would be gone altogether. She needed to do something.

Today, rain came down in sheets, and Claire shivered while she tried to cover Jimmy's trembling body as he sat in front of her on the horse. The only advantage of the rain was that it washed the grime from them. Gray clouds hung low and mist surrounded them. As they moved to the top of a hill, Claire saw an open expanse off through the pines to the left. They remained under cover of the trees, offering some protection from the wetness, but Claire longed to be dry and warm.

"We need to stop." The demand in her voice surprised her.

Sandoval's disinterest in his prisoners sparked an unnatural boldness in her. Lightheaded, she almost laughed. There had never been a time when she wasn't afraid of him. A thrill ran through her at the idea of defeating him.

"No. We are tracked."

Elation sprang into her heart. *Logan.*

"Claire," Jimmy whispered, straining his neck. "This looks familiar."

"Shhh. Don't let him hear you."

"The chapel." He nodded to the right.

Claire squinted, searching through the trees. "I think I see a building. How do you know it's a chapel?"

"That's what ma called it. She told me to stay out of it, but I went there and prayed anyway."

"For what?"

"For you, and your trip to Heaven. I told her you would kiss the stars and watch over us. But my prayers worked even better—they brought you back."

Claire swallowed against the tightness in her throat. Jimmy's gesture nearly broke her heart. Her mama *must* be crazy, she thought as she seethed with anger. Certainly it was madness to bring Jimmy out here and then lose him. In Claire's mind, that was unforgivable—as was much of what Maggie had done to hers and Jimmy's lives.

Claire glanced over her shoulder, trying to see anything, anyone. Sandoval had made sure she wouldn't jump off and run by tying her legs to each stirrup. Her hands were bound, as were Jimmy's, but her brother's feet were free.

If Logan tracked them, how far behind would he be?

Not far, Claire decided, since Sandoval had noticed.

She steadied herself and hoped to God she was doing the right thing.

"Jimmy," she said quietly into his ear. "I want you to escape. A man named Logan is tracking us. Go back the way we came and find him."

To Jimmy's credit he didn't flinch, or jerk around, or raise his voice.

"I'll let you down very carefully," she whispered. "Hide until we disappear from sight, then run as fast as you can."

Jimmy's slight shoulders rose and fell and he nodded, his head bumping her chin. Claire watched Sandoval's back as they moved through the muddy terrain, the rain pounding the ground. With her fastened hands she awkwardly pushed Jimmy's left leg over the pommel; he swiveled and faced the right side of the horse. Raindrops dripped into her eyes as she struggled to focus on a dense mass of shrubs nearby. She squeezed Jimmy's leg, alerting him to be ready.

In one fluid movement she shifted Jimmy to the ground. Arm and stomach muscles trembled in denial, spent beyond their limits, and Claire's heart pounded in her ears. She sat upright as if nothing had happened, all the while not taking her eyes from Sandoval. There was a dash of movement as Jimmy disappeared behind a clump of brush. Shaking, she struggled not to bring attention to herself. Every second that passed gave Jimmy a little more time to escape.

Claire blinked rapidly, her tears lost in the rain that struck her face. She needed to prepare for Sandoval's retribution when he discovered Jimmy was gone—to buy her brother as much time as she could. Hopefully, it would be enough.

But thoughts of what Sandoval would do sent a nauseating fear spiraling through her stomach. So much for feeling bold. Instead, she focused on Logan. She had dreamed of happy endings, and for a brief time her heart believed he'd brought one to her. Panic gripped her, mingled with regret. In the end, she'd been foolish to hope.

---

HARRY MYERS and Frank Griffin were a dangerous threat, but it was Dee who posed the greater risk to Logan. For the past day and night, he kept a wary eye on the two men, but it was Dee's sad countenance and inquisitive questions about him and his life during the last two years that tugged at him in a way far more hazardous than anything the men did.

Logan didn't love Dee—not exactly—but seeing her and spending time with her brought back a wealth of regrets he thought he'd laid to rest. He suspected he never would again trust her, but she seemed...in need. Her brother appeared to be a part of it—Frank didn't treat her well—and Logan felt a twinge of obligation toward her. An unwanted sentiment. He wondered if it was his lot in life to be played the fool twice.

Side by side with this confusion was a driving desire to find Claire. Once he had her at his side, he'd be able to think more clearly. Being without her, wondering if she'd been harmed, constantly gnawed at him and chipped away at his patience, pushing his mind to the edge of crippling frustration.

The rain let up, and in the gloomy aftermath of the storm the flat light gave the forest an otherworldly appearance, its hues drained to ashen colors. The damp smell of water-logged trees permeated the air and Logan's clothes clung to his skin. He glanced at Dee as she pushed at her wet hair. The moisture that hovered in the forest made them all uncomfortable.

Movement in the trees caught Logan's attention, and he withdrew his gun as Griffin dismounted his horse. A scrawny, wild boy ran from the mist and Frank grabbed him, the youth screaming from the rough handling.

"Jimmy!" Griffin yelled. "Goddammit! Settle down."

"No! No!" Jimmy struggled to escape Frank's grasp.

Griffin slapped the boy across the face, sending his slight body into a heap on the ground. Logan swiftly covered the distance separating him from Claire's little brother and hit Frank square in the jaw. *Damn that felt good.* Myers rushed him from behind, but Logan jammed an elbow into his face and yanked the man's gun from his hand. He kicked him in the stomach then aimed his firearm at Myers, who struggled to catch his breath amid blood running down his face.

Logan heard the click of a hammer, and a sidelong glance told him Frank had upped the ante. Holding Jimmy by the hair, Griffin pointed a pistol at the boy's head. Jimmy's hands were bound by rope, but the flash of defiance Logan saw in the boy's eyes made him realize the youth was foolish enough to take on Griffin himself.

"Drop it," Griffin said.

Logan dropped the guns he held.

Myers scrambled to pick them up. "I shur hope you didn't break my nose," he whined.

Taking one of the pistols by its long barrel, Myers cuffed Logan across the cheek, snorting with satisfaction. With sheer willpower Logan struggled not to retaliate, letting his anger pour into the look he gave Myers. With uncertainty, Myers stepped back.

"Tell us where Maggie is," Griffin said to Jimmy.

Logan watched the boy. There was a strong resemblance to Claire—the same blond hair, angular face and eyes haunted by a life neither of them wanted.

"I've been lookin' but I can't find her," Jimmy responded. His eyes shifted. "Are you Logan?"

Logan nodded.

"I've been prayin' but I don't think it's gonna help. He's gonna kill her."

"What the hell are you talking about?" Griffin demanded.

"Sandoval has Claire," Jimmy said.

Logan's blood ran cold. "Where?"

"Up ahead. I've been runnin' awhile, but if you go the way I came you might find her. But you gotta hurry!"

"Well shit, I ain't chasing after Claire if Maggie's not with her," Griffin said. "Sandoval can have her for all I care. Tell me where your mama is, James, and I won't have to hurt you." His grip tightened in Jimmy's hair, making the boy flinch.

"I told you, I don't know." Tears formed in Jimmy's eyes. "I lost her days ago, where the spiders were."

"That right?" Griffin replied. "That place is about half a days ride from here."

"See, I told you I knew where we was goin'," Myers piped in.

"That remains to be seen," Griffin muttered. "I doubt she's still there, Jimmy. Where is she now?"

"I dunno." The boy's face crumbled in desperation.

"This is bullshit!" Griffin struck the boy across the face again.

"Stop it!" Dee yelled. "Quit hitting him, Frank!" She spilled herself from the saddle.

When she stepped forward, Logan saw the gun in her hand. The weapon trembled as did her hands, both gripped tightly around the handle.

"Do you think beating him is going to give you the answer you want?" she asked. "We're wasting time. We should try to find Sandoval, and Claire, too. If Harry can't find Maggie then maybe they can. We can't let them get to her first, can we?"

Griffin stared at her. "Put the gun down, Dee. You wouldn't like the consequences."

Fear crossed Dee's face and she swallowed hard. "All right, I'm sorry." She slowly lowered her arms. "But he's just a child."

"Don't ever tell me what to do again." He shoved Jimmy toward her. "You like him so much, you take care of him."

Griffin stepped forward, eye level with Logan, and assessed him with undisguised malice. "I've tolerated you for Dee's sake, but if you hit me again I won't be so tolerant. I'll hurt those you care about the most."

"The way you hurt those closest to you?"

"Whatever it takes to keep them in line." He approached Dee and yanked the gun from her hand. "I think Myers and I'll keep the guns." He removed Logan's rifle from the scabbard on Storm's saddle.

Logan maintained his stance, hoping Griffin wouldn't do a body search.

"At least untie his hands," Dee said, her arm around Jimmy's shoulder.

Griffin paused and considered his son. He pulled a knife from a sheath on his waist and cut the ropes around Jimmy's wrists. "We'll look for Sandoval." He moved to his horse while Myers eyed the situation with suspicion.

"Jimmy can ride with me," Logan said.

Dee glanced up from her inspection of the raw skin around Jimmy's wrists and nodded. "Let me bandage these."

"You better be damn quick about it," Griffin's voice boomed.

Logan felt a surge of urgency as well. Every second counted for Claire. "Give 'em to me, I'll do it on horseback."

"I don't know why you're mixed up in all of this," Dee murmured. "Frank isn't an enemy you want to make." She retrieved a handful of white gauze from her saddlebag and handed it to him. "You're doing all of this for her?"

"There was a time when I would've done it for you."

The revelation hung between them for a moment, then Logan lifted Jimmy onto his horse and settled behind him. Although he still had Claire's horse, Jimmy seemed too weak to ride alone.

"Who are you?" Jimmy asked him.

Logan kicked his horse forward.

"Hold the reins while I bandage you. I'm Claire's husband."

Jimmy gripped the leather straps. "Then that would make you... my brother?"

Logan quickly wrapped Jimmy's wrists. "Yeah, that's about right. You're a part of my family now."

Logan took back the reins and Jimmy's hand came to the cheek Griffin had struck twice.

"That's good. I've been hoping for a new family for some time now."

"Things are changing, Jimmy. I'm here to see to that."

The boy craned his neck to look at Logan. "Claire must love you a lot, 'cause she always said she'd never get married."

Logan wasn't sure about the love part, but it gave him reason to hope.

# CHAPTER 17

Claire fell to the ground when Sandoval struck her face.

"Where is he?" he yelled.

Her head spun and the trees swayed. She knelt on her hands and knees, and struggled to suppress the images flying through her mind of the last time he'd done this. The fear, and the agony of that fear, caused her stomach to rebel, and with violent convulsions she vomited what little she had inside her.

Tears dripped from the end of her nose. With a shaking hand, she wiped the edge of her mouth and her wrist came away covered in blood from where he'd hit her. She stifled a sob.

Sandoval grabbed her by the arms. "You thought to send him for help? The whelp couldn't find his way around a shithouse. You've sent him to his death."

"You were going to kill us anyway," she said in a ragged voice, praying she had bought Jimmy enough time. The setting sun told her he'd been gone an hour, maybe more.

Sandoval stared at her. He laughed and shook his head. "*Puta.*" He brought his face close to hers. "Whore. You are nothing. You should get on your knees and beg for your life. You cast your *ponsión negra* on me all those months ago, but you don't have your potions now, do you?"

"You killed Luttrell, didn't you?" she asked, desperate to distract him.

"Luttrell was a stinkin' rat, and Maggie spread her legs far and wide for him. But that won't get her the prize. You want to spread your legs for me?" He grinned and caressed her cheek. He flicked his eyes downward. *"Sangre."* His hot, tobacco-scented breath burned her face, and she jerked her head to avoid the contact. "You bleed," he said with disgust.

She saw the bright red stain on her shirt and sucked in air as if she were drowning, suddenly aware of the ache in her ribs. She closed her eyes and wondered how quickly the end would come.

---

"How far ahead are they?" Logan asked Jimmy.

"A ways. I'm not sure. The sun's moved since Claire told me to run and look for you."

"Where's your ma?" Logan asked and scanned the ground for the boy's trail. He didn't want to waste time going in the wrong direction, and he wasn't about to trust Frank's tracking skills.

Jimmy was silent then spoke so low Logan strained to hear him. "I think the spiders got her."

"Spiders? Is she hurt somewhere?"

Jimmy shrugged, a flash of remorse crossing his face before he looked ahead again. "It's Luttrell's curse. The treasure has a curse."

"What did Luttrell leave up here?"

"I'm not sure," Jimmy replied. "Gold, jewels, money. My mama didn't know, but she's been crazy tryin' to find it." Suddenly he sat up taller. "Are we goin' the right way?"

"I hope so. I've noticed some of your tracks. You ran directly from Claire and Sandoval?"

Jimmy nodded. "He killed her once already. I don't like him. I thought she was a ghost when I saw her."

Logan's gut tensed. "Did Sandoval hurt either of you?"

"He was gonna hurt Claire, but I lied and said I could find Mama to save her, and it worked for a while. But I don't know where Mama is 'cause the spiders probably got her." Jimmy's voice wavered. "Comin' here's been nothin' but bad luck."

"There's no such thing in my book," Logan said. "And a curse is nothing more than a way to scare people. Scared people run away."

"I was scared," Jimmy said, his tone despondent. "I ran away."

"But you turned around and came back. Everybody gets scared, Jimmy. Everybody runs at some point in their life. It takes more courage to stop and try to fix the wrongs. It took courage for you to find me."

"I suppose. I just wanna go home."

"Me too."

———

CLAIRE OPENED HER EYES, the trees in her line of sight seemed askew. With her head hanging at an odd angle, she shifted her legs. They were numb and tucked beneath her while her arms were pulled behind her and tied around the trunk of a tree. In the dwindling daylight, shadows crisscrossed the orange mat of dried pine needles strewn across the ground. She moaned as she tried to sit back, her neck sore from the dead weight of her head.

She tried to remember what had happened.

Sandoval hit her with the butt of his gun. At least, she thought he might have. Her disoriented vision confirmed her left eye was swollen. He must have struck her, then tied her up once she was unconscious. *Where is he now?* She tried to moisten her dry mouth.

As she struggled to shift her position, she noticed her blouse was torn open, exposing her breasts, and her skirt was ripped.

Revulsion welled up inside her. Panicked, she couldn't breathe. A sob escaped her throat, an anguished cry, and she frantically looked around to see if Sandoval was there, watching, waiting. *He's raped me.* She couldn't stop the defeated shudders that wracked her body. Gasping for breath, the truth of what happened was more than she could bear. In near darkness, her head rolled against the tree. She stifled her sobs as she stared without seeing, her body as cold as the surrounding damp forest.

And out of the mist, came her mama.

*I must be dead.*

Her mama stopped a few feet from her, disheveled, not the standard appearance she normally assumed for the men and women of Las Vegas. She wore a long skirt, torn and ragged on the edges, once white but now streaked with dirt, and a heavy leather coat fell past her hips. Her hair was piled on top of her head—the way she had always worn it—and Claire thought it odd she would fix it while out in the wilderness.

"Who are you?" Maggie asked. Her eyes narrowed in suspicion. "Why did Sandoval take so much time playing with you?"

Claire was struck dumb. "You watched?" she whispered. "Why didn't you help me?" She could barely get the words out.

"I'm no fool." Her gaze was sharply bitter. Claire didn't think it was possible to be hurt anymore, emotionally or physically, but her mama's behavior toward her stripped another piece of flesh from her hide.

"Raul's a dangerous man," Maggie continued. "I don't step in his path for anyone."

"Then why are you here?" Claire was unable to keep the scorn out of her voice.

Seconds stretched into minutes. When Claire glanced up again, she saw her mama staring at her, the horror apparent in her eyes.

"Claire." Maggie's voice pierced the silence. "Claire?" She stepped forward and knelt down, her eyes searching. "We never found you," she said in anguish. "We looked, but we never found you." She brought a hand to Claire's face. "Where have you been? What happened to you?"

"I've been looking for you."

Maggie shook off her shock and produced a knife from inside her coat. She cut Claire loose and gathered her into her arms. Claire sank into the embrace, a child again, soothed by the touch of the woman who created so much ambivalence in her heart.

"I didn't know it was you," Maggie said frantically. "If I had, I wouldn't have stayed back while he hurt you."

It wasn't a few tears that dripped from Claire, but a torrent of emotion held back far too long. She couldn't stop it, the force of it consuming her. Somewhere in the maelstrom, she said the word. *Rape.*

"What did you say?" Maggie asked, pulling back to look at her. "Were you raped during the attack outside Albuquerque?"

"No. Here.... Now." Tears flowed in a steady stream down her face.

"No, Claire." Maggie took hold of her face. "Sandoval was rough with you, but he didn't attack you. Oh God, you thought I watched that and did nothing?"

"Are you sure?" she cried.

"I'm sure." Maggie's arms wrapped around her again.

The despair that consumed Claire began to slowly dissipate. Her mama may not have looked out for her, but someone had. *But by the grace of God do we all walk the earth*—Jack's words. Solace began to creep into Claire's soul.

"You're bleeding," Maggie said, examining Claire's ribcage.

"It's nothing. We have to get out of here. Jimmy was with me, but he managed to escape."

"Thank God. Where's he gone? I've been crazed since I lost him."

"We were being tracked. I sent him back to find help."

"Tracked by who?" Maggie asked, her tone both accusing and worried.

"A man named Logan Ryan. He followed me from Texas."

"Texas?"

"It's a long story." Claire sat up and wiped at her eyes.

Maggie removed her coat and gave it to Claire.

"I know about the land deed," Claire continued. "And the treasure that Luttrell left up here."

Maggie paused. "I don't suppose Shorty McClaren showed up?"

"Yes."

A light flickered in her mama's eyes. "Did you marry him?"

"No, I married someone else." Claire felt the edge of rebelliousness in her tone.

A voice echoed in the distance. "Mama."

Both Claire and Maggie turned toward the sound as Jimmy ran toward them.

Maggie stood and clenched her fists. "Sonofabitch."

Claire caught sight of Frank Griffin but directly behind him was Logan. Worry filled her, but seeing her husband also lifted a weight from her shoulders and she had to keep from running to him.

"Jimmy." Maggie hugged him tight to her side. "You scared me somethin' fierce."

"I'm sorry." He buried his face into her skirt. "I'm so glad the spiders didn't get you."

Claire stood and buttoned the coat to hide her nakedness as well as the dried blood covering her stomach. She saw Harry Myers and a woman she didn't recognize.

"Who's that man with Frank?" Maggie asked, as the group descended on them.

"That's Claire's husband," Jimmy said.

Maggie cast a suspicious glance in Claire's direction.

Logan dismounted and approached. "You all right?" he asked Claire.

She nodded, thankful beyond measure to see him, and a smile crossed her lips of its own accord. She wanted to fall into his arms but something about his stance made her hesitate. He took her hand and squeezed it. She noticed the bruise on his cheek, but Frank interrupted before she could voice her concern.

"Been lookin' for you, Mags." Griffin rested his rifle across his lap. His horse stopped several feet from them. Myers and the woman brought their animals side-by-side.

"You're not welcome here," Maggie said. "This is my land now."

Griffin laughed. "That so? Mr. Logan Ryan here seems to think it's his."

Maggie glanced at Claire and Logan. "Did you really marry him, Claire?"

"Yeah, she did," Logan answered. "And whatever greedy game you're all playin' is gonna stop now before someone gets hurt."

"Spoken like a man who's holding all the cards," Griffin said with a surly laugh. "Where's the money, Mags?"

"I don't know."

"Bullshit," he sneered. "You've been up here for weeks. Don't tell me you've found diddly-squat."

"Even if I had, I damn well wouldn't tell you."

"You've sure turned into a devious little bitch. You probably burned down The Dove, too."

"What are you talking about?" Maggie asked.

"Oh wait," Griffin continued. "Claire was in charge, except none of us knew she was alive and well. Really sent a piss-shiver through Sandoval when he found out." He laughed. "So, is it hardly a surprise the whole thing went up in flames a few days ago? You owe me for that."

"Is this true?" Maggie asked Claire.

Claire nodded. "I'm sorry. I don't know how it happened."

"Was anyone hurt?"

"No. Just Betsy and Ellie were there, and they got out."

Maggie turned back to Griffin. "How do I know you didn't burn it down? You could've killed someone."

"Like you killed Luttrell?" Griffin asked.

"I didn't lay a finger on him."

"Not after he was dead. But maybe the local circuit judge would like to hear how you seduced my sister's husband and stole all his money and land."

"You're one to talk. Don't think I don't know about you and Belle." Maggie's voice shook with anger.

"When one whore doesn't please you, you just gotta look for another one."

"I married you because I loved you, Frank."

"What?" Claire gasped. "You're married to him?"

"Best kept secret in town," Griffin added. "Just like your devotion, Mags."

"I don't take kindly to betrayals," Maggie said. "Whatever I did has been necessary."

"Empty excuses, broken promises. Those won't buy shit in this life." Griffin shifted his rifle and aimed it at Maggie.

Claire watched as Logan, with lightning speed, pulled a small handgun from under his shirt and pointed it at Frank. He pushed Claire behind him as Maggie moved in front of Jimmy, and Claire strained to see in the near darkness, the forest growing black.

"I want the money," Griffin said. "I wanted it months ago, but you thought you could toy with me. Sandoval nearly killed your precious Claire, but that didn't seem to spark a sliver of reason into your head. I don't care if Ryan owns the land. If I have to kill all of you, I will."

"Then I'll take you with us," Logan said.

"You think you're so clever," Griffin said. "I wonder if you even have bullets in that little pistol you had hidden."

"Only one way to find out."

A vision of Logan lying in a bloody heap seized Claire. "Give him the money, Mama," she whispered. "It isn't worth it."

"Wait." The woman beside Harry Myers spoke from atop her horse. "There's something you should know, Frank."

Claire looked at her—she was the woman she'd seen in the house outside of Cimarron. It was Frank's sister, Dee. She should have recognized her sooner.

"I've never spoken of this because there seemed no point," Dee said, her voice faltering. "When you forced me to marry Luttrell, I was already with child."

Claire sensed the woman's hesitancy, noticed Dee's horse snort and shift from leg to leg in agitation.

"Logan and I were engaged in Virginia City," she said, her gaze unfocused.

*Engaged?* Claire went cold. *Logan had almost married Griffin's sister?* A sickening realization sank into her bones.

"Dylan isn't Luttrell's son," Dee said flatly. "He's Logan's."

No one spoke.

Claire stood behind Logan, his broad shoulders shielding her from Dee, blocking the woman from his past. He was so dear to her —she even thought she might love him—but a bitter taste of betrayal began to take root and hope drained from her heart. She'd been so foolish to believe he might be different.

"What?!" Logan exclaimed in shock.

"I'm sorry. I should've told you." Dee turned toward her brother. "It doesn't make sense to hurt him, Frank. We can still get what we need."

"You're lying," Logan said.

Dee shook her head, grief clouding her pretty face. "No," she whispered. "I never thought I would see you again, Logan. But don't you see? We can work this out, we can all gain something. Don't you want this for Dylan, Frank?"

Claire's mind latched on to the boy's name—the youngster she'd treated at Belle's.

She wondered what else she didn't know; what Logan had never told her. He obviously had good reason not to share the details of his past with her, and she didn't want to acknowledge what that reason might have been. If it was as deceptive as her mind leaned toward, then Logan wasn't who she believed him to be. Had she been so wrong about everything?

"If I'm understanding all of this, then the most obvious plan of action would be to kill Claire," Frank said.

Claire jerked her eyes to him.

"Like hell," Logan growled.

Frank spoke of her murder as if he were putting down a horse that had outlived its usefulness. He smiled grimly. "You want them both? That figures." His eyes shifted to Maggie. "None of this'll be settled until you cough up the location of the loot, dearest. I'm even inclined to let The Dove be a wash between us."

Suddenly Jimmy ran. In horror, Claire saw Harry Myers draw his gun and fire. "Jimmy! No!" She threw herself forward, trying to shield him, but Logan grabbed her arm and pain lanced through her shoulder as he dragged her upright.

More gunfire ricocheted through the trees and in a split-second Logan changed his mind. "Run!" He shoved her away from him.

She struggled to move as she whipped her gaze to where her mama and Jimmy had been standing seconds ago. Both were gone.

"Run, Claire!" Logan bellowed as he pressed against her, crowding her, pushing her deeper into the forest. Despite the confusion, she noticed he didn't fire his gun.

Reality hit her. He didn't want to shoot Dee.

In the darkness everyone scattered, the air filled with shouting, gunfire, and the responses of unsettled horses.

Claire ran.

Her body moved in the direction she hoped Maggie and Jimmy had taken. The coat she wore weighed her down as she traversed a downhill route, moonlight guiding her in the eerie darkness. To her left, she saw her mama farther up the hill. Claire shifted direction to follow.

A quick glance over her shoulder confirmed she was alone—no one trailed her. Not even Logan. She looked again, upward then behind her. Should she double-back for him?

He probably went to help Dee. Maybe the woman was hurt, needed help, anything could have happened. She fought back tears. *What a fool I've been.* She went after her mama.

# CHAPTER 18

With Claire off to safety, Logan circled back to deal with Frank Griffin and Harry Myers. There'd been a third gunman hidden in the woods, and he didn't doubt it was Sandoval. Logan hadn't discharged his weapon since Dee had been in the middle of the gunfight. Despite his misgivings, and the questions that filled his head, he never would have forgiven himself if he shot the mother of his child.

*Dylan.* The boy at Southern Charm. A son he never knew existed.

There was a good chance Dee lied, but the timeframe of their affair played out right, as did the boy's age.

Rage and confusion consumed him, and a searing protectiveness burned in his heart. Logan didn't share what was his. The boy would not carry the Luttrell name all the days of his life. *Dee is lying.* Damn her. *She has to be.* But the seed of doubt had been planted, and he'd never be able to ignore it.

Logan skirted the area where the confrontation and revelations had occurred. No one there. Everyone had disappeared.

He found Dee's horse caught in a cluster of pines, untangled the animal's reins, and set him loose. Then he continued to stalk the perimeter. Finally, he sighted a smattering of blood across a boulder, as if someone had rubbed against it with his—or her—shoulder. From that he made out a faint trail and started after the men who would take everything from him.

---

CLAIRE CRESTED the hilltop and glimpsed the shadow of her mama weaving through the pines. She trailed behind, anxious not to lose her, and struggled to quiet her breathing as sweat broke out on her skin.

A small structure came into view, and she recognized it as the one Jimmy had called a chapel. It didn't appear to be a place of worship, but rather a simply made rectangular dwelling with one window covered with wood. At the back of the building, Maggie slipped inside. Claire hurried to the door, carefully pushed it open and was met with the musty smell of wet earth and moldy wood. Large, fully stuffed burlap bags covered the dirt floor.

Claire raised her eyes and looked directly into her mama's face. From a darkened corner emerged Dee.

---

LOGAN FOLLOWED THE BLOODY TRAIL—DIFFICULT under the cover of night but not impossible—and at the end found Harry Myers.... Dead. The man had been shot on the right side of his chest and had bled to death.

Logan stripped Harry's body of weapons—finding his own gun and two knives—but was unable to locate Myers' gun. He checked the readiness of the firearm and started off, but his further search of the woods turned up nothing.

"Where's Jimmy?" Claire asked, speaking in a hushed tone.

"He's run off again," Maggie answered. "But we'll find him. I didn't realize you were behind me."

Dee and Maggie appeared uncomfortable, the atmosphere charged with an awkward silence.

"What's going on?" Claire asked. She glanced at the bags. "Is that Luttrell's treasure?"

Maggie nodded.

"Tell me what's going on, Mama," Claire demanded.

"All we knew was that Luttrell had stashed some treasure in a chapel." Maggie's gaze flashed with purpose. "Of course, I expected something a bit more...ornate." She indicated their surroundings, then glanced at Dee. "That was my first setback, not realizing right off that this was the building he referred to."

"I described it to you," Dee said, an edge to her voice. "The chapel in the mountains, he'd called it."

"But you'd only been here once before, Dee," Maggie whispered in frustration. "You try living out here alone for a while. I'm the first to admit, I made some bad decisions during my search."

"Like the spiders?" Claire asked, trying to absorb the idea that her mama and Griffin's sister—Logan's ex-lover—were somehow working together.

"Yeah, well, Jimmy lost it when I started looking there," Maggie said. "The money wasn't in the chapel like Dee had said, so I started searching elsewhere. Remember Spider Hole, where I took you years ago?"

A vague memory surfaced of an abandoned mine shaft with wooden timbers perched unsteadily at the entrance. Claire had been a young girl at the time and hadn't liked the dank smell or the feeling of entrapment that permeated the atmosphere. "I don't recall any spiders."

"There really weren't that many. I think Jimmy's imagination was working overtime. It was the last place I thought to look, but it finally dawned on me that Teddy would hide the money someplace difficult. And I was right. I was so damn excited that I didn't notice Jimmy was gone at first, but I started looking for him as soon as I got all the money back to the chapel before Dee arrived." She turned to the woman beside her. "And why the hell did you bring Frank with you?"

"It wasn't my choice." Dee's anger filled the small space. "I was doing the best I could to lead them away from you."

"You told Jimmy it was gold," Claire said absently, dread building inside over the circumstances of Luttrell's death.

"It sounds more exciting to a little boy if he thinks he's going after some glitter." Maggie focused her gaze onto Claire. Her eyes gleamed with pride. "Before you go all proper on me Claire, just think for a minute. We can take our share and leave this place. We can go to San Francisco. You can finally study to be a real doctor, like you've always wanted."

"Our share?" Claire questioned.

"Dee and I split it fifty-fifty."

Claire wondered how far they had taken this partnership. "Luttrell's death.... What have you done, Mama?"

"Whatever I did, I did for us."

"You thought I was dead." Claire's voice shook. "You let Sandoval terrorize me, not once but twice. And what about you?" She faced Dee. "What about your son? If you both go to jail, how will that help Dylan or Jimmy?"

"I'm not without regret," Dee said with a fierce undertone. "But Luttrell was a bastard. He beat me every chance he got."

"Why didn't you leave him?" Claire asked, but she already knew the answer. It was the same reason she had never left The White Dove—not making a decision was a decision in itself.

"It wasn't that simple," Dee said. "I owed Frank. He always looked out for me. There were things that happened, when I was younger, that I'm not proud of. He said he wouldn't protect me if I didn't charm the pants off Teddy, and he told me Logan didn't have enough money."

"He does now," Maggie said. "How ironic is that."

"Luttrell deserved to die," Dee whispered. "He was determined to give me nothing. Maggie helped me get what was rightfully mine and my son's."

"No one's going to get it if we stand around here talking about it," Maggie said.

"You're going to drag all this money back to Las Vegas?" Claire asked.

"Is The Dove truly gone?"

Claire nodded.

"Then I say we head straight-away to San Francisco. Dee, you can come with us."

"I plan to go back to Virginia City. I have friends who will help me hide there, but first I have to find Dylan."

"You don't know where he is?" Claire asked.

"Frank took him from me to force me to help him."

"He did the same damn thing to me," Maggie said. "After Sandoval attacked you and I thought you dead, I was ready to go to the county sheriff since the town marshal would've been a complete waste of time, but Frank threatened Jimmy—his own son, for God's sake."

"Frank and Raul argued in Cimarron," Dee interjected. "Something about a shipment of stolen cattle and how Frank was fed up with all of Sandoval's skimming of the profits. God knows what else the two of them are involved in. When Sandoval left, I was scared. He's a man who holds a grudge and obviously he came up here to even the score."

Claire began to understand what the two women had been up against. "Dylan is with Belle Mason. She's got him at Southern Charm."

"You've seen him?" Dee's face showed the first spark of emotion since Claire had entered the so-called chapel. "How is he?"

"Fine."

Dee closed her eyes and breathed a sigh of relief.

"Instead of running, why don't you let Logan take care of all of this," Claire said. "He can present it to the circuit judge. Why not do all of this fair and square?"

"You don't understand," Maggie said. "Frank's influence is wide, and there's nothing fair about what happened to Luttrell. Truth was, it was an accident. The fool was sick and drank too much of that wild cherry bark you made for coughs. And before you accuse me of doing it, you should know neither of us overdosed him. I'll bet my bottom dollar it was Frank, though."

"If you knew he'd consumed too much, you could have helped him," Claire said, relieved her mama wasn't a cold-blooded murderer but still sickened by the fact she and Dee had done nothing to help him. "You could have given him ipecac," she said numbly.

"No, Claire." Maggie's tone was final, her expression resolute. "You'll just have to trust me on this." She changed the subject. "How much do either of you know about this Logan Ryan? Do you trust him?"

Claire didn't know how to respond because she wasn't sure about anything anymore.

"How do we know he didn't scheme to marry Claire?" Maggie asked. "Did he know about the deed beforehand?"

Reluctantly, Claire answered. "Yes."

Had Logan used her? A part of her found the idea incomprehensible, which undoubtedly was a sign of her ultimate gullibility. What a silly, romantic fool she was, hoping he'd love her and remain devoted to her all the days of her life.

"That solves it then," Maggie said. "We take the money and run. I've three mules nearby. We'll need to get these bags tied to them."

A gunshot pierced the wood of the cabin. Claire covered her ears and dropped to the floor as Dee screamed and did the same.

Maggie crawled around her and cracked open the door.

"No!" Claire grabbed her mama's arm.

More gunshots struck the exterior of the building.

"I've guns, too," Maggie said. "I'll be back." She crept from the building.

The gunfire ceased. For a brief second, Claire hesitated then took off at a dead run after her mother.

She raced with fear in her veins, praying she wouldn't be shot. They traversed through the trees, around the hillside, and quickly came upon the mules. Claire took the revolver Maggie handed her. With trembling hands, she checked it for bullets—the cylinder was full. Maggie carried a rifle and led two of the mules while Claire grabbed the third one.

"Stay alert," Maggie said quietly.

Within minutes, Claire lost sight of her. She tugged at her mule, but the creature balked at moving forward. She could hardly blame him. It was sheer lunacy to head back to the *chapel*, to risk being killed, all for a big pile of money that everyone thought would solve their problems.

*Where is Jimmy?*

Panic welled up in Claire's chest, and she glanced around. There had been no additional gunfire once she'd chased after her mama, and it was odd they hadn't been followed. The click of a gun hammer made her jump.

"Alright *puta*, where's the money?"

She jerked to a stop, her back to Sandoval. She held her own weapon in her right hand, out of his line of sight. Gripping the handle more firmly, she hoped he hadn't noticed it.

"I grow weary of chasing the cats," he sneered. "I grow weary of you."

She would get one chance. Her heart pounded in her ears. She wouldn't be afraid. She didn't *want* to be afraid anymore.

She swung her arm around, but a rush of movement pushed her to the ground with a jarring thud. Her mama screamed, landing on top of her, and gunfire blasted the air with explosive bursts.

In seconds it was over. Claire's ears rang.

"Mama?" she whispered. Claire rolled her to the side and struggled to sit up.

Sandoval lay in a contorted position, his face plastered with the surprise of his death. Logan approached the dead man and stripped him of his weapons.

"Claire.... He didn't get you, did he?" Maggie asked in a hoarse whisper.

Claire leaned over her mama as she lay on the ground. "No. Why did you come back?"

"To make up for all the other times, when I didn't watch out for you like I should've."

Maggie's sharp intake of breath chilled Claire. A quick inspection threw her into denial. "No, no, no." She shook her head.

"Well, I'm guessing it's bad, is it." Maggie's mouth trembled as she took several quick breaths. "There now, Claire. Be strong. You always were, you know. So strong, everything I always wished I could be."

"Shhh, don't talk," Claire said, trying to speak through her panic. "I'll help you. I can help you." She sobbed in helplessness.

"I don't think so." Maggie's eyes became glassy, and she moaned. "I know you always tried. You've been a miracle since the day you were born. I thought you were dead, stillborn. I was so young and scared, I didn't know what to do. And then you breathed." She stared at the stars as a smile played across her pale lips. Her body released a shuddering sigh, and her limbs sank farther into the ground. "You breathed and the room filled with light, and I felt such joy as I've never known."

Claire shook her head, crying. She grasped her mama's hand and desperately wished to turn back time.

Maggie gazed at her. "Tell Jimmy I love him."

Claire's body shook violently as the touch of death closed around them. Her mind screamed for it to stop.

Maggie closed her eyes. "I see a lavender sunset," she whispered. "Just like the ones when I was a little girl."

"No," Claire yelled. "Don't go! Don't leave me!" In desperation she wrapped her arms around her mama's shoulders, but Maggie didn't move.

Grief slammed into Claire. She couldn't be gone. Not her mama. How could her life end in just a few short seconds?

Clinging to the lifeless body, she knew it had to be some huge mistake. Maybe she could remove the bullet from her mama's bloody abdomen. With shaking hands, she began to examine the wound, but couldn't see with the darkness and tears blurring her vision.

It was all her fault. She should have shot Sandoval sooner.

"Claire, she's gone, and Griffin's still loose, we've got to go."

She ignored Logan and his hands that pulled at her.

*The bullet had been meant for me. Mama saved me.*

*Damn you, Mama.* Claire began to scream. It was an unbearable sacrifice and she wanted none of it. All she wanted was her mama back. The anguish and loss cut deep, so deep she suffocated from the pain.

Logan held her as she fought him, wrapping her tightly into his arms. "We have to go now, Claire. We have to find Jimmy before Frank does." The statement—and Logan's urgency—broke through her grief.

She stumbled as he dragged her away from her mama's lifeless body and said what she hadn't since she was a very young girl. "I love you, Mama." But the words had come too late.

# CHAPTER 19

Claire waited for Logan at Tia's cabin. Rain drummed on the roof, the steady thudding the only sound cutting into her numb emotions. The past three days had been a blur. She functioned as if she couldn't catch her breath, as if a train had hit her full-speed and all she could do was stumble from one moment to the next.

Unprepared for the aftermath of her mama's death, Claire was lost in a haze of grief, bombarded by memories and what-ifs. Her head ached from echoes of the past that afflicted her day and night. The funeral that morning hadn't given her closure, it simply added more salt on her wounds of guilt, anger, and overwhelming loss. Shorty McClaren's shattered countenance and Jimmy's unstoppable crying had only broken her heart more.

Following the shootings that fateful night, she had found Jimmy hiding in the chapel. He'd been the person firing at the building, having taken Myers' gun from the dead man's body. Fortunately, only four bullets had remained in the weapon and Jimmy had quickly discharged them, leaving Claire grateful beyond measure that her brother hadn't hurt himself in the reckless attempt to help them. Jimmy had thought Frank was inside the building and was horrified when he learned that Claire and their mama had been the occupants. With a heavy heart, she had given him the news of Maggie's death and then brought him here to Tia's to care for him.

During all of this she had ignored Logan's silent despair, rebuffing her husband, and burying any feelings she had ever harbored for him. She told herself it was for the best. He'd reluctantly taken a room at the Wagner Hotel.

With Harry Myers and Raul Sandoval dead, Frank Griffin sat in jail, nabbed by Logan when he attempted to sneak into the chapel. Logan showed little mercy or kindness to her mama's husband, suiting Claire just fine. Had Griffin truly cared for Maggie? If so, she hoped the pain of losing her would haunt him for the rest of his days.

Claire had no pity to give. Griffin was charged with the murder of Teddy Luttrell, and she prayed it would stick. While it was probable he'd done it, proving it in a court of law would be a different matter. Even though her mama and Dee had alluded to their culpability in Luttrell's death, Claire kept her mouth shut about their possible involvement. Frank Griffin deserved to take all the heat and she felt little remorse over it. And while she wasn't inclined to protect Dee Griffin from jail time, Claire would have wondered at her own motives if she had sent the law after the mother of Logan's son. That kind of vindictiveness wasn't Claire's style. Dee had disappeared from the Sangre de Cristos before any of them realized it, a bag of money in tow. She'd gone immediately to Southern Charm, held Belle at gunpoint, and demanded the return of her son. Then, she vanished without a trace. Apparently, her desire to protect her son displaced any bond she and Maggie might have had. Did Dee even know Maggie was dead?

Logan would surely go after them, and Claire wondered why he hadn't already. Ellie and Louisa told her he'd helped to arrange her mama's funeral, and he'd been present at the short eulogy this morning at the cemetery on the edge of town. Tia tried to draw

Claire out of her stupor, to get her to talk to Logan, but Claire knew fate was about to make a clean sweep of her life. And although she expected the outcome, she hardly looked forward to it.

When the sound of hoof beats signaled a rider's approach, Claire opened the door. The rain had stopped, and a white mist hung in the air. Logan dismounted then removed the damp slicker that covered his dark jacket, vest, and tie from the funeral. He came toward her, his face chiseled with a grim expression beneath the shadow of his hat. Thunder echoed in the distance, sending a shiver through Claire, and the vibration rebounded off the mountains and onto the plains below. The total sum of the man would always be what she remembered, despite the heartbreak and disillusionment, because Logan would always be worth remembering.

"It's past time we talked." He watched her intently.

Claire nodded and stepped aside as he entered the dwelling. She moved to a wooden stool near the cook fire and smoothed out the dark blue cotton of her dress as she sat. Logan removed his hat and also took a seat, separated from her by only a few feet.

"How're you holding up?" he asked.

"I'm getting through." She braced herself for the crushing conversation he didn't seem inclined to initiate. "I'm glad you've come—we need to discuss the terms of the divorce."

Logan's stormy gaze fixed on her and she could feel tension pour from him—it all but ignited the air in the tiny cabin.

"What are you talking about?" he asked, his tone sharp.

"Word has it Frank Griffin will walk any day. You'd best find Dee and your son before it's too late."

Logan's face became rigid, and his jaw flexed into a firm line. "I never meant to keep my past from you. There was never a good time to talk about it."

"It would appear everything played to your favor."

"I don't know what you're suggesting, but none of this was planned."

"But we play the hand we're dealt."

"We can re-stack the cards," he said.

"So you're saying you don't plan to find her, to claim your son?"

Logan's silence was answer enough. "I didn't marry you for the land or the money, Claire."

"Then you won't mind if I ask for half of it then. I'm not going to play the hand I was dealt anymore, either. I'll split the land and the money fifty-fifty with Dee."

"What if I don't agree to this divorce?"

"I'm not sure it's up for debate."

"What passed between us meant nothing?"

Claire fought back a rush of tears. She'd already cried a river. How could there possibly be anything left in her? "Of course it meant something," she said. "But you're not free to be in this marriage—you never were. And I won't settle for anything less."

With those words, her perspective underwent a drastic shift. She'd never known what it was to stand up for herself, to demand what she wanted in her life, what she *needed* in her life. She watched him with sadness and longing, aware that losing him would hurt like hell. But a faint voice called to her, still uncertain at times, but gaining momentum with each passing day. In the midst of the sorrow burned a surprising flicker of hope, a determination that she could face the future with conviction. She could make a life for Jimmy.

"Damn." He ran a hand over his face. "Honest to God Claire, I don't know what's going on with Dee. I don't even know where she is."

"Try Virginia City," she said.

He watched her, absorbing the information. It was clear to her what he would do. It seemed clear to him, too.

"Do you love me?" he asked unexpectedly.

The question caught her off-guard. If she answered yes, he'd still walk away from her, in search of the woman who had once held a special place in his heart.

"No." Through sheer willpower she held his gaze while she lied.

A flicker of pain crossed Logan's face. "What if you're pregnant?"

Claire hesitated. "It's too soon, we've hardly been together long enough." She hoped she wasn't pregnant, although a baby—Logan's child, no less—would be a precious gift.

"So that's it?" he asked. "That's the end of us?"

Claire stood. "Don't you dare blame all of this on me. I never expected you to marry me, but it certainly put you in the thick of things."

"I was trying to protect you," he said. "You sure as hell needed it. I'm not the bad guy you're making me out to be."

She was close to the edge of an emotional abyss of grief and misery, and she feared the slightest nudge would send her over. Not wanting it to happen in front of Logan, she reined in her sudden flash of temper. "I know," she said. "I never did thank you for taking care of Sandoval."

"After everything he'd done to you, he wasn't getting off that mountain alive," he said, his voice unwavering, his declaration absolute.

Claire gazed into eyes that had the power to draw her in and dissolve her defenses. Her body ached to be in his arms one last time, to feel his strength and his response to her. But that wasn't love, and it wasn't enough. God, how she wished she was the kind of woman who could settle only for the needs of the flesh. But her selfishness was also absolute—she could never share him with another woman.

"I'll make arrangements for the divorce," she said. "I'm sure you'll want to ride at first light."

Suddenly needing to be alone and in her own space, she opened the door, but Logan rose and pulled her to him.

"This wasn't how I saw it," he said. "This wasn't how it was supposed to end."

She averted her gaze, knowing how easy it would be to slide into his arms.

"Everything ends," she whispered. "It's just a matter of when."

Without a backward glance, she walked out of the cabin. Sunlight filtered through gaps in the thunderclouds as Claire walked into the forest, the same haven she had occupied as a child when dreams held promises of the future and kept the demons at bay. It was here that a dove had come to her, white-feathered and pure, the bird so precious and sweet that Claire had felt truly privileged. But no magical feathered friend would come to her today. Today was the end of a dream.

She walked mindlessly through the pine forest as pain tore through her. Tia and Jimmy appeared, and Claire realized they had been waiting out here to give her time alone with Logan. She hugged them both as tears flowed down her face, knowing they'd spent part of that time in the rain.

"It will not always be this hard, *Palomita*," Tia murmured.

Claire prayed she was right.

# CHAPTER 20

*Three months later*

Claire sat down in the parlor of the main house at the SR Ranch, Jimmy at her side. Their hats and coats had been taken by Rosita, a stout Mexican woman whom Claire had become acquainted with several months earlier during her brief stay at the ranch of Jonathan and Susanna Ryan, Logan's folks.

Rosita excused herself to find Mrs. Ryan and Claire took another deep breath, wondering if she'd been wrong to come. Nervously, she adjusted the dark wool dress she wore. The flame crackling in the fireplace was a welcome sight after their long ride from Fort Richardson in the chilly, late-October weather. A cattleman, conducting business at the fort, had aided her and Jimmy in locating the Ryan's ranch, but Claire's general questions about Logan had been met with a shrug from the young man.

"What do you think's gonna happen?" Jimmy asked.

"I don't know," she replied.

Jimmy had taken their mama's death hard, as had Claire—as she did still—but he'd been holding up well. Following their mama's burial and Claire's divorce from Logan, there had been no money with which to live—Luttrell's stash, what was left of it, had been placed in temporary legal custody—but surprisingly Belle had approached her and offered to pay for Claire's medical services. It hadn't been much, but it had kept her and Jimmy afloat while they awaited Frank's trial—Jimmy had wanted to know the fate of his father.

Belle, in what Claire decided was the woman's bid to make amends, had also offered her and Jimmy a place to live, but the Hyman family likewise had come forward with a generous offer of room and board at a minimal cost, which Claire had gratefully accepted. The support extended—both emotional and practical—by the townsfolk who knew them had made her feel, for the first time, as if she was a part of something, as if she *belonged*. It comforted her more than she could have ever imagined. She and Jimmy soon settled into a welcome routine, but when Logan contacted her at long last about the proceeds from the sale of Luttrell's land, she'd felt her world slide out from under her again and knew she would have to face him.

Susanna Ryan appeared at the threshold. "What a surprise." She crossed the room, her skirt brushing the floor, and took Claire's hand. Susanna was much as Claire remembered her—tall, dark haired, with a strong face softened by a warm gaze.

"Mrs. Ryan, it's good to see you again." Claire rose from the couch.

Susanna smiled. "I thought I might never see you again."

"This is my brother Jimmy."

"How do you do," Susanna said.

"Ma'am." Jimmy stood and took the older woman's hand.

"I had no idea you were coming. Please sit down."

When they were settled again, Claire spoke. "I apologize for dropping in unannounced. I wasn't quite sure I would come, even as we traveled."

"How did you get here? By buggy?"

"No. I purchased horses in Fort Richardson. They're outside." Claire regretted leaving Reverend behind, but the old gelding never would have survived the trek. Hopefully, he was happy at Tia's place. "Doug Callahan directed us the right way."

"The Callahans have long been our neighbors. I'll have one of the hands see to your horses."

"Thank you." Claire pressed her lips together. "Is Molly here?"

Susanna shook her head. "She and Matthew have a place about five miles away. We can send for her in the morning, although she's been a might ill recently."

Confused by the slight smile on Mrs. Ryan's face, Claire waited for an explanation.

"She's expecting," Susanna said.

Claire shifted uneasily. "That's wonderful." She truly was happy for Molly but couldn't get past her apprehension over seeing Logan again. His letter said he was back in Texas—she could only assume Dee and Dylan were with him. Any minute, she expected one of them to enter the parlor and make her discomfort complete.

"You'll stay the night, won't you?"

Claire knew there was no alternative—it was too far to return to the fort tonight—but she hardly looked forward to staying under the same roof as Dee and Logan. Claire glanced at Jimmy, but her brother was engrossed in twiddling his thumbs. "Is she here?" she heard herself ask.

"And who would that be?" Susanna replied.

"Dee Griffin."

Susanna's countenance changed, becoming more circumspect. "No. And I would venture to say you didn't come here to see me. I'll send Dawson to find Logan. He spends far too much time on Storm chasing beeves anyhow." With consideration she added, "I think it will do him good to see you."

Dee wasn't here? Claire didn't know what to make of that. "About everything that happened...."

"No." Susanna put a hand up. "The heart is an ornery thing and oft times as blind as a bat, but it always finds its way home." Susanna stood. "James, come with me. I'll fetch you a snack."

Jimmy looked at Claire, and she silently gave permission for him to go ahead.

"How old are you?" Susanna asked as they left room.

"Eight years old, ma'am."

Claire focused on the fire and wondered how Logan would react to her sudden appearance. She longed to see him, but at the same time had dreaded confronting him with Dee at his side. But Dee wasn't here. Claire's heart pounded at the thought.

Although she arrived fully expecting to see him with his new family, a part of her hadn't cared. During the past three months she'd come to miss him so much, so thoroughly, that seeing him became a matter of survival. She was lost without him.

The letter he'd sent had given her the excuse to meet with him—although she wasn't certain about anything anymore, least of all her own motives—but she questioned if she could truly handle visiting with him, only to walk away again.

Anxiously, she waited for him to return to the house and wondered how to tell him the truth.

---

LOGAN CHECKED the cattle clustered into a group a few miles south of the SR. Their tails flicked in agitation as their bawling and mewing filled the cool night air. The wind howled across the plains and Logan wrapped a scarf around his face and pulled his hat lower on his forehead. Winter would be upon them soon enough.

He thought of Claire and wondered if she'd received the money. He thought of Claire too damn much of late. He ought to find her, try to see her. Each passing day brought the thought closer to reality. But she'd told him she didn't love him. His luck with women was one for the books. He was better off with the cows, which was where he spent most of his time these days. Evenings at the ranch house with his folks, and occasionally with Matt and Molly, had turned his loneliness into physical pain, driving him out to the flat plains of Texas.

He'd taken to riding the SR from dawn to dusk, using hard labor to tire his body and exhaust his mind. It was the regrets that hit him the hardest, circling his thoughts like vultures waiting to pick the choicest morsels.

It rankled how much he'd tried to attribute a greater depth of character to Dee that simply hadn't existed. She blindsided him again with the truth that Dylan *wasn't* his son, his heart still smarting from her last and final confession. In her attempt to defend herself, she'd stated how devoted Logan had been to law enforcement, how she'd felt neglected, how difficult it had been to resist the attentions of John Moore, Dylan's real father. She'd cheated on Logan, then dumped both him and Moore when Frank threatened her, forcing her to marry Luttrell.

With disgust and disillusionment, Logan had ridden away from Dee and a past he had held on to for far too long. She had hurt and betrayed him then lied to him—giving him brief hope that Dylan was his son, then snatching it all away in the span of a short conversation. Moore could have her for all Logan cared, if the man could stomach all that she'd done to him.

Logan was finished with her.

His eyes burned as a gust of wind blasted him. Storm whinnied and Logan knew she wanted to head back to the ranch and a warm stall with a bucketful of grain. He started toward the main ranch buildings, with too much to occupy his mind as the days grew shorter and the nights colder. He lost far more than a son—he'd lost Claire. He'd chosen Dee over her, and in doing so had undoubtedly killed any possibility of regaining Claire's trust. Maybe he and Claire could've had a chance if they'd had more time. Maybe he could have made her love him.

At the main house, he had just settled Storm in her stall when Dawson caught up with him. "I've been lookin' for you. Your ma wants you at the house."

"I'm headin' there. Anything wrong?" he asked the foreman.

"You got a visitor." Dawson veered his stiff frame back to the bunkhouse.

Logan strode across the clearing to the front porch, taking the steps two at a time. He slammed into a woman in the entryway, knocking her off-balance onto her rear-end.

"Pardon me, miss." He reached down to help her, and she turned her face to his. "Claire?" No black wig or revealing dress this time, just strands of blonde hair escaping her braid and a dark gown that covered every inch of her.

Stunned, he stared at her as if all his hard thinking had conjured her from the howling wind that whistled around them.

She gazed at him with apprehension and regained her footing, removing her hand from his.

"What are you doing here?" he asked.

She straightened her gown and took a deep breath. "I've come looking for you. Actually, I was headed outside to find you."

He ushered her back into the house, closed the front door, and removed his coat and hat. He gestured for her to return to the parlor, hardly able to believe she was here as she sat on the overstuffed couch.

"It's good to see you," she said, but her face conveyed concern and Logan braced himself for a difficult encounter. Who was he kidding? It was difficult just looking at her.

Color blossomed across her cheeks, and he wondered how deep her reaction to him went.

"Where's Jimmy?" he asked, standing like a sentry across the room.

"He's here...with your mother, in the kitchen I think."

"Is everything all right? Didn't you get the money I sent?"

Claire nodded. "Yes, and that's why I've come. You said in your letter that it was all the proceeds from the sale of the land, and...." She wrung her hands together. "It's too much. I meant for Dee and Dylan to have some of it. You don't have to give it all to us." Her green eyes flashed at him.

"No. As far as I'm concerned, you and Jimmy are entitled to all of it. Anyway, Dee lied about Dylan."

"She did?"

"He's not my son. When I found her in Virginia City the two of us finally sat down and had a long talk."

"If Dylan is really Luttrell's, then he's entitled to everything from that land," Claire said, pleading her case.

"No. Dylan was fathered by another man, a man I knew. He owned several stores and saloons in town and as soon as she could, Dee ran straight to him. She hadn't been certain he would take her back, but it was clear she wanted him, not me. She said she'd lied about Dylan being mine to try and save me, to save you, fearing what Frank might do to us. In some twisted way, she thought she was helping."

"I'm sorry. I'm still not certain Jimmy's entitled to the land though, especially in light of this."

"Dee told me Frank and Luttrell had been set to buy the property from the Maxwell Land Grant when Frank's funding suddenly dried up, despite having recently bankrupted Maria Chavez's husband. Luttrell offered to float him until he could buy back his share, but as insurance Frank pressured Dee to marry Luttrell, just in case. It all backfired when Teddy went back on his deal with Griffin, and Dee wanted out of her marriage. To make matters worse, Luttrell inherited a sizable chunk of money from a deceased uncle in St. Louis and Frank thought to get it through his sister. But Luttrell got paranoid and dragged all the money into the mountains to hide it. Maggie entered the picture because she wanted revenge against Frank, who was having an affair with Belle Mason. So Maggie romanced Luttrell and got him to deed the land to her through you. Dee was the one who told her about the money."

"The local authorities were never able to pin Luttrell's murder on Frank," Claire said. "Do you think he did it?"

"Probably."

"Will Dee be safe from him?"

"That's no longer my concern. Luttrell gave the land to Maggie, albeit through you, so I can only assume that was his last wish. I checked and he has no immediate living relatives. It only seems right it should all go to you and Jimmy, what with your ma gone. In the end, the two of you paid the highest price."

"I'm not so sure about that," Claire said quietly.

"Is that the only reason you've come?" He tried to hide the longing in his voice, but it was there nonetheless.

"No." She gave a slight shake of her head, her expression pensive. "I've something else to tell you and thought I should do it in person."

Her eyes met his, the deep color of the forest, and he was struck by how much he'd missed her.

"I'm with child."

A vision of Dee flashed in his head, her faithlessness and manipulations still fresh in his memories.

"You're telling me it's mine?" he asked.

Surprise registered on Claire's face. "You think I'd travel all this way to tell you it wasn't?" She rose and moved to the fireplace. "Maybe this was a mistake. I agonized whether to come at all considering I thought I'd walk in on a cozy little setup with Dee and

Dylan. But it wasn't right when she'd kept knowledge of Dylan from you, even though it turned out to be a lie, so I thought you deserved to know we were going to have a baby together."

"There hasn't been anyone else?"

She spun around with a fire in her eyes. "Anyone else?" she demanded. "How could there be when I can't stop thinking about you? No matter that I thought you married me for the land, that you deliberately didn't tell me about your history with Dee because you were still secretly in love with her. I want you anyway, and it's taken all my willpower not to grovel and beg you to take me back now that I know you didn't marry her." Tears filled her eyes. "I've lost my mama, but life does go on. But losing you has been like losing a piece of myself. The past few months have shown me how truly miserable I can be. This child is a blessing and a curse, because to have a part of you is better than nothing, but to be reminded of not having you makes me despair in a way I never have before." She stifled a sob.

Stunned by Claire's words, Logan felt as if he'd taken a horse-kick in the gut.

Did she really mean it? Hope clawed at him, but he refused to give it free rein.

"You asked for the divorce." He couldn't afford to be dragged through the mud again.

"I thought I was doing the right thing."

"Did you lie to me when I asked if you were with child?"

She shook her head. "No, of course not. It was too soon to know. And with everything that had happened...losing my mama and dealing with your betrayal.... It was several weeks after you left that I realized...."

"After my betrayal?" he asked, incredulous.

"You never told me about Dee! What was I supposed to think when she suddenly showed up and you started protecting her?"

"A necessary end to a chapter of my life. I would've told you about her, in time. Unfortunately for us, there never was enough of that."

"I didn't come here to fight with you." Claire's voice was hollow and weary. "I wanted you to know about the baby and I couldn't put it in a letter. But Jimmy and I will be heading out tomorrow."

"Like hell," Logan said. "You're not leaving this house."

He crossed the room, took her face in his hands, and kissed her. She tried to resist, but he wouldn't let her.

"You think I'm manipulating you," she said, her lips against his.

"Are you?" His mouth devoured hers.

"No.... Yes." She yielded to him. "I want this baby to have a father, not to grow up like I did, and I miss you and I love you." The words came out in a rush.

She clung to him and Logan felt a void in his life disappear, an emptiness that spanned such a depth he'd had no idea until he'd been without her, no idea until he heard her say how much she needed him, how deeply she felt for him.

"We'll get married again," he said.

"What if we can't make it work." Claire buried her face into his shoulder.

"Promise me one thing."

"What?"

"Don't shut me out again."

She gazed up at him, her eyes filled with worry but also longing —and love. "I won't. I've missed you so much. I was afraid I'd come here and you'd be married to Dee."

"I was prepared to make it work for Dylan's sake. And you made it easy you when you asked for the divorce and told me you didn't care. I convinced myself loving you had been a mistake."

"Do you still feel that way?"

"No, but my pride kept me from finding you and telling you. Eventually I would've picked up my brains from the dirt and come after you."

"I hope that's true because I never stopped wanting you, but you needed to be free to choose. And so did I."

"I told you I don't believe in sacrifice."

"It wasn't sacrifice, Logan," she whispered. "I finally came to know I had to follow my dreams, but it took me three months to realize it. It took me all this time to gain the courage to come here and tell you about the baby, not to bind you to me but to share it with you." Her face held an expectant gaze. "Did you mean it when you said you loved me?"

"I never say anything I don't mean. I thought I told you that once." His lips came gently to hers. "And if you remember, I said I wanted a babe. Or two."

"There's something else you should know. I've heard tell there's a women's medical college back East in Philadelphia, and...."

Logan considered her rosy face and the spark of excitement in her gaze. "And you want to go," he finished.

"Yes." Her eyes became glassy. "It frightens me, but yes, I want to go. Or at least I want to try, after the baby's born."

Logan's wandering tendencies had come to the fore. Roots had never been tied to a place—although he certainly felt at home here at his folks' ranch—so following Claire made an odd sort of sense.

"Then I say we go," he said.

She gripped his hand. "Is that truly what you want?"

"Well, if I could get you alone, I'd show you what I *truly* want."

Her blush returned in full force, and she smiled at him.

He folded her into his arms and knew that God had made his journey to the woman of his heart a difficult and painful one, but she'd come back to him.

He wouldn't let her go again.

# CHAPTER 21

Three days later, Claire sat with Molly in the parlor. A fire burned in the hearth as they both took a much-needed break from the festivities at the end of her second wedding day. Susanna pulled the event together in record time, a small crowd of friends and family gathering to celebrate. Already exhausted from her pregnancy, the ceremony—while a much sweeter affair than her first one to Logan—managed to drain the last of her reserves.

"Are you as weary as I am?" Claire asked.

Molly agreed as she leaned her head back and sighed. Her dark hair escaped the pins that held it in place, but it was clear she didn't care. Molly never stood long on decorum—it was one of the traits Claire liked best about her. That, and her innate fortitude. She had shared tales of her time with the Comanche in a humorous tone that often opposed the tragedy behind her abduction. Her strength never failed to inspire Claire.

She decided pregnancy agreed with Molly, her friend's face glowing and a slight bulge showing beneath the lacy dress she wore today as Claire's matron of honor. Molly's baby was due to arrive a month sooner than Claire's.

"I think I could sleep until tomorrow night," Molly said.

Claire contemplated the woman who had become her sister. Not only had Molly saved her life after Sandoval had beaten her the first time, she had brought Claire to Texas—she'd brought Claire to Logan.

"Did I ever thank you for finding me?"

Molly smiled. "Yes." She rested a hand on her abdomen. "I haven't told Matt yet, but I've a feeling the baby will be a boy."

"Truly? I haven't felt an inclination either way." Claire had been quite ill in the first few weeks and only now was able to get some needed rest. Lying next to Logan every night was the best medicine she could envision.

Her dreams had come true, but they were far from the innocent longings of the girl she'd been. She understood now that walking away from difficulties was too easy. She and Logan weren't perfect, they'd both made mistakes, and they could have easily lost one another. It would take work to build trust, to compromise and mold their lives together, but she took heart in the knowledge Logan wanted a life with her as much as she did with him.

Molly squeezed her hand. "Are you all right?"

"Everything has happened so fast. My head is still spinning."

"I've felt that way, too. Matt says I blew his world apart, like a stick of dynamite."

They both laughed.

"He does need to work on his sweet-talk a little," Molly continued. "But that's all right. He makes up for it in other ways."

They giggled again.

Molly's expression became serious. "The pain of losing your ma won't always be so sharp."

Claire knew she spoke from experience. Molly's mother had been murdered when Molly was a child.

"Susanna's helped to fill the gap in my life," she continued. "I'm sure she'll do the same for you...when you're ready."

So many changes, so many unknown opportunities to come.

Claire worried over them but felt comforted by the fact that Logan would be with her. They would make a new life together.

There was a knock at the door, and Rosita came from the kitchen to answer it. The men were still in the barn with several of the wedding guests, and Jimmy was afoot somewhere.

"I wonder what's wrong," Claire said when Susanna's voice became audible. Both she and Molly stood.

Susanna came from the foyer with a young woman, and Claire thought she appeared familiar. Chestnut hair hung in a braid, and her face and hands were darkened from the sun. A heavy wool shawl covered a dirt-stained white blouse and a ragged cotton skirt. She appeared cold and utterly exhausted, but more than that, she seemed defeated at some basic level.

Recognition hit Claire. The girl resembled Molly.

The young woman spoke first. "Molly? Is it really you?"

Molly nodded slowly, clearly shocked by the sudden arrival of the stranger. But Claire knew this was no intruder. It had to be the youngest Hart daughter, Emma—Molly's sister. They'd been separated for ten years since the night their parents had been murdered and Molly had been captured by the Comanche. Everyone—including Emma, who had been raised in San Francisco by an aunt during the ensuing years—had thought Molly was dead until this past spring.

"Emma?" Molly said thickly. She moved quickly to embrace her sister. "I've missed you so much. I didn't think I'd ever see you again." Her voice hitched on a sob. "How did you get here? We received word from Aunt Catherine that you'd gone to Grand Canyon."

"I can't believe you're alive." Emma buried her face against Molly's shoulder. "I dreamt it over and over, but when Nathan told me I could hardly believe it."

Molly leaned back. "Then he found you?"

Emma nodded.

"Is he with you?"

Emma's eyes filled with tears. "No, he's not. I thought he might be here, waiting, with you."

"Shhh, it's alright." Molly smoothed away wisps of Emma's hair that clung to her wet cheeks. "We'll figure it all out." She put her arms around her sister once again, hugging her fiercely. "Thank God you're here, and that you're safe and well."

Claire saw the concern on Susanna's face. Logan had told her that Nathan Blackmore, an old friend of Matt's, had gone in search of Emma Hart after the Ryan's had received a letter from Catherine —the Hart's aunt—that Emma had run off to Arizona Territory.

"Mr. Blackmore is a Ranger," Claire said, her tone hopeful. "He can certainly handle himself in any situation."

Molly nodded. "This is Claire, Logan's wife, and she's right. I'll talk to Matt. He'll know what to do." Holding her sister close, she said fiercely, "I'm so glad to see you. Where have you come from?"

"You look worn to the bone," Susanna said. "Let's get you cleaned up and fed. You can tell us everything after you've rested. Nothing can be done tonight."

Susanna led them upstairs and Claire started to follow but stopped when Matt and Logan appeared through the front entryway.

"What's going on?" Matt demanded. "Whose horse is that outside?"

"It's Emma," Claire replied. "She arrived just moments ago."

"Is Nathan with her?" Matt asked.

"Apparently not. But she did say he found her."

"Then where is he?" Logan asked.

Claire shrugged helplessly. "Emma doesn't look well, but maybe once she rests we can learn what happened. I'm going to see if Susanna needs any help."

She kissed Logan then hurried up the stairs to join the other women. She had a pouch of dried passionflower leaves with her medicines—she would offer to make a tea for Emma to help her rest.

―――――――

MATT'S SILENCE WAS DEAFENING.

"You think Nathan's in trouble?" Logan wondered the same thing.

"He wouldn't let Emma come here by herself. Not all the way from Arizona."

"Let's talk to her first before jumping to any conclusions."

"You're right. But if need be, I'll ride at first light."

"I'll go with you," Logan declared.

"You don't have to. I'll take Dawson or Hicks. I owe Nathan—he risked his life when Cerillo had me. And you just got married today."

"Yeah." Logan was a happy man, and he certainly had no intention of jeopardizing that happiness needlessly. Claire carried their child, and the thought made his lips twitch into an almost-smile. He had much to be thankful for. "But you're right, Nathan wouldn't have sent Emma out on her own at this time of year. Don't ride without me."

His brother looked at him with gratitude. "I'd appreciate the backup."

"I'll find Pa and tell him what's goin' on."

Matt agreed. "I'll check on the ladies." He paused for a moment. "I'm glad Emma's here. It's weighed on Molly a lot lately, wondering when, or if, she'd ever see her again."

Logan saw the relief in his brother's gaze and realized he hadn't noticed in the days since his return how much Matt had been concerned about his wife. As he went to find his pa, he hoped all would be well.

WARM LIPS NUZZLED HIS EAR. Logan woke, still in the parlor, having dozed off while waiting. He pulled the warm body close, and Claire wrapped her arms around him. A quick scan of the room told him they were alone.

"How's Emma?" He buried his hand in her hair. God, she felt good.

"She's more than just tired, she's seems almost hollowed out inside. It's heartbreaking." Claire laid her head into the nook of his shoulder. "We fed and bathed her, and I gave her a sedative tea to help her sleep."

"Did she say what happened?"

"They got split up somehow, and she was very upset when she learned he wasn't here."

"Matt may ride out tomorrow to look for him." Logan twined his fingers with hers. "I'm gonna go with him."

Claire moved closer. "I thought you might, and you should, but please be careful."

"Always, darlin'."

"Can we go to bed?" she whispered, her breath hot on his neck.

He kissed her, his mouth aching for hers. A thought flitted through his mind. *Claire Waters couldn't possibly be here.* But she was. She was here beside him, in his life, in his home, and she would lie beside him tonight as his wife, for good. His mouth moved over hers with a hunger that needed privacy to be appeased.

He carried her to his bedroom. Their bedroom.

"It's a good thing your room isn't upstairs," she teased.

"It wouldn't matter." He pushed the door shut with his foot. "There's no doubt in my mind that no matter how tired I was, I'd still be able to make love to you all night long." He laid her on the bed, and he saw the acceptance in her eyes along with a need that matched his own.

He had her stripped and beneath him in no time, reminding him that he'd had as little patience on their first wedding night. Claire matched his hunger, and the coupling left them both panting and clinging to the other. He ran a hand across her ribcage and felt the scar tissue from the bullet she'd taken in Cimarron.

"Your wound is healed?" he asked.

"Yes, but it took a long time."

He leaned down and pressed his lips to the knotted flesh, savoring every part of her.

Much later, after he'd had her twice more, they lay together, sheets twisted around them and Claire's hair in a mess across his chest. He thought of the child in her belly, and a sense of peace and excitement engulfed him.

There would be more children, God willing.

He reached over to his nightstand, opened a drawer, and withdrew the item he'd kept all this time.

"I have something for you," he murmured.

"What's that?" Her sleepy voice stirred him.

He handed her the wood carving of a dove she'd made as a child. She looked up at him in bewilderment.

"Where did you get this?"

"Tia gave it to me for safekeeping." He'd been unable to part with it, this piece of Claire's soul. "We'll give it to the baby."

"All right." She scooted against him to bring her mouth to his, revealing an enticing view of the valley between her breasts.

*Palomita.* The dove had come back to him.

---

I'M so pleased you chose to read *The Dove*, and it's my sincere hope that you enjoyed the story. I would appreciate if you'd consider posting a review. This can help an author tremendously in obtaining a readership. My many thanks. ∼ Kristy

Don't miss THE CANARY, featuring Logan and Claire's daughter, Sarah. Paleontologist Jack Brenner enters a fake marriage with Sarah Ryan to protect her in the Arizona desert, but he never expects to fall for her ...

kmccaffrey.com/the-canary/

READ THE NIGHTHAWK, featuring Logan and Claire's daughter, Sophie. U.S. Deputy Marshal Benton McKay must contend with reporter Sophie Ryan while trying to locate an outlaw gang in the wild and wooly mining town of Jerome, Arizona Territory.

kmccaffrey.com/the-nighthawk/

READ THE SWAN, featuring Logan and Claire's eldest daughter, Anna. In Oklahoma Territory Malcolm Hardy has created enough distance from his questionable family name to find a quiet purpose to his days, but then Dr. Anna Ryan walks back into his life, and his hard-won peace is in jeopardy.

kmccaffrey.com/the-swan/

*Don't miss THE WREN*
*Wings of the West Book 1*

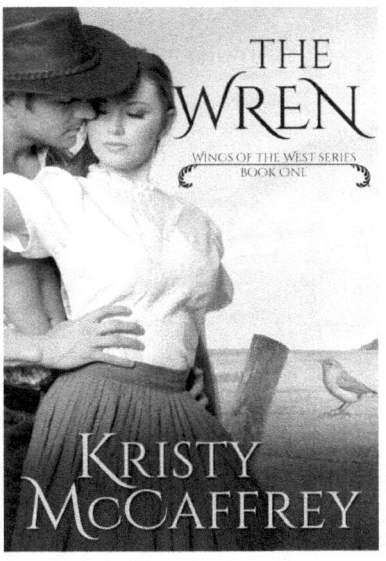

Ten years have passed since her ranch was attacked, her folks murdered, and Molly Hart was abducted. Now, at nineteen, she's finally returning home to north Texas after spending the remainder of her childhood with a tribe of Kwahadi Comanche. What she finds is a deserted home coated with dust and the passage of time, the chilling discovery of her own gravesite, and the presence of a man she thought never to see again.

Matt Ryan is pushed by a restless wind to the broken-down remains of the Hart ranch. Recently recovered from an imprisonment that nearly ended his life, the drive for truth and fairness has all but abandoned him. For ten years he faithfully served the U.S. Army and the Texas Rangers, seeking justice for the brutal murder of a little girl, only to find closure and healing beyond his grasp. Returning to the place where it all began, he's surprised to stumble across a woman with the same blue eyes as the child he can't put out of his mind.

kmccaffrey.com/the-wren/

## The Sparrow
## Wings of the West Book 3

In 1877, Emma Hart comes to Grand Canyon—a wild, rugged, and, until recently, undiscovered area. Plagued by visions and gifted with a second sight, she searches for answers about the tragedy of her past, the betrayal of her present, and an elusive future that echoes through her very soul. Joined by her power animal Sparrow, she ventures into the depths of Hopi folklore, forced to confront an evil that has lived through the ages.

Texas Ranger Nathan Blackmore tracks Emma Hart to the Colorado River, stunned by her determination to ride a wooden dory along its course. But in a place where the ripples of time run deep, he'll be faced with a choice. He must accept the unseen realm, *the world beside this world,* that he turned away from years ago, or risk losing the woman he has come to love more than life itself.

kmccaffrey.com/the-sparrow/

### The Blackbird
### Wings of the West Book 4

Bounty hunter Cale Walker arrives in Tucson to search for J. Howard "Hank" Carlisle at the request of his daughter, Tess. Hank mentored Cale before a falling out divided them, and a mountain lion attack left Cale nearly dead. Rescued by a band of Nednai Apache, his wounds were considered a powerful omen and he was taught the ways of a *di-yin*, or a medicine man. To locate Hank, Cale must enter the Dragoon Mountains, straddling two worlds that no longer fit. But he has an even bigger problem—finding a way into the heart of a young woman determined to live life as a bystander.

For two years, Tess Carlisle has tried to heal the mental and physical wounds of a deadly assault by one of her *papá's* men. Continuing the traditions of her Mexican heritage, she has honed her skills as a *cuentista*, a storyteller and a Keeper of the Old Ways. But with no contact from her father since the attack, she fears the worst. Tess knows that to reenter Hank Carlisle's world is a dangerous endeavor, and her only hope is Cale Walker, a man unlike any she has ever known. Determined to make a journey that could lead straight into the path of her attacker, she hardens her resolve along with her heart. But Cale makes her yearn for something she vowed she never would—love.

kmccaffrey.com/the-blackbird/

## The Bluebird
### Wings of the West Book 5

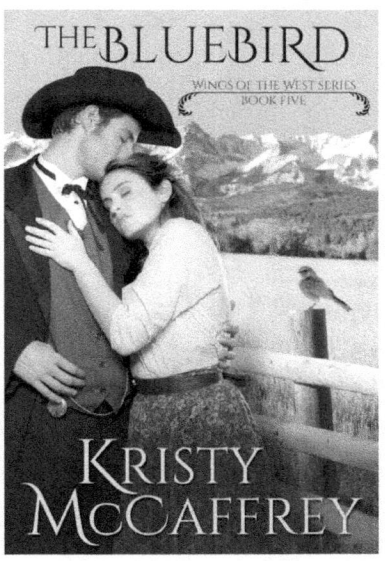

Molly Rose Simms departs the Arizona Territory, eager for adventure, and travels to Colorado to visit her brother. Robert left two years ago to make his fortune in the booming silver town of Creede, and now Molly Rose hopes to convince him to accompany her to San Francisco, New York City, or even Europe. But Robert is nowhere to be found. All Molly Rose finds is his partner, a mysterious man known as The Jackal.

Jake McKenna has traveled the bustling streets of Istanbul, exotic ports in China, and the deserts of Morocco. His restless desire to explore has been the only constant in his life. When his search for the elusive and mythical Bluebird mining claim lands him a new partner, he must decide how far he'll go to protect the stunning young woman who's clearly in over her head. A home and hearth has never been on The Jackal's agenda, but Molly Rose Simms is about to change his world in every conceivable way.

kmccaffrey.com/the-bluebird/

## *Into The Land Of Shadows*
## *A Stand-Alone Novel*

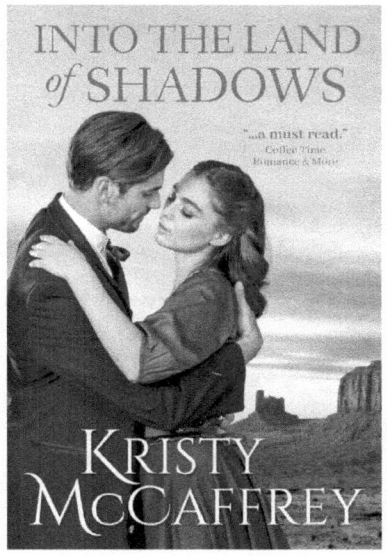

This book was previously published in 2013 under the same title. While the text and cover have been updated, the story remains the same.

It's been five years since a woman came between Ethan Barstow and his brother, Charley, and it's high time they buried the hatchet. When Ethan travels to Arizona Territory to make amends, he learns that Charley has abruptly disappeared after breaking more than one heart in town. And an indignant fiancée is hot on his trail.

When Charley Barstow abandons a local girl after getting her pregnant, Kate Kinsella pursues him without a second thought. She's determined he set things right, and even more determined to end her own engagement to him, a sham from the beginning. But an ill-timed encounter with a group of ruffians lands her in the company of Charley's brother, Ethan, who suggests they search together.

As Ethan and Kate move deeper INTO THE LAND OF SHADOWS, family tensions and past tragedies threaten to destroy a love neither of them expected.

kmccaffrey.com/into-the-land-of-shadows/

# ABOUT THE AUTHOR

Kristy McCaffrey has been writing since she was very young, but it wasn't until she was a stay-at-home mom that she considered becoming published. A fascination with science led her to earn two mechanical engineering degrees—she did her undergraduate work at Arizona State University and her graduate studies at the University of Pittsburgh—but storytelling has always been her passion. She writes both contemporary tales and award-winning historical western romances.

An Arizona native, Kristy and her husband reside in the desert where they frequently remove (rescue) rattlesnakes from their property, go for runs among the cactus, and plan trips to far-off places like the Orkney Islands or Machu Picchu. But mostly, she works 12-hour days and enjoys at-home date nights with her sweetheart, which usually include Will Ferrell movies and sci-fi flicks. Her four children have all flown the nest, so she lavishes her maternal instincts on Jeb, an American Bulldog her family rescued in 2021. He has his own Instagram account at @jeb_therescue.

Connect with Kristy
    Website: kmccaffrey.com
    Newsletter: kmccaffrey.com/subscribe/
    Facebook: facebook.com/AuthorKristyMcCaffrey
    Instagram: instagram.com/kristymccaffreybooks/
    BookBub: bookbub.com/authors/kristy-mccaffrey
    TikTok: tiktok.com/@kristymccaffrey

www.ingramcontent.com/pod-product-compliance
Lightning Source LLC
Chambersburg PA
CBHW070920180626
46817CB00003B/1145